Queen Victoria's Bomb

Queen Victoria's Bomb

Ronald Clark

C

CENTURY PUBLISHING
LONDON

Copyright ©Ronald Clark 1967

All rights reserved

First published in Great Britain in 1967 by
Jonathan Cape Ltd
This hardcover edition published in 1986 by
Century Hutchinson Ltd
Brookmount House, 62–65 Chandos Place
London WC2N 4NW

ISBN 0 7126 9478 1

Printed in Great Britain by
WBC Print

Contents

London   *September 12th, 1967*

My dear Richard,

You probably read the notice in *The Times* about Geoffrey Huxtable. I think he was at Cranwell one or two entries before your time, but you'll no doubt remember him. He was big, blond and boisterous, and we always said that any idea which found its way into his head would curl up and die of surprise. Nevertheless, a war or two ago he would have been called good officer-material, and it's a pity he came to grief on such a typically hare-brained exploit.

When the news of his death was at last confirmed I found that I was his Executor. There's not been much to it. Not much, that is, with the exception of a manuscript among his effects. You'll recollect how he used to claim that there would have been no Charge of the Light Brigade if the Queen's Ministers had not boobed over his great-uncle's advice. Some of us thought he was bonkers – or a secret drinker. Now I'm not so sure.

The manuscript, which I am sending you, was written by the said great-uncle, Professor Franklin Huxtable, who died at the turn of the century. You'll have to riffle through the reference books quite a while before you find him, as he doesn't seem to have made much of an impression on his age. The reason will become clear as you read what is really an account of his life.

Your first reactions will probably be the same as

mine: that the Prof could not have been so far ahead of his time – and that, anyway, it just couldn't be done. All the same, it's unwise for amateurs to get too cocksure, especially when a genius like Rutherford was claiming in the 1930s that nuclear energy would never be used. And there is, of course, the 'frightful possibility' to which Huxtable refers in the second and shorter document which I am sending along.

I wondered about the existence of this second document when I had finished reading what the old boy had written on his journey back from Africa in 1886. Had there, I wondered, been a later addition which had for some reason been removed from his effects – although the earlier and longer MS. had somehow been missed? I had more than a suspicion about where to look. And in a place which I had better not disclose I came upon the final pages I am sending – dated 1899 and also in Franklin Huxtable's writing.

To these final pages there was attached a short, colourless record of his public life, obviously prepared from official sources and apparently intended for publication in *The Times*. Pinned to this obituary was a sheet of Government notepaper on which there had been made three remarks. The first merely said: 'Passed as suitable for publication.' The second had been written by a Civil Servant whose pen had spluttered (with indignation?) as he had asked: 'Why did we never make use of this man?' The third, with a Ministerial signature, said: 'Suggest do not encourage publication. Let sleeping dogs lie.'

Well, here are the two documents, and with them the note which Geoffrey had attached to the longer one. 'Send this along to Richard,' he says. 'If he doesn't want to publish Uncle Franklin's story he can't have the guts

I credit him with. It's time we let the Huxtable out of the bag.'

Now it's over to you.

Yours,

RONALD

1 : Conception

Off the African Coast, 1886

It was the sight of the veterans who had fought at Waterloo which first made me conceive of a weapon to end all war – the ultimate deterrent, as His Royal Highness was later to call it.

I must have been only six or so at the time, but I can see them now: on stumps, in rags, broken things that were no longer men. Some had pensions of a sort, although a handle to one's name, Court interest, or a hatful of votes for some ambitious politician were the normal requirements for that. The rest of them begged. An extraordinary number of them also survived – one outcome, it was said, of being schooled to follow the Duke and live through that experience.

They were hard times. Even now, two-thirds of a century later, the tinkle of metal on metal reminds me of a coin thrown into a tin cup and the hesitant nod of thanks from a remnant of an army that had saved Europe from an Emperor.

My father's family had come from the West of England. During the Protectorate they had moved, for reasons of which I know nothing, to the outskirts of Edinburgh; so I can claim that there runs in my veins the blood of men who saved England from the Armada and of those who later threatened her with a king from over the water. My mother's kinsmen also came from Scotland but had been unlucky in the aftermath of the '45; had fled to France; and had then formed recruits to the party that helped settle Kentucky with Colonel Boone.

My grandfather on this Stuart side had barely established himself when the troubles that followed the Stamp Act blazed up. And while he felt too old to move again, he sent his young daughter, born only in 1773, across the Atlantic with a relative, in what must have been one of the last vessels to reach England before America became the United States. They had travelled north across the Border to join their own people, and to her last moments my mother remembered how at the age of fifteen she had gone through a trap doorway into a darkened room, to drink over a sheaf of black ribbons a last toast to a memory who had died in Italy – Prince Charles Edward Louis Casimir, an old man once known as the Young Pretender.

Three years later she met and married my father – half soldier, half scholar, and ten years her senior. He was almost immediately caught up in the French war; was given up for lost, and returned home only years later, a one-armed man who pursued his quiet life on little money and much hope, and who helped to produce me a year before he died from the result of French prisons and too much cold in the stone rooms of Edinburgh. My mother, her thoughts across the Atlantic, insisted on calling me Franklin.

I was seven when my grandfather died in the United States. My memories are only of a long succession of lawyers visiting our house above one of the narrowest and foulest wynds of Edinburgh, and of our translation to more substantial quarters in the New Town.

At the same time, the fortune which my grandfather had made in the Blue Grass country brought a change in my schooling, and it is he whom I must therefore thank for the chance of altering history. For without the support of my grandfather's money I should never have received adequate instruction in Edinburgh; without this, I should never have started, let alone completed, my studies at Cambridge; and without this background I would have been unable to concentrate my speculations on a device so terrible that its mere existence would banish the monstrous waste of war.

At Cambridge I indulged in the usual follies, and due to my Scottish accent and bellicose manner became involved in more brawls than my fellows. Yet I spent as much time as most in the inconvenient and ill-arranged buildings erected on the old Botanic Gardens for those who wished to probe into the mysteries of the Natural Sciences.

Today the Cavendish Laboratory stands on the same site, and who knows what wonders will not be discovered within its walls. Yet when I read of the latest mysteries being unravelled within the physical sciences I think of an old colleague who clambered about the Alps twenty years ago. At the club he would listen intently as young men discussed forthcoming 'first' ascents. When they moved away there would come a booming chuckle dissolving into, 'When they *do* get up – if they do – they'll find a cairn; and, if they trouble to look, my card beneath it.' Now, as science marches on towards whatever goal destiny allows, I think of how its great men will, when the truth comes out, find my card awaiting them.

I can date from a certain afternoon in the year 1833, when I was still an undergraduate, the moment when mere speculation began to crystallize into the faintest hint of possibility.

That year, my enthusiasm caused me to attend the meeting of the British Association in Cambridge. As you will know, it was the occasion on which Dalton's grant was officially announced – a stipend of £150 a year wrung from the Crown. I was personally interested, since much of Dalton's work had deeply affected me. So I was bold enough to follow the great man at a distance, and to surprise him as he conversed with a number of companions, sitting beneath the trees by the Backs and discussing, as I realized when I approached, the interrelationship of science and the State. Here my boldness failed and I stood at a distance, watching as the changing patterns of the leaves moved across their faces.

Dalton was already an old man, roughly built but neatly dressed in his Quaker costume of knee-breeches, dark-grey stockings and buckled shoes. His countenance was kindly if reserved. Suddenly he looked up.

'Come in, young man, come in,' he said. 'We are only settling the fate of the Government.'

I joined the group, literally sitting at Dalton's feet, a prophetic event for a man of my future, and listening as he and his companions mulled over the problems of arousing interest in the natural sciences. All at once Dalton looked down and asked what I was studying.

'Atoms, sir,' I replied.

The great man looked at me, saying nothing. Then he asked what I hoped to achieve by my study. Even five years later I would have been more circumspect. As it was, I said that I wanted to change the world.

'Only that,' he said. 'A common enough ambition.'

Then he looked at me again. 'You must tell me of your studies,' he said, rising from the bench, putting his hand on my shoulder, and half-leading me away from his companions.

As we talked, he repeated his famous conclusion: 'That every species of pure elastic fluid has its particles globular and all of a size; but that no two species agree

14

in the size of their particles, the pressure and temperature being the same.'

He had reacted as I had desired. And I then put to him the question which I had prepared.

John Dalton was a dour man. I knew this, yet was surprised by his reply. He stopped in his tracks and for a moment remained still, slowly passing his large and rough hand back and forth across his under-jaw.

Then he looked at me piercingly. 'Do not tamper, sir,' he said. 'Do not tamper.'

From that day on, I began to believe that I might not live in vain. Whether I have or not is a matter on which you must make up your own mind. And it is to help in your judgment that I am now setting down my personal story, sitting on the deck of Her Majesty's latest gunboat as she steams back through the Indian Ocean, returning from the brief campaign in which my weapon was at last, and with such strange consequences, deployed on the field of battle. Although, after all these years, I may be confused on minor details, you will discover as you read my story that about important events my mind is as clear as when I first met Dalton.

Do not tamper! Indeed for a while I saw little chance. But Dalton and his simple seven words by the peaceful Backs set me thinking even harder than before.

But I was still in my early twenties. I knew that a fortune was tied up in my mother's name and would eventually come to me; and I knew that I would never have to bear the drudgery of mere work for money. So I mixed with the fellows of my time, one of whom was to play a part in my story. This was Alfred, Lord Tennyson.

The man whom you will think of only as the Poet Laureate went up to Trinity two years before me. We

15

were different in almost every way – he gentle and loving the landscape; I prone to pick a quarrel for the fight that would result, and more interested in the hard substance of matter itself than in his airy imaginings. Yet we became friends. More than once I visited the vicarage at Somersby; and it was from Somersby that one spring morning in the mid-1830s I rode out with Alfred to Wainfleet, where we left the horses for a long meditative stroll along a coastline of sedge and fallow.

I can see him now as he was then, and I can understand how the local fishermen, coming upon him as they often did while he wandered alone, declaiming the words he had found and searching for those beyond his reach, believed him to be mad.

That morning he was jubilant, with some great epic bubbling in his mind, and it was only by chance that when he started upon the future state of the world I mentioned that wars might one day end.

At first he laughed unbelievingly. But I said – I realize now what risks I took – that man might some day contrive a weapon so fearful that no despot would dare to use war as policy, so great would be the fear for his own kith and kin.

'This,' he said, 'would be another side of the vision.' I did not understand him.

'But men will fly,' he continued. 'Maybe not within our lifetime, but in the future. I already have it here,' and he tapped his head, 'great argosies of airborne ships, dropping their costly bales wherever the industries of the world need them.

'And now you –' he looked at me and, striding on, kicked indignantly at a heap of pebbles, which spluttered out across the islands ' – you have filled in what I always knew must be the other side of science. The warriors of the world will no longer keep their feet on the earth or their ships on the oceans. If your dream comes true we shall hear the heavens filled with shouting . . .'

He was slightly ahead of me, and now he stopped and looked back. The picture of him, dark against the golden sands, with the wide wastes of the Lincolnshire flats behind, was something never to be forgotten.

'The heavens filled with shouting,' he declaimed, 'and if you are right, Huxtable, as I am afraid you may be, there will rain a ghastly dew.'

I tried to calm him down as we walked on, but without avail. He repeated the words again and again. 'Hear the heavens fill with shouting, and there rains a ghastly dew – from the world's – no, not the world's – from the nation's flying battle fleets . . .'

I realized that I was watching a wonder of creation. I could not see where the war of the future came in, but when Tennyson persisted I would not presume to complain.

Soon we were coming up to Gibraltar Point. He looked across to the grey line cut clear against the spring sky.

'Not battle fleets,' he said. 'Navies, the navies of the world – the nations' airy navies grappling . . . grappling . . .'

He turned to me perplexed, as though it were my fault that his words were running out. All unconsciously I looked up to the sky where, for all I knew, Tennyson's airy navies might be grappling even before my life was spent. As I gazed, two huge cathedrals of white cumulus began to part. Between them, widening as we watched, was the light blue of the upper atmosphere, to the scientist but a prelude to the deeper hues of space itself.

'Of course!' Tennyson brought his hands together in what was almost an attitude of prayer. 'Of course ... the nations' airy navies grappling in the central blue.'

Then he was away again, with the words tumbling out and almost pleading to be put into proper order.

I have never forgotten the impact which that morning's walk made on me. In some ways it took me past a milestone, for from that day the impetus of my efforts increased. I think it may have been due to Tennyson's wild eyes and his belief that there are some men who can see into the future.

Henceforth, overcoming those problems which barred the way ahead was to be the main object of my working life. I say 'working', but that is hardly the word. For within a short while of my coming down from Cambridge two important events took place. My mother died – and with her death there came to me a wealth that had been accumulating for years. Secondly, I launched out on to seas quite as perilous as those of science – I mean the seas of matrimony.

Amelia, who was to help me through the worries of a troubled life – even if she could not, for reasons of security, be said to share them – was only slightly older than myself, well endowed not only with good looks but with that other helper-along of a happy marriage, private means. Her estate in Wiltshire became our estate, while to my town establishment in Hanover Square I was able to add my own laboratory. This was most helpful; poverty may, as Napoleon said, be the best school for a soldier, but it is a great handicap to a scientist.

However, marriage brought me more than Amelia and

her ample competence. It brought me Dobbin, then a young retainer on her estate and by now almost an extension of myself – half hero, half buffoon, a man who appears to act without prompting from the mental processes, yet who in practical matters can be, I must admit, a dozen steps ahead of me.

Dobbin sits beside me as I write these words, still gimlet-eyed and keen, almost as old as I am, slightly disreputable as men of his kind are apt to be when they age; yet one who might have been an inventive genius had he been born into another class – ex-Sergeant Dobbin, the eternal sergeant down the ages, always confident that he knows more than his master.

On that morning when he first appeared in Hanover Square, his silhouette was almost quadrilateral in the open door of my laboratory. He had been sent with some papers I had forgotten during our recent visit to Ovington Tracey, but I did not know what manner of man would be bringing them.

'Dobbin, sir,' he said. He looked at me somewhat critically as he held out the package. 'Ex-Sergeant Dobbin. 95th Rifles and La Haye Sainte, sir.'

He was of indeterminate age, but even then I thought he looked far too young for Waterloo. He was almost as broad as high, yet well-built in spite of the disproportion, and with fine, almost beautiful hands. He seemed to have been carved by the winds rather than to have grown, a natural product of those Western Downs on which he had been reared.

He was intrigued by the apparatus on the nearest bench, and perhaps he was a little perplexed. I was a little perplexed myself, since I had spent two days trying to assemble the complexity of test-tubes and draining devices as I wished. Nowadays the matter would be simple; fifty years ago, all a man's ingenuity was required.

Dobbin looked at the large retort on the far end of the bench and followed with his eye the path of the material which seeped from it. He knew nothing of the process, yet he could see that I wished a product to be heated here, an essence to be drawn off there, the result to be treated in such and such a way.

I watched him. A hand half stretched out and he looked at me.

'If a bracket were supported here, sir,' he said, 'It might carry this tube, and then . . .'

I nodded, for the idea was about to occur to me. Material was to hand. I indicated it and Dobbin brought it. He held, while I fixed. 'If, sir,' he said, 'you were to move . . .' I looked at him and nodded again. He was exceedingly bright to see what I had in mind.

Without asking, he took off his jacket. Almost hypnotized, I removed mine.

'There was a time in the East, sir, when we needed water badly,' he said as we worked away. 'We had to construct a wooden pipeline . . .' He handed me a piece of tubing; I obediently held it as he talked on. Within half an hour we had re-modelled my apparatus. Amelia found us mightily pleased with one another.

I quickly saw that Dobbin would be invaluable. So he was, although I grew a little tired of his old soldier's tales and have never discovered exactly what campaigns he really served in. Unless he was a drummer-boy in baby-clothes he never saw Waterloo – except from a stage-coach years afterwards.

However, Dobbin was transferred from Wiltshire to London. He became my manservant – or, to be more accurate, my manservant-cum-laboratory-assistant – who would always respond, when the machinery of research became odious, to the request: 'Carry on, Dobbin.'

During the months that followed I often did need a helpful response in the laboratory, since my mind was now packed full with developments of the possibility I had hinted at to Dalton. I worked hard, although most of my contemporaries, who knew nothing of the matter, no doubt considered that I was a dilettante, pirouetting along the border of science. I approached my task purely from the theoretical side. I pushed my chemical researches no farther, tackled only the mathematics of the riddle as I saw it, and eventually arrived, expectantly, on the far side of the problem. And I then saw that if all my prognostications were correct they would be proven so by the potentials of a material greatly different from any which were among the common coins of science.

I turned back to the Records, to the Transactions. There, of course, was the answer. About half a century earlier Martin Klaproth had discovered a new heavy material; he had named it after the planet which Herschel had recently discovered. And although Berzelius and his supporters were putting new constructions on the subject, I felt that my answer must lie here – in uranium.

Klaproth was long dead, his son but recently so. I noted that one of Klaproth's books was in translation – *Observations Relative to the Mineralogical and Chemical History of the Fossils of Cornwall*. Until now I had paid no attention to it; yet now it drew me and I searched it for significance. As I re-read the *Observations*, one phrase lodged in my mind. For the peculiarity of Cornish fossils provided, it was claimed, 'rich materials for the increase of geological and mineralogical knowledge'. Perhaps the phrase was a chance one. Perhaps it hinted at more than even Klaproth knew. I determined to find out.

With the spring we were to make a leisurely tour of the West and it would be easy to include the land beyond the Tamar. Included it was, although of our journey to the farthest west and then back through the follies of Bath to Ovington Tracey and so to London I will recount only two incidents. Both were vital to construction of the ultimate weapon.

The first of these seminal events occurred on our return through Penwith from the Land's End, up that rocky finger of desolation whose tin mines I made it my business to inspect. They stood then, as they still stand, with their tall stacks bleak against the breakered Atlantic as though the Midlands had been moved two hundred miles south-west.

It was on the cliffs – even now I am reluctant to be more specific – that I stood hearing the piston-beat of the rollers surging up through the chasms of the rocks below and the rhythmical clank of machinery as it lowered the men into the workings. The owners had pushed the adits out dangerously and well, had lost only a few lives in the process, and rightly disregarded complaints that the men below ground could hear the waves beating above them. It must have been unpleasant but no more – 'Better,' as Dobbin put it, 'than the hum of the cannon-ball.'

I had already got my specimens during the preceding few days, and was reluctant to take more. Yet as we passed the spoil-heap, returning to the carriage which would take us to Amelia and her maids, securely sunning themselves in St. Ives, Dobbin insisted on fingering a piece of the curious material that lay there. It was pitch-like in quality and I almost dissuaded him from handling it.

'Only a small piece, sir,' he begged. 'I have known

times when the smallest mite was of use for an unexpected purpose.' He winked without apparent reason; before I could stop him he had kicked off a lump as big as a man's fist and, our canvas collecting bag being full, had slipped it into his pocket.

Being careful in all such matters I noted the locality, the time and the date.* But I thought no more of it, neither when we rejoined Amelia nor on our journey back to Ovington Tracey.

On our way we stopped at the Fox Talbots', where my old friend, master of the magnificent Lacock, was already engrossed with his project for outlining nature not with pencil or with pen but with rays of natural light.† Now that photography is established, it will be difficult to understand our wonder at Talbot's little hobby, our disbelief of his claim that he could make the sun do the artist's work and imprint on paper, without visible means, the lines of the actual world. It was, of course, easier for me than for Amelia to comprehend the art. As Talbot exposed the shapes of leaves to his sensitized paper, produced their silhouettes for us, and then went to the contrivance with which he was recording the actual shapes of his home, I could understand what he was about. The chemical processes were comprehensible, and we discussed much that went far beyond the women, or for that matter beyond Dobbin who made frequent appearances on one pretext or another, as

*By 1850 uranium had been found in Saxony, Bohemia and Cornwall, usually in patches. In 1889 a continuous lode containing it was found in Cornwall's Union Mine.

†William Henry Fox Talbot (1800–77), whose early photographic discoveries were first reported to the Royal Institution by Faraday on Jan. 25th, 1839, was also a considerable mathematician whose 'Researches in the Integral Calculus' had been published in the *Philosophical Transactions* three years earlier.

though fearful of missing some fact to be garnered and stored for future use.

Before we left I handed over to him two plates with which our host had entrusted me: plates duly sensitized by a new process of which he seemed to be certain, and with which I promised to record the form of some leaves which as I explained – though I was really anxious to see if the process worked in my hands as well – could be found only in the grounds of Ovington Tracey.

We left Lacock in the morning. We were home by noon, and in the afternoon light I exposed my carefully wrapped plates according to the instructions of Mr. Fox Talbot. I waited the exact time, I took the necessary precautions, I applied the chemicals in the correct order. And as I waited for the results to appear, I knew that something was wrong. Each of the plates which I had treasured and processed so carefully was completely and irremediably, as we would now say, 'Fogged'.*

Dobbin slowly shook his head. 'It just can't happen, sir,' he said, perambulating his head as though it were a Chinese doll's about to come loose.

He looked at me. 'Mr. Fox Talbot would not lie, sir,' he said. 'You would not err.' He stretched back into a corner of the little workroom and held up the small bag in which he had carried the plates. He delved and drew from it the carefully wrapped black lump from the spoil-heap in Cornwall.

'The logic of it is, sir,' said Dobbin, 'that this must be the cause.'

Simple, honest Dobbin. He had, I realized as the tea-bell rang, stumbled on the secret – or, to be more accurate, he had enabled me to stumble on it.

*Much as Becquerel's plates were fogged in 1896, giving the Curies the clue to radioactivity.

'How curious,' I said. 'How very, very curious' – disguising the excitement I felt welling up within me as one realization tumbled into another. In less time than it takes to describe, I saw that chance had kicked open the penultimate door.

As I left Dobbin to join Amelia I realized that the solution of one problem had merely set an even more difficult one. We talked of our successful journey, of country management, and I explained that there had been some misadventure with the plates. But I knew that I was confronted with the greatest riddle of all.

My prognostications had been correct. It was clear that in some materials the elemental forces of the world were in a state of constant disintegration. Yet why, I asked myself for many an hour, did they allow the world itself to continue? How was it possible that they had not exploded in a fury which might be the world's salvation could I but harness it?

During the next few weeks, as I returned to my study and mulled over the incident – which I was careful to repeat with a second set of plates after a specious story to Talbot – as I did this, I realized certain facts.

It became clear that this peculiar substance, present in some infinitesimally small amount in the Cornish material, must itself be locked to another, very like it in composition but somehow moderating in its effect.

That was the way I saw it, and if there were vast gaps in my theoretical knowledge it was a chasm in my practical knowledge that worried me more. For these two substances, I postulated, must be so similar, varying in a way of which we knew so little, that to separate one from the other would be impossible. And without that separation there would be no explosion, no weapon. Differences there must be, but to utilize these differences, I foresaw, would be quite beyond what Jeremy Bentham had called, half a century earlier, the technology of the day.

Good fortune had brought me thus far, before the stoutest door of all. I had no suspicion that better fortune was to show me the way through.

That summer we spent much time at Ovington Tracey, riding about the glorious downland, travelling as far afield as Gloucestershire or Dorset, and vastly enjoying ourselves. At least, Amelia enjoyed herself. For me, much of the pleasure which I simulated was overborne by the black shadow of increasing frustration. I had come so far. I was certain that only one problem remained.

The solution came during a magnificent September. We were staying with Amelia's fashionable friends in Dorchester and I made an excuse – scientific, I hope – to ride out for the day with Dobbin. He had travelled much of the world – or so he said – but had never visited a natural wonder that existed so near his home county. I mean, of course, the Chesil Bank, that sixteen-mile beach of stones that runs from Portland to Bridport. Its pebbles to the east are the size of roundshot; the farther west one goes the smaller they become, in proper order.

By noon we were sitting above the sea, Portland standing high like a mountain on our left, the sweep of Lyme Bay before us, and I ready to instruct Dobbin to whom I had already shown the beach.

'In the dark, sir,' he said, 'a man would know his part of the beach by pebble-size.' As I told him, many smugglers had done so.

'The current, sir, sweeping in, must hold the stones as a magnet holds filings,' he went on. 'The heaviest in one place, the next heaviest next door – and so on.' He nodded as though agreeing with Nature.

'Why, sir, at Bridport they must be no more than sand in size.' They were indeed – Golden Pea Gravel, the very best of its kind.

I assented approvingly as Dobbin looked at me with great knowledge in his eyes. 'I remember years ago, sir,' he said, 'we had reached the Danube and found sand as white as snow. The very horses began to shiver and we had to separate them . . .' He babbled on.

To separate them. A current. As a magnet holds filings. The heaviest first, and then the next. I looked up towards the sky and in my inspiration I thought back to Tennyson and *his* inspiration on another seashore.

We rode back, I still silent and Dobbin still talkative. 'You must be thinking, sir,' he said, 'of the stones and the magnetic current.'

I was indeed. And of much else.

That evening Amelia noticed a new excitement about me. I will explain why.

Even today the force of magnetism, that primeval power from the farthest past, still maintains the grandeur of its ultimate mystery; fifty years ago it retained still more. But I had often thought that there might be some new and unsuspected connection between this force and the electricity which Faraday was beginning to harness to the wants of mankind. So far I had seen no reason to test my idea, nor method of utilizing it were I right. Now I could either make or mar my theory – and, if it were 'make', might break through from theory to practice in my plan to produce a weapon such as the world had never contemplated.

Dobbin with his simple analogies had wrought better than he knew. The explicable current of the sea could select pebbles according to their weight; if the link which I suspected did exist in nature, might it not be used to turn the force of magnetism back upon itself, to act upon the very particles of matter and thus separate, into its components, the material which had ruined Fox Talbot's plates?

There was, indeed, such a link. I found it. And although men have advanced far since those distant days, that link still remains unfound by any other. Long may it remain so.

We returned to Ovington Tracey. We returned to London. And I knew that I had some four months of difficult work before me, months during which I would be sucked of energy and left prostrate by the intellectual exercise still required.

Considerable apparatus was needed and here, as always, Dobbin was invaluable. Naturally I told him nothing of the enterprise – only that I was, as I put it, experimenting with a device which might, if successful, control the weather. His comment was queerly apposite.

'Weather needs altering, sir,' he said. 'But don't make it too good or you'll give the world good campaigning twelve months a year. That'll never do, sir. If you could go the other way, make it selective, give a twelve-month frost where you wanted it, why then, sir, you could stop all wars.'

Would I, I wondered, do just that?

The servants were accustomed to being shut from my laboratory, but as my work moved towards its climax, it became the turn of Dobbin as well. He was not resentful. 'You can pass on, sir, all it is necessary to tell,' he said. 'No more and no less, sir, as the Duke said when it came to setting troops at a town. Enough is enough.'

By mid-December all was ready. I did not, of course, intend to build a bomb in my home. But I knew that all now hung on one experiment. If I had been correct, the process would work; and I already had grandiose plans as to what I should next do.

I went into my laboratory and locked the door. I looked about me, and I could congratulate myself that before the age of thirty I had come so far. On my right the tall double windows which looked out on to the square were well curtained. On my left were the shelves of those books which were of little account in my study but which here, in my workroom as it were, formed the tools of my trade. Before me were my benches.

There was much to be done.

Two hours later I was nearing the decisive stage.

On the centre of a bench, alone in the place which I had cleared for its occupation, stood my especial piece of apparatus – a cylinder only some three foot long, and but two high, constructed in glass of a green, almost metallic consistency, which at times reflected from the light above a scintillating sparkle as though it had some great secret to unfold.

I now came to the crux of my experiment. It was not only that I had various ingredients to mix together; of such is but the stuff of alchemy. I had also to subject them, as only I knew how, to the natural forces whose key had been delivered to me.

I looked at the glass and I experienced a sudden shock as its whole appearance changed, in an instant, for no apparent reason. I glanced back towards the curtains; what had astounded me was but the result of the lamplighter on his evening round, reaching up with his long pole and setting fire to the gas-lamps in the square below.

I was nervous, of course. Who, in such circumstances, could hope to be otherwise? Yet I thought back to my ancestors, and I thought of Montrose. I did not think that my deserts were small. I did not fear my fate too much. I had come to the turning point of my life and I was not only willing but determined to win or lose it all.

I connected two wires. I began to turn a handle.

I was still looking through the green glass. The cataclysmic explosion that I had most irrationally half-feared had not taken place. Instead there showed, in the heart of the green world before me, just what I had hoped to see: a narrow, transitory and almost invisible line of light, as though a comet had passed through a miniature sky – and I thought of the countryman's saying: 'a life come and a life gone.'

I felt that I had witnessed a tremor in the heart of nature. It was a tremor which was to shake the world.

As I stepped back from my bench, I was sweating in the cold of that late December evening.

I glanced at my watch and was astonished to find that I had been four hours at my task. As I did so there descended a good augury for the future. Through the long purple curtains came the voices of children in the square outside, bringing the sounds of that carol so encouraged by Prince Albert.

'Silent night,' they sang. 'Holy night.'

Holy night, indeed.

I looked once again at my green glass cylinder, turned out the lamps, locked the doors behind me and descended the stairs, well satisfied, towards what I knew would be an excellent dinner.

2: Birth

I had looked into the very arcana of Nature. I knew where duty lay.

Although I had scarcely dared to believe that such a situation might arise, I had always hoped for it; and I had taken such steps as I felt might be necessary to exploit it.

I had contributed to the learned journals. I had cultivated the acquaintance of men of utility. And there can be little doubt that in the events which were now to take place I was assisted by the social activities of my dear wife – even though she herself knew nothing of the essential matter. For I was able to secure, without too much difficulty or delay, that first necessity, an interview with the Prime Minister. The work of the study had been completed; now I was to thrust myself out into the world.

I dressed with particular care, well knowing how much can depend on appearances in even the gravest concerns. What sort of man was it, I asked myself, from whom Sir Robert, back in the saddle again, was to hear an account of how war could be stopped for ever? The mirror gave me my answer. I was of moderate height and build, well set rather than graceful, and I had never tried to condition myself to the dandyism of the times. My features were bold rather than beautiful, though I was glad to note the dark eyes which I inherited from my mother and the thick raven hair which I wore as long as the age demanded. I bowed to convention so far as to wear the short 'sides', as thick and dark as my hair, but adopted the fashion of being clean-shaven, not wishing to conceal my lips under a bush of hair – or for that matter the jaw which I set to the world with a fair measure of determination.

My stock was new, and of a lustre which almost shone. My clothes were sober, as befitted a man of science, but as I scrutinized them in the full-length mirror of my room I was well satisfied by the fact that they were cut in the latest manner. I had never been ambitious of fashion, but from the earliest days of a hard childhood, before fortune came from the States, I had been taught to make the best of myself. Sir Robert, I knew, would be seeing no hole-and-corner professor from some undistinguished laboratory, but a man who could stand on his own feet.

What is more, there was my manservant – or call him my retainer, for I by this time thought of Dobbin in almost feudal terms, a part of the joint human enterprise which we were together pressing forward.

For the occasion I had re-accoutred him, so that while Dobbin was but a man to be left at the postern gate of great events he would yet show to the guards what manner of man it was who had entered.

Pompous words, you may think. But although I have had less respect for such things as I grow older I have learned that the rest of the world does not agree – and I chuckle as I realize how much the fools set on the flummery.

However, I knew that all this presentation, necessary though it was, counted for little when weighed against the essential. I believed. I believed that my work had shown me a method of creating a device so destructively powerful that it would banish the idea of war from our planet. And I believed, also, that the confidence which all genuine men of science should have in their ideals would illuminate our interview and convince Sir Robert not only of my sincerity but also of my ability to do what I promised.

I had not before seen the Prime Minister at close quarters. When I did so I found him more impressive than I had been led to expect. He was lofty in stature and large in make, tending to be portly but still handsome. Above such a full body, his head appeared small although well formed, with regular features below a broad forehead. His movements still betrayed, in spite of the sense of power which infused them, that slight hesitation or nervousness which I had heard compared to that of a cat. His manner was somewhat shy, more awkward than I had expected of a politician, yet it became clear from our opening exchanges that he was a man of ripe culture and varied information.

The room into which I had been shown was long and narrow, made even more so by the bookshelves with which it was lined and which, together with the half-partitions of the farther part, produced a certain gloom.

Sir Robert was at this period bearing heavy burdens, but he did not hurry on to the subject of my visit. Instead, he asked my views on his proposal to introduce an Income Tax – and took it in good part when I said that the suggestion appeared revolutionary; and only after a general discussion during which we ranged over the affairs of the world, did he come to the subject I most dearly desired. He had, I later surmised, been testing the soundness of my opinions – for reasons that were to become evident.

Knowing that politicians are frequently practical men

of little vision, I concealed the mainspring of my enterprise, the abolition of war. Instead, I merely repeated what I had outlined in my initial letter – that I had discovered a method of producing a new weapon of almost unimaginable power.

The Prime Minister asked how many men it would kill, and I told him that it would kill as many as he wished. He then asked me to explain further, and I did my best to enlighten him on the general principles of the processes involved. It was here that he seemed to evince but small interest, yet all at once took down a folio volume, brought it to the table beside me, and opened it to reveal a large-scale map.

'Professor Huxtable,' he said, 'am I to understand that if your device was left or thrown here, then all would be killed within a quarter of a mile?'

I followed his outstretched finger and found myself gazing at a representation of the country south of Waterloo. It was obvious that my attempt to explain the nature of the device had been unsuccessful.

'Sir,' I explained, 'the matter is of totally different order. If you wished, a complete destruction might be confined to as little as a quarter-mile. But it could quite easily be to one mile, two miles – perhaps even ten.'

The Prime Minister then brought a folder from the far side of the room, and sat opposite me.

'Professor,' he said, tapping what I saw were copies of various papers I had written during the last few years, 'when I received your request for an appointment, I instructed my secretary to obtain details of your various works. Otherwise I should by now be quite certain that you are mad. As it is, I must merely consider the possibility.'

Then, half-turning, Sir Robert asked, 'What does the Duke say? Is it really possible?'

I saw, to my surprise, that we were not alone. From the far end of the room, from between the shadows provided by the half-shut doors of the Private Secretary's room where he had been standing immobile, there emerged a familiar figure. Much as I deplored the carnage which had been so necessary at Waterloo, no one in his proper mind could but admire Wellington.

He advanced slowly, tight-lipped, with across his mouth a thin smile of belief.

'Possible? Is anything impossible? As I've said before, read the papers.'

For a moment I wondered what his reaction would be. Then I remembered a phrase from his dispatch from the field – 'nothing except a battle lost can be half so melancholy as a battle won.'

He regarded me intently for a moment, as if he wished to see not the calculations within my mind but whether I had the light of battle in my eyes. Then he spoke.

'You will put all us military men out of business, Professor Huxtable. At least, I hope you will, although I still doubt the common sense of the human race.' He nodded towards Sir Robert as he said to me: 'Tell him what you want for Her Majesty's bomb.'

I explained that my device must be made and tested. That it would require money, and men. And I demanded secrecy also – for my own sake as well as for theirs. For there was always, though the prospect was too frightful to contemplate, the remote possibility that my calculations might have been wrong – even that my experiment might lead only to a distressing catastrophe.

Sir Robert nodded gravely, said that there was already

enough on his mind to keep a regiment of men busy, and enjoined me to be patient.

It was, perhaps strangely, with the Duke that I felt most in accord. As I turned to leave he took me by the hand. Looking at me from beneath those craggy brows, he said merely: 'Good fortune, Huxtable.'

I left Downing Street in high fettle. Dobbin saw me into my carriage and joined me there, for by this time he had become a privileged indispensable.

For once it was I who could start first. I turned to him, with a remark I have never let him forget. 'Dobbin,' I said, 'as I was saying to the Duke a few moments ago . . .' After that, I felt him bow whenever I entered the room.

Peel had enjoined me to be patient, and my patience had to last so long that I feared the moves over slavery and the Riots had caused my proposal to be forgotten in the wash of what were considered to be more important things. Then, unexpectedly, the Summons came. I was to present myself before Her Majesty.

It was with interest, as much as with trepidation, and bearing in my head a mass of instructions from Amelia who wished to know many trivial details about the Queen, that I drove down to Windsor on a morning rich in possibilities.

It was a fine warm day and the river was a good sight with its watermen and its pleasure-seekers. More than one may well have been mourning a loved one lost in Afghanistan and I had difficulty in staunching Dobbin's views on the subject.

I need give no more than a brief account of my Audience. I was much impressed. The Queen was really quite beautiful; not tall, of course, but with eyes which followed all one said.

'We understand, Professor Huxtable, that you have invented a device which would be of use to our Army,' she began. 'We wish you to tell us about it.'

I did my best, and it was somehow easier than with the Prime Minister. Her Majesty showed no sign of scientific training. Yet she had a facility for asking pertinent questions. Thus at one point she turned from her seat by the window and with the frankest of expressions asked. 'What exactly, Professor Huxtable, are we to understand by . . .?' And here she pronounced a single word which lay at the very kernel of my explanation. I realized that she had been understanding me even better than I had imagined.

When I had ceased speaking, Her Majesty remained motionless, and for what must have been two full minutes I could hear only the solemn ticking of a fine time-piece in the room behind me, and the sound of the common people on the river beyond the open window.

'Professor Huxtable,' said Her Majesty at last, 'you have discovered something of great moment to our country.'

I was about to thank her as she added, 'And to the peoples of all the world. We are not certain that it is a *good* thing.'

With a woman's intuition she must have sensed the disappointment that I tried to keep from my face.

'Professor,' she said, 'you may well be a benefactor to mankind. That is one of the things we must try to discover. Prince Albert tells me that we stand upon the margin of a great sea, an ocean of discovery, and that the voyage which our age will make upon it will alter the prospects of the world. He tells me, also, that there will be dangers as we learn to understand in more detail the workings of the natural laws.

'We cannot be certain, Professor Huxtable, that the consequences flowing from your device will be as simple as you believe. However – ' and here she turned and looked at me in the most friendly manner ' – however, we must surely first be *practical*. We must first ensure that your device has all the properties which you attribute to it. We think that you should build it. Then we can ensure, by means of an experiment, that you are correct.'

I realized that the Audience was over.

I thanked Her Majesty and left. The next stage of my enterprise must now be put in hand.

It was clear from the inquiries which I had already made that the spoil which had confounded Fox Talbot's invention was available in large quantities at low cost. But I did not wish to arouse suspicions; and since there was money available I thought it wisest to acquire an interest in tin.

Quite apart from my main ambition I thought there might truly be financial possibilities in the chemical exploitation not only of the metal itself but of the waste products of our expanding industrial age. Even were I wrong, such activities would help to disguise the vital work. As I told Amelia, science applied to industry as well as science pursued for its own sake might bring awards, letters after one's name, or even that dubbing on the shoulders that is so delightful to a man who can expect nothing else, and is therefore doubly delightful to his wife.

It was necessary for us to have our own factory, which we set up at a convenient spot between Cornwall and the capital and which did conjure up a great variety of useful products from the material which we handled. Perhaps Dobbin, whom I used to keep matters up to the mark, was of greater worth than I even now imagine. Perhaps we were lucky. Whatever the reason, our enterprise prospered. More important, there was not the slightest suspicion that after one pound of the dross had been rendered down the product was itself diminished to a much smaller quantity by Professor Huxtable in the private laboratory of the little works. It was then taken in the same Professor's own private pockets to his London home. And here, in his own private time, what had been reduced to fractions of an ounce was submitted to the tensions of his own apparatus and reduced still further.

It was lengthy work. It was also complicated, and I can see future investigators grubbing around to find out exactly how I had done what I had done. I wish them luck. They will need it.

Eventually my device neared completion – or, for the sake of accuracy, the two complementary halves of my device. For its immense capabilities were only to be transmuted from promise to reality when more than a certain quantity of its vital ingredient was assembled in close proximity. Thus it had been necessary for me to plan the weapon in two halves, each containing a quantity less than the critical mass. When the moment for detonation arrived the two halves would be brought together, the male portion united with the female, thus producing the desired quantity of essential material and with it an explosion which my calculations convinced me would be of gigantic proportions.

When, therefore, I had acquired half the essential poundage, I used this to fill one-half of the device in the laboratory I had built at Ovington Tracey in the form of a two-storey tower, still known as Huxtable's Folly. In Hanover Square, safely distant from this male half of the device, I went on with the work of separation; and when the second half of the required poundage had been prepared, I poured this into the female half of my weapon.

So far so good. There was, however, an impediment. For while I knew that the most cataclysmic explosion produced by man would result from the union of the male and female halves, one question remained unanswered: how close to one another could they be brought before the influence of one impinged upon the influence of the other?

How close, indeed! My work suggested that this critical distance might be virtually non-existent – that it would be necessary for the male half to be butted up firmly against the female half before the prognosticated effect took place. Yet I was not certain. It was possible that the explosion might be set off if the two portions were brought within a few inches of one another; perhaps a few feet might be dangerous. Perhaps even a few yards.

Herein lay my trouble. For to eliminate any possibility of disaster I had to ensure that male and female were kept at least some hundreds of yards apart until the time for detonation arrived, a requirement which added much to my work.

When all was ready, I informed the Prime Minister, with whom I had had more than one meeting. Then, for the first time, I was brought into contact with the gentlemen of Whitehall.

The question of secrecy had naturally been raised at an early stage. It was the Duke, subtle but outspoken even in old age, who had provided the solution to this vexatious problem. 'To attempt complete secrecy is the resort of fools,' he said. 'In this case it would be idiocy.

All the business of life is but a reflection of the business of war, an endeavour to find out what you don't know from what you do – a guessing about what's on the other side of the hill.'*

Peel nodded as though at the words of a master.

'Someone,' Wellington continued, 'always does know something.'

I thought of Dobbin as Wellington looked round and smiled. 'You must ensure that it is enough to lead people astray.'

There was thus official blessing for my idea – that in the minds of those few who did have to know of the experiment, the scheme should be fogged by suggestions of a purely meteorological device.

Even so, such was the nature of the weapon, matters would surely arise which would be questioned in Whitehall?

'When those matters do arise,' said Wellington, brushing my remarks aside as his cavalry might have overrun a piquet, 'then, my dear Huxtable, you will obtain the Prime Minister's intervention. You will have his support. Paths will be smoothed. You will get what you want.'

All I had to do, he went on, was to send a brief note. 'There will be no questions asked,' the Duke continued. 'All doubts will be set at rest by a mere suggestion; a suggestion that the Prime Minister is grateful to you for help in extricating him from one of his entanglements.'

For a moment he seemed sincerely shocked at the expression on my face. 'Good God, Huxtable,' he exploded, 'all men have entanglements.'

So be it.

*See *The Correspondence of the late Right Honorable John Wilson Croker* edited by Louis J. Jennings (John Murray, 1885).

My first meetings with those who were to smooth my path were hardly propitious. When I explained that an area some ten miles by ten would be required for my experiment I was treated as a madman – until a note to the Prime Minister encouraged them to humour me.

I had thought of the wilder places of Scotland or Wales, but in the new and democratic age that had arrived it was not possible to clear such areas with ease. And there was also, as always, the question of compensation.

The Under-Secretary concerned, a young gentleman of no particular ability and believing my device to be within the normal run of life, was gravely concerned about all that hung on the word 'responsibility'. He thought of my weapon as hardly more than a penny firework, yet had lathered himself into a fine state of worry by the multitudinous problems which he feared he might, in some months' time, be called upon to settle.

Poor fellow, he was at his wits' end when he uttered, as a sudden bright thought, the one word 'Skindling', pulled the bell-rope behind him, and asked the messenger to send for the man.

The figure which now entered the room was more skin than flesh, more bone than skin. His tall frame was the stuff of skeletons and one expected him to rattle as he walked. The long narrow fingers, once beautiful, now seemed to be permanently grasped round some invisible quill. Skindling looked as though he had been weaned on parchment.

'We have a problem,' said the Under-Secretary. 'We wish to test a new device which Professor Huxtable has been perfecting at Woolwich' – I did not correct him – 'and his insistence, or perhaps I should say the insistence of the Prime Minister, on certain circumstances, has raised a difficulty.' It was, he said, a matter of responsibility.

As the position was explained, the Civil Servant stood almost motionless, merely moving his hands up and down the sides of his polished trousers much as a farm labourer cleans his hands at the end of a day's work. All the while, one realized, his brain was working.

Slowly, like the moon rising, a smile began to alter the contours of his face. He spoke in a high voice, hoarse but slightly hushed, and as he bent over his master's desk all I could catch were the words 'the Company', repeated more than once by the Under-Secretary with a mixture of awe and relief.

He relaxed, and settling more comfortably in his chair, he exclaimed, 'How ingenious! How very, very ingenious, Mr. Skindling.'

Ingenious maybe, but also aggravating. For when the man had been dismissed, the Under-Secretary, beaming as though the solution were his own, began by uttering the single word 'India'.

India it was in fact to be – that great sub-continent where, as I was to learn, the diminishing powers of the East India Company still lingered on, side by side with, or in some cases overlapping, those of the Crown. This uncertainty, as to who was responsible for what, was of course the reason, in the eyes of authority, for India's great charm as a demonstration site. Yet their advantage was my distress. The plans involved a lengthy period abroad, and it thus became necessary for me to concoct a story with which to deceive my poor wife. Yet herein there lay, unknown to me at the time, a great benefit for the future.

For as I speculated on how I could embroider my

story, I remembered Dalton – not Dalton with his new ideas about the atom but the very same Dalton who had studied Lakeland weather for years, the Dalton who had published his *Meteorological Essays* almost half a century before, and whose speciality thus contributed to my ideal camouflage. I was surely to take meteorological readings in the remoter parts of India, accumulating data with the help of the explosives in my two black boxes and hoping that I might one day be able not only to record but also to control the weather. This was but an expansion of the chance remark I had first made to Dobbin. This was the story told to my wife and to all except the favoured few – who knew that for 'meteorological' they might substitute 'military'.

Should anyone without authority penetrate this outer meteorological cover, they would find beneath it merely the trial of a slightly more powerful explosive – a deception locked within the deception. For even the selected few thought only of a bigger weapon; I thought of an apocalypse. All this was well conceived; three decades later, moreover, it was to help extricate me from one of those difficult corners into which my work was to thrust me.

Eventually all was ready. Although I was confident of success, it was impossible to remove the last niggling doubts. My calculations ordained that when my two black boxes were brought together, a phenomenon of an entirely new kind would be produced. But they were only calculations; when I stopped to consider, I had worries enough, though they were to be alleviated when I eventually acquired the two volumes of Tennyson's 'Poems'.

As I read the lines of 'Locksley Hall', for the first time but not for the last, I realized that on that Lincolnshire morning a few years before, Tennyson and I had touched on the same noble theme. Now it was my brain which was quickly leading to those times when

> ... the war-drum throbb'd no longer, and the
> battle-flags were furl'd
> In the Parliament of man, the Federation of
> the world.

Had I only known!

I studied the lean but determined face of Sir Archibald
as his punkah-wallahs tried to dissipate the Indian heat
which crept even through the blinds into the cool
marbled room. And I realized that yet another obstacle
had to be overcome – by deviousness, by manipulation,
by those actions which are so distasteful to a serious
scientist. I call him 'Sir Archibald' though I must admit
that he bore another name; but in my story there will
come times when an innate respect for the proprieties
induces me to alter the name of a man or a place.

'I really cannot see, Professor Huxtable, why we
should be submitted to such inconvenience,' he repeated.

I looked up at the gorgeous ceiling of the room, its
inlaid mother-o'-pearl iridescent even in the half-light.
I pretended to be deliberating how I could best present
him with the facts of life; yet as I determined that no
one should hinder the Queen's enterprise, I was also
remembering the events of the previous months.

We had sailed in a teak-built Bombay Indiaman of
nearly 1,000 tons. I say 'we', although the second half
of my weapon followed me a fortnight later, travelling
separately in Dobbin's good care – as it continued to
travel until the two halves combined to meet their destiny in the most remote part of Her Majesty's realm.

We crossed the line, when I, with others, was ducked,
shaved and made uncomfortable for the next week,
which I took in good part although I found the affair
frivolous. We neared the Cape, meeting great flocks of

albatross while still days out at sea. Then we sailed east on the last leg of our voyage, until I awoke one morning to find the azure blue of the ocean replaced by a ship's wake as muddy as a duckpond. That day I found a butterfly upon the cabin window, and soon after the watery horizon was fringed by the tops of palm-trees, by the pinnacles of distant lighthouses and other land-marks sailing on the horizon. The post-boat pulled to-wards us and I then perceived how we sailed between converging though still distant shores.

A Sampson steamer arrived. We were made fast to it and were drawn in on the flood tide, followed by a train of fishing boats and fruit boats, past mud-banks where the alligator could be discerned basking tree-trunk-like, past the occasional body which formed a raft for the devouring vultures, onward past the drifting sound of native music from the banks, and into the Hoogly which flows from the heart of the continent.*

Garden Reach and its villas came into view, and mo-ments later we were anchoring off Fort William, with Calcutta and its palaces shining before us in the morning light, bleached white and how like Venice, I thought. Now came the fuss of disembarkation, and I was im-mediately grateful for the foresight of the Duke, and the advices which he had sent ahead. For here, waiting to help me beat off the importunities of coolies and palan-quin-bearers, was the Honourable Henry Lane, A.D.C. to the Commander-in-Chief of the distant province where my device was to be tested.

Lane was in his early twenties, a well-proportioned young man. His family connections and his experience

*For further details of Indian life, see *Five Years in India*, by H. E. Lane, A.D.C. to the Commander-in-Chief, India (Col-burn, 1842).

of India combined to give him the entrée both to military society and to the prosperous civilian milieu which still lingered on as a memory of those days when the East India Company had been run by daring merchant-venturers. Thus during the next few weeks I was to be granted a most extraordinary experience.

For I – a scientist with little connection with commerce and even less with the Army – was to be drawn into an amazing world where 'John Company', that relic of Clive's time, still lived on in uneasy partnership with Her Majesty's administration. Its officials still 'shook the pagoda tree' from which there fell rich and ample rewards; its own troops still numbered many thousands, and Lane was but one among many officers who constantly lavished praise upon the Company's horse-artillery, the finest arm of its forces. And during the weeks that followed I was to enjoy – if that is the right word – many adventures which must sound strange to modern ears. Thus I breakfasted one morning with the head of the Company's opium factory; watched on another a parade of the Company's forces which would have done credit to the Horse Guards; and, as I shall explain, found great areas where Her Majesty's writ ran, when it ran at all, only with the thinly disguised permission of John Company.

How wise of Mr. Skindling, that desiccated figure from Whitehall, to shoulder off my enterprise into a land where success could be claimed for oneself – or any trouble neatly planted into another's lap!

The unloading of the male half of my device, securely boxed, was accomplished without trouble, and in the Garrison Mess I explained to Lieutenant Lane how the second half would be arriving with my man in a few days; how it was essential that the two boxes should be kept at least a quarter of a mile apart; but how, with this exception, I would require neither the facilities nor the great quantities of transport which he appeared to have envisaged. Lane, like many military men I have met, was more intelligent than one might expect from the popular idea of the soldier. He accepted my stipulation, though completely ignorant as to its reason, and within a few hours had arranged that we should be followed throughout the first stage of our journey by a second vessel which should remain one day behind us during our passage up-river.

I had expected to find in India a life of great strangeness. Yet I still was astounded by the vigour and the richness of the existence into which I was now swept, a life which began, at least in the cantonments, with the morning gun, fired at daybreak and the signal for rising. My boyhood with the Pentlands on our doorstep now served me well, and I noted polite surprise among the officers that a man of science not only was able to ride with them on their morning constitutionals but also knew how to handle a horse in open country.

It is no part of my story to tell how we travelled up the river in easy stages, moving comfortably in the almost draughtless 'flat' through whose Venetian blinds some welcome breeze was usually blowing. But I could feel that in spite of my peculiar position – sponsored by the military, as it were, yet obviously not of them – I was accepted into such company as an equal. At the cantonments, we hunted through country in which deer, antelope, wild hogs and peacocks rose before us in such numbers that I began to think all the continent's game must be concentrated in one spot. More than once we were invited to native durbars where the gaudily decorated elephants, the gold-embroidered saddle-cloths of the horses and the jewellery of the nabobs, loaded as they were in precious stones which would have kept a city in food for a week, all bore testimony to the splendour of Her Majesty's realm.

And behind us, stage by stage, day by day, there followed, strictly according to Lane's admirable plan, a vessel containing the female part of my device, a phrase which greatly amused the officers. With it came Dobbin, 'chaperoning the lady' as the military put it. He had wished, for reasons which I did not at once perceive, to be known throughout the journey as mere 'Dobbin', dropping the 'Sergeant' by which he was known in England; and it was as my assistant, a scientific technician, that he dutifully followed with his precious load. Only on my return did I learn of the court he had held, keeping duly secret on the essential in hand, as he had been enjoined, but enlarging on those wonders of weather-control which he and his master had already perfected. His own part in these proceedings was, I gathered, both spectacular and of considerable bravery.

So we came to Firzapore, an Indian city near the fringe of Her Majesty's domains, and one whose garrison was to provide us with the necessary column of escort troops. Here I met Colonel Swyre, a man as different from Lieutenant Lane's lithe boyishness as a bulldog from a greyhound. The Colonel did not display the scars of conflict; indeed, he had no need to, since his every movement, his every utterance, the way he held himself and no doubt the manner in which his brain worked, betokened the man of war – professional, adamantine, as tuned to the demands of battle as an instrument is tuned to a player's ears.

When I saw him first he stood at the opening of his tent, brightly lit by the sun against the dark interior, of middling height, immaculately dressed, but not so immaculate as to make his uniform an impediment. His face was all features – hawk nose, protruding chin, full cheeks, bushy eyebrows, each prominent as though his Creator had lacked time to smooth them into a coherent whole.

He thrust forward an immense hand with the one word: 'Swyre.'

I had no wish to be subservient to the military, so I thrust out mine with the one word: 'Huxtable.'

His eyes, I noticed at once, were of a burning intensity, as though their very fierceness would dissuade an enemy from attack. He motioned us into the cool interior of his tent, beckoned for a servant to fill the glasses and, almost ignoring Lane, turned to me.

'There seems,' he said, 'to be considerable mystery about your visit. But I gather you are to test a new weapon – although for some reason the work is to be described to all except the privileged few as meteorological rather than military. You are, I assume, a gunner.'

I explained that I was a man of science, and wondered what his reaction would be.

'If you can help us, so much the better,' he said after a pause. 'There is no point in hitting the enemy for two when one can hit him for six.'

Here was a man cast in Wellington's mould, one for whom the dire horrors of battle, when unavoidable, were horrors to be disposed of as quickly as possible. How sincerely, I felt, would he uphold the reasoning that lay behind my weapon; how galling that the needs of security made it impossible for me to give him more than the broadest of hints as to what it would accomplish. All this passed through my mind within the first few minutes of our talk. As he questioned me and as there came through the open tent door the sounds of horses and artificers, of rifle-stacking and the tramp of boots, I was filled with admiration for this man. I had no inkling then of the trouble he was to cause in years to come.

To Swyre I explained that the second half of my weapon would arrive and be unloaded the following day, after the first half had been brought a safe distance from the river. Swyre came with me to supervise the unloading and was greatly impressed at the way in which Dobbin handled this, supervising the strapping up of the black box, ensuring its safety and ordering the labourers and bearers as though born to it. And yet – how different he seemed from the Dobbin I knew.

'Excellent,' said Swyre as they met. 'Careful handling. Attention to detail. Much experience.'

'Mainly with glass, sir,' said Dobbin. 'The most fragile commodity, sir. Very great experience indeed is required. I expect the Professor has told you of our difficulties, sir.'

It was with some surprise that I heard this, and with still more as Dobbin reeled off a list of words and phrases he must have picked up from books in my laboratory. He turned to me with a deferential, 'Was that not so, sir?'

To Swyre all this was gibberish, but I had no wish to disappoint him. 'Exactly, Dobbin,' I therefore replied, 'and very well handled it was too.'

Swyre nodded, as though in perfect comprehension, and I think that from that moment I knew my Dobbin better. To me, the scientist ignorant of all military matters, he was the old soldier; to men such as Swyre he was the civilian expert, one step ahead in the march of science.

That first morning I discussed my needs with the Colonel. As I explained, the demonstration site must be free from inhabitants over an area some ten miles by ten.

I had expected protests, but none came. Swyre knew his job as I knew mine.

He called over his shoulder towards an ante-room: 'Mr. Stacey, bring me the maps of the Chenaba area.'

The maps were brought and unrolled. 'I was told simply that you would require a desolate area,' said Swyre. 'I knew no more. I have selected certain possible sites.'

As he smoothed out the canvas-backed paper he looked at me questioningly. 'Does height matter?'

I explained that height was immaterial – all I required was an area ten miles by ten in which there were no inhabitants; and one along whose perimeter there would be no spectators.

'The size of the area you demand is, of course, quite extraordinary,' said Swyre. 'It seems that the only suitable place is the Jubila Plateau.'

He used the words casually enough. They rolled off his tongue without significance. Only I knew that he was giving to this isolated outpost of Her Majesty's dominions a place in the history of the world as important as Runnymede is to England or Bannockburn to Scotland.

Swyre tapped the map meditatively. 'There might be difficulties,' he said, half to himself. Turning to Lane he added, 'Chlorister is apt to be touchy.'

Lane's understanding 'yes' meant nothing to me, and my two companions turned towards me as if to explain the alphabet to a child.

'Sir Archibald Chlorister,' said Swyre.

' . . . of the East India Company,' added Lane.

'He is largely responsible for the territory on whose north-east fringe the Jubila Plateau lies,' the Colonel went on. 'The Company works well, but it works in its own way. I doubt if Her Majesty's troops have gone near Jubila for two decades.'

'If there were any – misfortunes,' explained Lane, 'Sir Archibald might feel that any explosions in the area over which he has a paternal though not a legal interest, would be held to his account. It is not too clear on whom responsibility would rest.'

'On us,' interrupted Swyre.

My mind went back to Whitehall, to Skindling, as Lane politely disagreed.

'The position, sir, is somewhat confused,' he said. 'Only recently the Commander-in-Chief . . .'

Swyre held up his hand with the resignation of the eternal field commander at the eternally superior knowledge of the Staff.

'The point at issue,' he elucidated, turning to me, 'is that we do not wish Chlorister to hamper us. Jubila is undoubtedly the best site. We must utilize it. We must deal with Sir Archibald when the time comes. Now, gentlemen . . .'

And so, for the next half-hour, we were all three engrossed in the details of baggage-animals and starting-times, with that meticulous attention to detail which unites the higher levels of the military and the scientific worlds.

The journey to Jubila epitomized the delights of travel. We rode by native pathway and by river-track, from the forest towards the hills. We mounted gradually, through country increasingly rugged, until at last we might have been in the wilds of Wester-Ross, although here all was on an even grander scale. At times, our path was only a yards-wide passage above a roaring torrent. At others, the long white tongues of the winter snow-slides still stretched across our route so that the horses had to cross with careful steps.

We had made one such passage when a serious incident took place. We were following a fast mountain river, along a mere nick cut in the hillside, a route that followed almost exactly the sinuosities of the waters. I was momentarily with Dobbin at the tail of the column. Around a distant bluff, but across the unseen river roaring away hundreds of feet below, there approached a line of horses and men.

Almost too late I called out to the riders to halt. Had it not been for Dobbin's warning shout it might, in fact, have been too late. It was certainly he who, with the sharp tongue he could command when necessary, helped in the emergency.

For as I looked across the void, with the shimmer of the air making detail a little difficult, I realized that what I saw was the head of our own column, brought round by the great U-bend of the river so that, as it came forward and we progressed to meet it, head and tail would pass within two hundred yards of one another, even though divided by a double stretch of waters!

Swyre had done his best. He had faithfully obeyed my command that the two halves of the device should remain separated by the length of the column. But he had not realized – how could he? – that were they brought within a few hundred yards of one another by the geographical vagaries of the river, then disaster might end our expedition before it had truly started.

For a moment there might have been confusion.

Dobbin spurred his horse forward, taking it to the

very brink as he jostled his way past the baggage animals and their astonished escorts, sending a flurry of stones tinkling and tumbling down the slope before they shot over the drop that separated them from the waters below.

Then the crisis was over. The animals, turned round, were moving back from the danger point, and a messenger had been sent forward to halt the head of the column.

It was impossible to make oneself heard above the rush of the waters and there was some delay before Swyre and I rode to meet one another, he coming back along the track while I went forward, leaving Dobbin to maintain order in the rear. I confirmed that the female half of the device was sufficiently far back from the narrows; the head of the column was taken past this dangerous point; the rear was brought up; and, once again in good order, we resumed our progress.

From the tail of the column I looked across the narrows, this time from the other side. Even less than two hundred yards, I now estimated!

How close, I wondered, had we come to disaster?

I glanced at Dobbin. He looked to the far bank and then looked at me in a strange way. How much, I asked myself, did this simple man really suspect?

It was a week's march before we reached Jubila, remote in its isolation, a rocky jewel clasped in a mountain setting. The small town clung to the hillside, dominated by the Palace. To the north, there rose the grey shape of the plateau, twenty miles away, thousands of feet higher, a conveniently uninhabited wilderness that stretched to the roof of the world.

Sir Archibald Chlorister was awaiting us, a man stiff of bearing and sanguine of expression, with a countenance that would have fitted the picture-frame of an ancestral home far better than the luxuries of the Palace, where he lived with the influence if not the power of a potentate. He was courteous, though not effusively so, and he hoped that we would dine with him after we had assured ourselves of the comfort of the troops, and had been shown to our quarters.

It was an uncomfortable dinner – despite its splendours. For me, translated from my scientific world, the surroundings had the quality of fantasy. For much of the time we talked generalities, as course after course was borne in, and as the magnificence of our host seemed to be equalled by the variety of Oriental table-delights. Then, all at once, I sensed that we had reached a dangerous corner in the conversation.

Sir Archibald turned to Swyre with a brusqueness at which I could only wonder. 'This incursion which you are proposing to make is most unfortunate,' he began.

I watched Swyre searching for the most tactful way

of turning the phrase. 'Not exactly proposing...' he started awkwardly. 'My orders ...'

Thus was the wrath diverted on to the humble Huxtable.

'Of course.' Sir Archibald shook his head as though reprimanding himself. 'I should have appreciated, Colonel, that with you, as with us, it is the ignorance of those in England which is responsible. Ten years ago ...'

He rambled off into a discourse involving the supply of merchandise through territory, the payment of rupees in what seemed to be phenomenal amounts, the necessity for complex bargaining which only he could understand – a discourse as shot through with the ignorance of the authorities in England as a good Stilton by blue veins.

'I understand.'

He turned to me and I realized that Swyre, Colonel though he was, commander of a thousand though he might be, was now by-passed in all Sir Archibald's calculations. It was the humble civilian, bearing bad tidings from the Mother Country, to whom all attention should be turned. In some ways I was dismayed; in others I felt that this was a minor victory in my battle. For science, rather than the military, was now being wooed. I turned to Sir Archibald quite confident that I could convince him.

It was not to be easy. 'I suggest that you visit me tomorrow morning,' he said. 'Then we can talk in confidence.'

I was astonished that the commander of Her Majesty's troops was so sharply excluded, and was about to protest. But I refrained; and I thought back to Skindling and the wisdom of the Civil Servant who had picked the place where responsibility might so easily slip down the crack between two authorities.

I thanked Sir Archibald. The following morning I rode round from the cantonment, marvelling at the sights and well decided in my own mind how best to deal with him.

At first all was pleasantry. I seated myself and tried to ignore the surroundings as though they were the commonplaces of life in Hanover Square.

'I do not profess to know a great deal about your enterprise,' he began. 'But it is clear from what Swyre tells me that you plan to march deeply into my territory. Of course,' he continued as though noticing the questioning glance I had purposely given him at his phrase, 'of course, you may find it curious that I should use the word "my". Yet it is the area through which the Company's trade passes; trade rests on goodwill – a fragile commodity, Professor, easily broken by those not acquainted with the long years necessary to acquire it.'

He turned to the large map behind him; a map, I felt, which had some similarity to those of medieval geographers, who so happily filled the empty spaces with imaginary dragons.

'So far as goodwill is concerned,' he went on, 'what we have here is the product of the Company over the centuries. I have nurtured it. I have so far kept it free from the troubles which have ravished other parts of the sub-continent. I have done so only with the help of the Company. An intrusion by the forces of Her Majesty, even though carried out with the greatest circumspection, will nevertheless be – an intrusion.'

He repeated the phrase of the previous evening. He could not really see why the territory should be 'submitted to such inconvenience'. And he then continued in a manner which for the moment astounded me.

'Swyre tells me,' he went on, 'that your task is to test what one might almost call a meteorological weapon. Since you are a man of science, and science now presumes to meddle in such things, you may be personally involved. I do not know, and I do not inquire, under whose auspices you come. But in manufacture there is always money. And I do not see why an honest man of science should suffer from the circumstances which have brought his path across the amiable administration of territory.'

'He sat back in his chair, rested his elbows on both of the wide arms, placed his hands together as though about to pray, and looked at me in a kindly fashion.

'I must point out that your experiment may well cause us difficulty. If you should desist, make other arrangements or so decide that our territory is not involved, no doubt we could come to an arrangement – that would be only just.'

It was the first time in my life that any man had tried to bribe me.

I had decided, as I had considered the matter during the night, that I would take the strongest possible attitude in any argument which arose, and I now told Sir Archibald that those in the service of Her Majesty, for such I was, even though not in uniform, were in no habit of being bribed, whatever might be the practice in the Company.

I expected him to launch an attack on an innocent who knew little of the world; or, perhaps more likely, to appeal that his words should be forgotten and that the matter should go no further.

Instead, he took the matter quite differently.

'I understand your feelings,' he said. 'You do not

know the East and you are a young man. You will learn.'

He rose and walked to the window, moving slowly and considering, I felt, how much he should tell me. He turned and as he did so his brown face, its wrinkles as numerous as the lines on a map where the streams of a delta divide and sub-divide, looked as old as Egypt.

'You may find it difficult to believe,' he said, 'but when I came to India, Napoleon was preparing for his first campaign in Italy. It was not the India you know today, safe within its cantonments . . .' He could see my thoughts of the recent risings and quickly dealt with them. 'Safe, in spite of the troubles, in a way that we never knew. There were a score of us, all under the age of twenty. Half died of fever within the first few years. Three were killed. Two disappeared, going to we know not what unfortunate end. When men married, or their wives came out, the wives were apt to die too. Death was a constant companion; after a while we got used to him. And we made India.'

He looked at me, I thought, almost pityingly. 'You have come with the military. But a man should know more than the art of killing. Whatever you may believe, men cannot govern for ever by the sword.'

His face crinkled for a moment. 'I know you will say we govern by . . .' and as he spoke he rubbed the fingers of his hand together in the eternal sign of man taking money. 'That helps. But it is the custom of the country and you must not judge it too harshly. And all the while trade grows – from our hills and forests it goes out to feed and to clothe the peoples of the world. You may conquer men with weapons, but you will win them only with trade. But it is a delicate growth, easily harmed, its veins easily ruptured.

'If your column passes up through our territory, men will believe, whatever I tell them, that Her Majesty's forces are once again on the way to war. There will be delays, non-deliveries. You, Professor, will have brought great harm to an area the size of southern England.'

I think he was being honest. Perhaps we might disrupt for a while the profits of the Company. But I had steeled myself to meet such protests. Sir Archibald was wasting his time.

'I am sorry,' I said. 'I would gladly go elsewhere. So, no doubt, would Colonel Swyre. However, the decision is not ours. You must understand, Sir Archibald, that I come under the express orders of the Queen herself. Indeed, it is not only Her Majesty who approves of the venture. You see . . .'

And then, I fear, I used methods of which in normal circumstances I would have been ashamed. I spoke of a prominent Director of the Company, and I spoke of him as an old friend, although I had met him but once. Although it was merely an Under-Secretary in Whitehall who had been responsible for the machinery of my visit, it was the Minister himself of whom I spoke. As for Wellington, whom I had met only twice, I spoke as though we dined together regularly – and as though it was a common practice of the Commander-in-Chief to seek the society of Franklin Huxtable.

I was aided by the fact that Sir Archibald knew nothing of me. I was aided by the fact that he had been so long from England that England was a foreign country. But I could tell by the changing expression on his face that he felt it unwise to challenge me further. And when I saw that the battle was won I dropped a hint that when I returned to Britain I would be glad to commend his services to the ears of those who mattered.

What repercusions that innocent remark was to have, both on the private life of Britain's monarch and on affairs of State! For Sir Archibald now picked up my rash offer and transformed it.

'I want nothing for myself, Professor,' he said, ' – although you may find that difficult to believe of a member of the Company. What I want is something for my son.'

I was surprised to hear that he was married, and my surprise must have betrayed itself. 'My wife died bringing him into the world, only a few months ago,' he said. 'She was young, hardly out of girlhood – too young for India. My son, also, is too young.'

The boy had already been sent to England, that promised land where he would grow up free from the trials and tribulations through which his father had been forced to fight.

'He will live with distant relatives,' Sir Archibald went on, 'with men and women of his blood, but men and women whom I have never seen. My life is here. I wish someone to keep a kindly eye on him. Do that, Professor, and we will say no more.'

We said no more, but merely shook hands.

The following morning, as we set out from the town, I hardly realized how my future would be burdened with the fortunes of Charles Chlorister. Indeed, my thoughts, as we passed through the gates and out northwards towards the distant line of high country, were set solely on the great adventure ahead.

It was beyond the gates, where the last shabby hovels stood on the edge of the vegetation which seemed about to enclose them, that there took place an incident I was long to remember.

Colonel Swyre and myself were somewhat ahead of the column when a bend in the dust track brought us to a turbanned figure, squatting cross-legged by the roadside. Something in the man's aspect, perhaps the character of his clothes, put him apart from the plenitude of beggars with which the country is cursed. What is more, as we approached he did not extend his hand for money, but raised it as if in demand.

I reined in my horse and Swyre, looking quizzically on at the interest of a visitor to whom such things were still new, did the same.

The old man slowly raised his head and I looked down into a dark face from which there gazed out two eyes almost completely white, so light was the colour of their irises.

'You travel to the plateau,' said the man in a thin but steady voice, and in an English of remarkable culture.

'We do,' said Swyre, with something of contempt and amusement.

'In peace or in war?' persisted the soothsayer.

'The trouble,' remarked Swyre, ignoring the man as he turned to me, 'is that once a native learns the mother-tongue he gets impertinent.' He looked back over his shoulder as he spurred his horse: 'Let the column proceed.'

As I glanced downwards, I thought that the Indian was smiling. He moved both hands in a form of salaam. 'The column must always proceed, my masters,' he said, 'though we know not where we go nor why; nor to what strange destiny our journey leads us.'

As he spoke, the dust from the horses' hooves rose in miniature clouds; when I looked back they had surrounded him.

Our march took two days. Then we camped in a

clearing among pines, below cliff-like ramparts which rose for some hundreds of feet and beyond which the flat plateau stretched for miles.

The troops, and the junior officers, had been informed only that an invention, said to be concerned with the weather, was now to be tested.

As Her Majesty had insisted that the demonstration should be carried out without loss of life, it was necessary for troops to cross the plateau to ensure that no natives were there – an operation which was explained by our reluctance that our weather-making should be witnessed.

The next day, certain military material which I had selected was taken up to the plateau and left there in chosen positions. We returned, and I realized that all was at last ready. I slept confidently that night and the following morning set out for the plateau, accompanied only by Swyre.

I had been torn between taking Dobbin with me for the use which he would undoubtedly be, and leaving him behind because of the danger to security that his presence might create.

Dobbin himself solved my problem. He knew, of course, that we had come to the crux of the matter, but he also knew his place.

'You can, sir,' he said as he nodded to my instructions to remain in camp, 'you can tell all in detail on your return.'

As so often, I wondered just how much he had guessed.

He looked at me with a mixture of interest and affection. 'What is more, sir, it will be proper for one to remain should there be any calamity.'

So Dobbin remained, having checked that both

Swyre and myself had all that we needed and then holding high above his head a lamp that I could for long see shining in the darkness of the camp as we rode up to meet the dawn.

Swyre went first with one black box on a baggage animal, and leading two horses which had been decreed as surplus to establishment. I followed nearly half a mile behind with the second black box which, the Colonel being safely away, I had brought from the far end of the camp. And I led two more horses.

The chill morning air soon passed, and it was warm by the time we reached the higher open ground and started on the narrow track that slanted diagonally across the ground ahead. Then came the arduous pull up a steeper path that laced its way through the cliffs, rising and ever rising until we could see back not only across the camp and the nearer ground but over the first ridges towards a smoke-blue haze that covered the plains of India.

Finally I reached the crest and saw thankfully that Swyre had moved on, according to our pre-arranged plan, so that he was by this time only a distant figure, hundreds of yards away and already almost lost in the immensity of the plateau.

The hard morning light was reflected back with great intensity from the buff-coloured schistose rocks that spread away in front of me. The scene stretched to eternity, it seemed, a flattish sandy desert, broken only intermittently by rank scrub, a few stunted trees – and, away in the distance, by the loads which the troops had deposited the previous day.

We rode on until we were some miles from the edge of the plateau, I carefully keeping my distance. Then we set about our work. Not the least strenuous part of this was the final assembly of a miniature track, an equipment which might be compared to the lines of a child's model railway. For, strangely enough, one of my greatest difficulties in bringing the device to perfection had lain outside the complex calculations. It was possible to solve the scientific problems, but I for long remained perplexed at what might have been considered a much simpler matter – how to bring the two halves of my device together with sufficient speed. This difficulty I finally overcame by enclosing each half in a small box which could be mounted on a diminutive trolley; these trolleys were set upon a length of track a few hundred yards long; and clockwork mechanisms, operated by simple timing devices, were all that were needed to bring the two trolleys together.

Between us, Swyre and I completed the work started by the troops, and I placed my two black boxes in position at either end of the track, each mounted on its trolley. From the cases which the troops had left we took equipment which I arranged at varying distances from the central point on the track, being anxious to discover the effect of my device upon it. Then we tethered the horses, also at different distances from the black boxes.

I carefully set the clockwork mechanism, much to Swyre's amusement, and we rode back in the glare of the afternoon.

Before we dropped down from the plateau I turned to take a last look at the scene – a wilderness in the far distance of which my two boxes could hardly be seen, with the horses strung out at intervals, whinnying by now and peculiarly disturbed at being left alone.

That evening I dined in the Colonel's tent. My mind was not untinged with anxiety, for my device had been timed to operate at midnight. There is no need for me to describe that evening; to detail how I returned to my own tent; or to dilate on how anxiety turned to despair as midnight passed and the silence of the night continued to be broken only by the distant sound of jackals.

I did not sleep, and it seemed an eternity before the dawn brought Dobbin. He did not speak. He merely pursed his lips, shrugged his shoulders and, good man, went about his work. He was busying himself outside the tent when Colonel Swyre arrived, a not unkindly look upon his face, for he was a decent fellow. He made one comment: 'No detonation, Professor.'

He was also a brave man. For when I explained that it would be necessary for me to visit the plateau to discover the cause of the impediment, he made great efforts to accompany me. But, as I explained, we had our different duties in life: mine lay with my device, his with his men.

Poor Dobbin was most moved. He did his best to accompany me, but I was adamant. As I left he insisted both on saluting me and then holding out his hand in such a way that I could not forbear to shake it as he so obviously wished.

'Thank you, sir,' he said.

It was clear that Dobbin did not expect to see me return. I had my own apprehensions as I rode back along the track up to the plateau.

I could not understand it. After all my labour. After all those intricate calculations. After all my checking of the results and of the double-checked results. The silence from the space in front of me was almost more than my mind could bear. The heat was intense and I was acutely uncomfortable. But my brain was still incredulous and critical of itself.

Eventually I was able to see the crest of the track which rose before me, and I almost wished I would suddenly be destroyed by the greatest explosion mankind had ever created. If that were the case, at least I should not have been travelling up a scientific blind alley for the last few years.

At the crest I dismounted and, holding my horse on a long rein, crossed the skyline almost crouching against the ground. I soon realized how unnecessary this was; that my attitude was determined not by reason but by the stories I had listened to from veterans of the wars against the French, those men who had so often told me, in their cups maybe, how cannon-balls struck level, horizontally across the ground, and that a man well flattened would have the best chance of survival. For long I had believed this to be the talk of cowards – until one of my more rational colleagues had said: 'But, Huxtable, you have overlooked one fact – the evidence comes only from one group: the survivors.'

Once over the crest of the plateau I had to raise myself before I could see, in the far distance, beyond the tethered horses, the dark outline of the tracks, deep black against the piercing midday glare.

I realized my situation, and almost laughed as I straightened up. For if the ideas on which I had mortgaged my reputation had been but the passing illusion of a fool, then I was in no danger. But if there had been some unexpected interruption of the mechanism which might right itself without intervention as I approached – then I might crush myself into the earth and would yet be unable to avoid destruction.

Nevertheless – for as my medical colleagues are always affirming, we are frightened creatures – I went forward with a good deal of anxiety. But in spite of it I mounted my horse and rode on until the track was only a few hundred yards before me.

Then I saw with relief that it was not, necessarily, my equations that were wrong. From the eastern end of the track the little trolley had moved forward on its wheels, as I had planned, to its appointed spot. To the west, the second trolley had run but a matter of yards.

I dismounted and, with the sun beating down with increasing ferocity but with a heat that worried me no longer, I walked forward to discover what had prevented the success of my research.

Had there been, after all, some inner force of nature which had stopped these two halves of the apocalyptic device from meeting? Had there been some secret of matter which had escaped me and which had held these two halves at some pre-ordained distance? Had some Will, of which I had so far seen no evidence, held them apart on this isolated desert plateau of a great subcontinent, placing between them a limited ocean of frustrating space just as, we are told, the waters of the Red Sea were held apart for the passage of Moses and his followers?

It was nothing of the sort. As I leant down I saw that the cause was but a minute grain of sand, an unconsolidated example of the country's timeless sediments, a particle of petrographically expected quartz. It had lodged in the mechanism and had thus endangered the whole enterprise.

I bent again to the machinery, which was so hot in the glare that it was painful to touch, and as I did so I started back with horror as a snake, sinuous and flecked with orange markings, slid silently out from beneath the trolley and glided off to the cover of the neighbouring rocks.

Now I knew what to do. It was strenuous work pushing back the trolley which had dutifully played its part in the operation, but finally the task was done and the mechanism re-wound. I returned to the recalcitrant trolley, cleaned it with some difficulty, and re-set this mechanism too. Then, and only then, did I remount my horse and return to camp. That night, I knew, our labours would be repaid.

We dined as before. But I felt that Swyre knew my suspense, and after a very brief round of the glasses I returned to my own tent, walking back through the bright light of an almost full moon which lit up the surrounding ridges as though they had been carved in ivory.

Again and again I anxiously consulted my watch, but I must have failed to synchronize it with my mechanism. For it was with surprise that I saw the pale canvas of the tent, half-lit by the moon, suddenly lighten. From a faint primrose yellow it bleached to white, and from white it shone for a moment with a huge exterior glare as though the most dazzling of suns was illuminating it.

I could hardly believe that this could be the result of my device. Then, as I looked at my watch, I felt a gentle heaving of the ground as though Mother India herself had taken to the oceans. It was a most frightening experience.

I hurried through the tent-flaps; as I did so there came in what sounded like Dobbin's voice a startled shout of 'Meteor!' followed by another of 'Earthquake!' Then the ground began to rise and fall tremendously as a huge rolling reverberation filled the air.

From all around there came the curses and exclamations of the men, the wild shouting of servants, and from the lines the sounds of terrified horses. A wild crashing came from the compound where the elephants were staked, and from the officers' tents the crackle and smashing of chairs and crockery as everything untethered was shaken by the lurchings of the earth.

Then, with the thunder, there came the wind.

As I happened upon Swyre and we both shouted for calm amid the confusion I looked westwards to where, only a few miles away, a forest-clad mountainside was lit by the moon. As I watched, the whole regiment of pines was bowed as by the passing of a giant hand.

A moment later, as the earth still surged, a hurricane swept through the camp, sending tent-pegs like smallshot through the air, curling up the ropes and adding to a confusion in which the shouts of the men mingled with the cries of the natives, and above which there rose an insistent whinnying from the panic-stricken horses.

As I spat the blown sand from my mouth and staggered with Swyre through the murk to help restore order, I realized that we were seven miles from the point of explosion.

The movements of the earth did not last long. Through the subsiding veils of sand and dust it again became possible to see one's companions, and to move without risk of suffocation from the drifting debris. At some places fires had been started by overturned lamps, and the men were soon busy stamping these out while others calmed the animals and yet others began re-erecting the tents and setting the camp to rights once again.

Officers and men – and I myself – were still busily

engaged on this work when first light came.

An hour later we gathered for breakfast, served in an impromptu mess-tent, and the officers began to take stock of the damage. But it was not their details of ruined equipment which intrigued me: it was their un-awareness of what had really happened.

'So much,' commented one of the subalterns, as we sat down together on the hastily prepared benches, 'so much, Professor, for your two black boxes.'

At first I was surprised at the calm acceptance that a weapon detonated more than seven miles away could produce such results.

'If you have no others,' he continued, 'you must, I imagine, say farewell to the prospects of an experiment.'

For a moment I did not know whether to protest or to laugh. Yet I could see that the very success of my device had itself aided my plan of passing off the explosion as the fall of a meteor. There had indeed been some consternation at the blinding flash which had illuminated the night and by a lucky chance more than one officer had taken up those cries of 'meteor' and 'earthquake'.

Meteor I let it be, and as the conversation jumped back and forth across the table, I could see that no problem of security would arise. 'Earthquake' and 'meteor', and man's reluctance to imagine any cause that lay outside his own experience, combined to solve a problem which those in England, possibly believing that I had exaggerated my claims, had refused to face.

Only Colonel Swyre had doubts. He did not express them, but I could see that he was watching me carefully, obviously unable to make up his mind about what had really happened a few hours before.

As we rose from our meal he came across to me. 'I

imagine, Professor, that you will want to see if the earthquake has left anything of your two black boxes intact,' he said. There was a slight smile on his face as he spoke, and his fellow-officers thought him to be joking. I was not so sure.

As we reached the plateau, later that day, I noticed that the wind, as on the previous occasion, blew from behind us, down towards the distance where there dwelt some tribes whose name escaped me.

It was an awesome sight which met our eyes. Within a mile of the spot where we had left the device, nothing whatsoever remained. The few trees, the nearest animals, the scrub – all had disappeared; some of the rocks themselves had melted, so that in places the ground was covered with huge panels of a substance resembling recently hardened lava. Beyond the area of immediate destruction, interesting phenomena were to be seen.

Even the animals most distant from the explosion had been stripped of their coats by the heat, and these Swyre dispatched with his revolver. A most instructive morning was spent as I filled my notebook with data, and we approached nearer to the centre of the explosion.

Before this was reached, however, I noticed an unusual effect. The nearer horses, unprotected from the full effects of the device, had been completely transformed into their original elements and had, of course, been entirely eliminated. But their shadows had in some curious manner been implanted on the rock around them in unmistakable silhouette.

This was not all. Some few yards away there was another dark patch upon the lighter ground. Swyre and I rode towards it, he doubting, I fearing, how the shape would resolve itself.

We reined in our horses a short distance away. Swyre said no word. Neither did I. Outlined before us on the shelving ground that sloped towards the scene of the explosion was the unmistakable silhouette of a trooper, distinguishable down even to the outline of his boots and forage cap.

Swyre turned away with a comment into which I could read no inflexion, no prior knowledge.

'Scorched to death by the meteorite, no doubt, Professor,' he said.

We exchanged no words as we slowly returned to the crest of the cliffs. Swyre looked back as he motioned me to lead the way down. 'It must have been an exceedingly large one,' he added, continuing the sentence he had begun some miles back.

Once again we continued in silence. It was some while later, back in the camp, that we learned of the missing trooper. He had been unhappy at having the redundant horses taken away to some unknown fate. A few hours before the descent of the meteor and the resulting earthquake – for as such I was now careful to speak of the occurrence – he must have made his own way back up to the plateau. At the time of his death, therefore, he was a deserter from duty. His death must have been quite painless; nevertheless, if it was necessary for him to make such a sacrifice it was unfortunate that he was not much farther from the explosion. Then he might have survived, at least for a while, and thus been able to provide useful information.

However, in the Army of those times men did disappear, leaving no trace, without undue concern or fuss, and the incident was soon forgotten.

During the days that followed we returned to Jubila, where I deplored to Sir Archibald the sad fate of our expedition and whence, as promised, I dispatched a message to Her Majesty. It was essential that she should be informed of our success and as essential that the message should be senseless to all others. I solved the problem neatly, sending Her Majesty a one-word message, 'Jubilate' – a device used by Napier with his much publicized 'Peccavi' on the capture of Scind.*

From Jubila we travelled on to Firzapore and then, by stages, back to England. It had been discreetly arranged that Colonel Swyre should follow in due course. In the organization of affairs in London his name had been suggested to me as that of a man whose discretion was never in doubt. But it had been decreed that he should be returned to London for preferment as soon as possible, for some distinction of a not too obvious kind, and for subsequent appointment to one of those positions where responsibility, if no more, encourages a man to keep a sharp rein on his tongue.

The fate of Colonel Swyre, let alone of the trooper, was soon overborne in my mind by the shadow of the weapon I had found it possible to create. I returned to England believing, in my too innocent way, that the world was now to enter upon a millennium of peace and expanding prosperity.

*Following the defeat of 20,000 troops by Napier's force of about 3,000 at Hyderabad in 1843.

5: Her Majesty's Prerogative

As we returned round the Cape, beat up through the heavy seas of the South Atlantic, and made our way into the homely Channel once again, there should, I know, have been but one thought dominating my brain. The coming repercussions of that instant's release of energy upon the Jubila Plateau should have driven all else from my mind. It was not so. Instead, I thought only of Amelia who would be waiting, as she has been waiting on my return from other journeys, and as she will once more be waiting in a few weeks' time.

Our joy at reunion was intense, and marred for me only by the dissimulation which I had to practise, with my talk of meteorology and of the unfortunate manner in which my two black boxes had been destroyed.

This was bad enough. Worse was to follow. For I now had to prepare a report on the demonstration and present it to the Queen. This, in its turn, meant that I had once more to deflect the questions which came from my wife. I did my best, but Amelia could not comprehend Her Majesty's concern with a mere meteorological device.

The evening before my visit to Windsor I was, after dinner, engrossed in the Transactions. My wife was equally engrossed in the womanly task of embellishing a cover with brightly coloured silks. At least, I thought she was engrossed; yet when she broke the silence of the room, it was not merely to speak but almost to accuse me.

'There is some important business with the Queen which you have not felt it proper to reveal,' she said, 'and I have suspicions about your journey to India.' Indeed, she spoke no more than the truth, though I could hardly tell her so.

Today, in what may or may not be a more enlightened age but is certainly a different one, it would have been more difficult for me to handle the situation. As it was, I had merely to inform her that this was an affair of State, that it was not a woman's business, and that I felt great surprise that she should speak on such a subject.

'I am sorry, Franklin,' she said. 'Perhaps it was unseemly intuition. But recently I have sensed some mystery. I have felt that there were things untold about your work, and that they were different from those marvels of science which I could never deem to comprehend. But I must, of course, rest upon your judgment.'

That was more than forty years ago. Since then, I have often noted a sideways glance from Amelia, at times almost a smile. But she has been a good wife; she has never raised the subject again.

There were, of course, worries enough. Writing my report for the Queen stretched both my literary ability and my ingenuity. It was first necessary, I decided, that no hint should be contained in it of the real secret. I decided, therefore, to include a 'Technical Appendix'. But it was, in the nature of things, unlikely that such a report would ever fall into the hands of any but laymen; none of those, I judged, would have the knowledge to observe that the one essential set of facts was missing even from the Appendix.

Just how necessary such a precaution really was, will become apparent as my story unfolds – even though I decided that only five copies of my report should be prepared, each in my own hand. The first was to be delivered to Her Majesty and the second to the Prince Consort. The Prime Minister and the Duke were each to have one, while I myself would keep the fifth and final copy.

I headed the document 'Report of an Experiment on the Jubila Plateau' and I then described how I had taken out my device from England. I described how the two boxes had been placed at their separate stations and how they had been brought together. I then came to the most important part of my report. My whole aim and object was to make war so terrible that not even the most ignorant would wish to engage in it, and I therefore felt justified in describing the effects of the explosion in great detail. My notebook was full of data, and from it I was able to extract the necessary graphic details. All within a radius of a mile or so had been utterly destroyed, rendered back to the elements from which it had come; all within three miles or more, destroyed within our limited meaning of the word; while at even greater distances destruction was considerable.

This was the main burden of my report on which I worked with much zeal, and which was eventually ready for presentation to Her Majesty. I informed her, through the channels which we had earlier decided upon, that the final part of my task was completed, and I once again found myself driving down to Windsor, passing through the grey gateway and being announced into her presence.

It was the same room in which I had been received less than eighteen months previously, before the test on the Jubila Plateau, before I knew that my equations had been correct. But now it was winter. Across the windows, through which I had heard the laughter of the people on the river, thick curtains were drawn, and only my imagination could conceive what lay outside in the darkness.

And now we were not alone. Beside Her Majesty, who glowed with even more radiant womanhood than at our first meeting, there stood Prince Albert.

'We received your message,' was her first remark, 'and we duly rejoiced.'

I bowed also to the Prince and was then motioned to sit on the far side of the long table, so rich and brown in the lamplight.

His Royal Highness, pacing the room, half-hidden in the outer penumbra of shadow, stood still for a moment. The top portion of his face was bathed in green light from the shade; the bottom half lit by the flare of the lamp below. I have always remembered him thus, as though he might have been split two ways about the significance of my discovery – or as though mankind itself might be half green satyr, half human being.

I can still see his mouth, its line opening like a wave breaking on a sandy beach, the set of his perfectly formed teeth, and I can still hear his slow, firm and guttural voice.

I shall never forget his first words.

'Professor Huxtable,' he said, 'we have here a question of moral choice.'

The next half-hour was one of the most memorable of my life. I had discovered, as I knew only too well, something more dangerous than the secrets of Pandora's box, something more valuable than the mysteries of the alchemists. Only now, in the quiet of this room, broken when a servant far away opened a door and momentarily released into our inner sanctum the sounds of a great establishment about its business, did I realize how my discovery had swept me into different waters.

For a moment my mind slipped back some years and I thought of how I had interrupted Dalton's discourse upon the impact of science on government. Now I, master of my profession as I was, felt adrift and inexperienced, a mere untutored artificer compared with those accomplished practitioners, Her Majesty and Prince Albert.

It was he, I felt, who struck most surely towards the essentials of the new situation I had created.

'I conceive it,' he went on, 'to be the duty of every educated person closely to watch and study the time in which he lives, and, as far as he is able, to add his humble mite of individual exertion to further the accomplishment of what he believes Providence to have ordained.*

'Professor Huxtable, Providence has ordained your great discovery.'

I could not deny that this was so.

'This discovery,' the Prince continued, 'has opened wide the gates to a new age; but it will be an age which increases rather than decreases moral responsibility. There can never, of course, be any question of our employing such power in combat, even against savages; yet its mere demonstration, in suitable circumstances, will denude opposition of reality.

'However, we must be practical. The mere fact that your apparatus consists of two halves which must be brought together to induce detonation, itself involves a limitation. We would never consider the use of such a weapon, even so, use must have credibility. Apart from demonstration, agreeable to all, how would it be done, Professor?'

*Quoted in *Prince Albert's Golden Precepts, selected from his addresses* (Sampson Low, 1862).

This was a matter which had exercised me from an early stage of my experiments. Yet it was a problem to which there was a solution.

'Your Majesty, Your Royal Highness,' I said, addressing them both, 'there are numerous solutions; they depend on the size and the weight of the two separate pieces of equipment. As I have described in my report, these pieces are each but the size of a small valise. They are, for the sake of convenience, housed in black boxes only a few feet in length and even less broad. It is unlikely that these sizes could be reduced. Their weight is another matter. It might not be impossible for this weight to be so reduced that each piece of equipment could be carried with ease by a soldier. Two men, each with his own half of the device, would merely need to meet at a point suitably close to the enemy's forces and suitably distant from our own. For each, death would be certain, but for such valour Your Majesty might provide a special award.'

The Prince, humanitarian as always, rubbed his chin as he suggested, 'Even artillery, Professor, might surely be utilized?'

I explained the difficulties of ensuring the necessary accuracy and, turning the problem, stressed that the simple mechanism used on the Jubila Plateau would be sufficient for a demonstration – all that would be needed.

I then made a serious error.

'However, should such a demonstration not deter,' I continued, 'a warning that the weapon might be used unexpectedly, in unthought-of circumstances, would certainly be adequate. A great advantage of the device is its unique flexibility.'

I then went on to point out that two civilians, brave and dedicated men, might with comparative ease enter an enemy capital from opposite points of the compass, each carrying what would appear to be no more than a valise. They would walk nearer to one another unnoticed, through the streets of such a city. They would approach one another, and when separated by a distance of which I was still ignorant but which was surely measured in yards – then 'Pouf!'

'There would,' I explained, 'be no more city.'

'Professor Huxtable,' said Her Majesty, 'that would be murder. We will not discuss it.'

Instead, for twenty minutes I listened as Prince Albert, intently watched by the loving eyes of Her Majesty, expounded on the fundamentals of the new situation. At times the Queen would interpolate a comment, ruminating on how such and such a point might be illustrated by the situation in Europe or Asia.

And yet I was perturbed. It was not only the impact on existing alliances and balancings of power which was involved. There was also the attitude of mind summed up by the Prince in one phrase as he soliloquized.

'But one can wonder – in fact, one must wonder,' he said, ' – whether it is right to exercise such absolute power.'

Of course. I had wondered about that a good many times myself, and I had come to a conclusion. I speculated, for a moment, on what a sheltered life Prince Albert must have led. How much, I asked myself, would those veterans of Waterloo have questioned any moral purpose that succeeded in keeping their limbs attached to their persons?

However, it was soon apparent that there were qualifications about the reception of this bounty of science. The end of all wars had seemed such a natural consequence of my work. Now, for the first time, I began to doubt. For it was soon clear that the complexities of politics precluded what I had most hoped for, a public demonstration attended by the military representatives of the Powers. There appeared to be grave objections to such a course.

'Prior knowledge removes surprise,' the Prince stated, 'while such a demonstration might well set alight the minds of other scientists in other countries.'

Only thus did I slowly comprehend that though my device might be used to safeguard the peace of nations, the manner of this would be very different from what I had expected. My weapon would not be given to the world.

Her Majesty must have appreciated, with that quickness of mind so characteristic of her, the thoughts which passed through my brain, for it was now that she looked at me with great penetration.

'How many people,' she asked, 'know the secret of your discovery, Professor Huxtable?'

This was a most difficult question to answer with the complete honesty to which I am accustomed. I explained how the natural laws were open to inspection by any man of the right ability and sufficient perseverance; how no cloak could ever be drawn down to conceal an understanding of the innermost secrets.

'They are there, Ma'am,' I explained. 'Only understanding is needed. But I have no reason to believe that any other investigator has considered the facts as I have considered them, has written down in the right equations the correct symbols which have been presented to his eyes and to his imagination, and has drawn from them what I felt – correctly, as we now know – to be the inevitable conclusions.'

All this, I could not help feeling, was well received

by His Royal Highness, who stood opposite me as I spoke, nodding his head gravely and stroking his chin with a somewhat nervous movement. I felt that the great difficulty was past, that I would not be called upon to advance further towards the critical point from which I shrank. But it was now that Her Majesty turned her sweetest gaze upon me and asked:

'We understand perfectly, Professor Huxtable. But *what* symbols? *what* equations?'

I then realized, for the first time, something of Her Majesty's character. She was not yet twenty-five, yet it was her personality, her regal authority, which made her so difficult to resist. There was only one person who could do that – Prince Albert. He now came to my rescue.

'There are two secrets,' he said. 'The first lies in that combination of chemical and physical knowledge of electro-magnetic possibilities, without which Professor Huxtable would have been unable to produce his remarkable results. He alone has that secret and I do not doubt that he will guard it well. The fewer who are able to peer through the door which he has opened, the better it will be for the world. There is no need for us to look beyond the laws we know. There is no reason why we should inquire . . .'

He turned to me as he bowed slightly and said: 'That is Professor Huxtable's privilege and it belongs to him alone.'

He drew back and pursed his lips. The lines of his face set into a determined expression as he continued:

'The second secret is that such a secret exists; in some ways, that is the most important aspect of the matter.'

Even this, it soon became clear in our discussion, was more complex than at first appeared. Only I and perhaps Colonel Swyre knew the full measure of the secret. Sir Robert and the Duke, as well as Her Majesty and Prince Albert, might speak of a weapon which could end all wars, yet I felt that in spite of my explanations all looked upon my device as merely a yet more powerful explosive.

Beyond this small circle, and at a lower level as it were, there existed the Secretary of State for War who believed that I had been experimenting with a new invention of which he knew little and, I fear, cared less. And at a still lower level there were various members of the Government who vaguely knew that something had been afoot.

'Thus it is true, is it not, Professor Huxtable,' the Prince continued, 'that while rumours may exist, and may continue to exist, there is little chance that the true nature of your secret need ever be prematurely released, and that it should be possible to deflect unauthorized inquirers with harmless words?'

I agreed that this was so.

All this was, of course, very different from what I had expected. Yet I saw, in the light of the worldly wisdom of the conversation, that the same ends would have to be achieved by other means. And so it was agreed that the greatest care should be observed in speech, in letters, even in the most private of documents.

'Indeed,' said Her Majesty, 'I will make no reference to it, Professor Huxtable, even in my diaries. It will be difficult. But then all worthwhile things *are* difficult, and we must so bear ourselves that we do not, because of that, *shirk* them.'

'There is one other matter,' the Prince went on. 'Her Majesty and we men of science must ensure, above all things, that word of this is not bandied about among the politicians.'

The Queen nodded. 'We would not be happy, Professor Huxtable,' she said, 'if hints of such a secret were dropped about even among my Ministers. Politicians are apt to be garrulous. It may well be that at some future date, when we feel that a decision of moral significance is at stake, there will no longer be a need for the secret to be kept. But until then we must remember that for every one of these men who is informed, even indirectly, there is a little group around him who will also hear the news.'*

To deal with any such further extension of knowledge the Prince now proposed an ingenious plan. 'These two copies of your report,' he said, indicating the sheets on the table, 'will remain for ever amongst our most private papers. Your own, Professor Huxtable, will, of course, be kept with equal security. There are two others.'

He stopped in mid-step, pursed his lips and looked at the Queen as though expecting her to continue.

'We have confidence in Sir Robert Peel,' she said, looking at me so candidly that I realized the Prime Minister had recovered from the repercussions of the Bedchamber Affair, 'and in the Duke. And of course the Prime Minister *whoever* he may be, and the Commander-in-Chief of our forces, whoever *he* may be, must be informed that a weapon of the most significant magnitude lies within our armoury. But we live in difficult times, Professor Huxtable. We never know to what exigencies

*Compare with Churchill to Ismay, April 19th, 1945: 'It may be that in a few years or even months this secret can no longer be kept. One must always realize that for every one of these scientists who is informed there is a little group around him who also hear the news.' Quoted in *Tizard*, by Ronald Clark (Methuen, 1965).

we shall be driven by Parliament – or by the unwisdom of our people.'

She looked up at Albert with a mixture of love and admiration. 'The Prince has made a suggestion. It is one with which I am certain Sir Robert and the Duke would most willingly agree. It is this: that the copies of the Report which you have delivered to them, should be regarded as their own personal property; that arrangements should be made for their destruction when the Prime Minister and the Commander-in-Chief pass on to that eternal peace they have so surely earned; and that you, Professor Huxtable, should provide for transmission in their official papers an account of your experiment which is less revealing.

'Perhaps it would be possible for you,' she went on, 'to describe the explosion in lesser terms – not "of unparalleled magnitude", for instance, but "of great force". Perhaps it would be best if you omitted the more frightful details – and your alarming suggestions as to what might happen should the device be exploded against an army in the field. Sir Robert we *know*. And it is as well, of course, that a Prime Minister should understand what power lies within his hands to be given to the Army as he may direct. But in the hands of even enlightened Prime Ministers, power can corrupt. We dread to think what absolute power might do. Therefore we believe it best if knowledge of this device continues to be restricted.

'However' – and she appeared to sigh – 'we must be constitutional. We must observe the proprieties. And we must therefore insist, however abhorrent the idea, that if circumstances should ever arise in which you are asked to speak of your device by my Ministers, then speak you must, and freely. The Queen's prerogative continues to exist, but I am afraid that its stature diminishes.'

The Prince, who had been pacing the room as though still troubled, now turned to Her Majesty.

'It is necessary to be practical on one other matter,' he said. 'There may well be occasions on which messages regarding this device will have to be conveyed – between us two should we be parted, between either of us and Professor Huxtable; perhaps even between a Prime Minister and the Professor. It would surely be wise that no hint of its most intimate and secret nature should escape from such correspondence.'

The Prince, as so often, was correct. As so often, Her Majesty was aware of it.

'We must, then, refer to it by another word,' she said. 'I think that the Professor . . .' and she turned to me with an expression of great charm, 'I think that the Professor, after all his labours, should be allowed to name it – and in such a way that it will never be recognized.'

I had not foreseen such an honour. For a moment possibilities coursed through my mind. It would be impertinent to suggest 'Victoria' and it would be tactless to suggest 'Albert'; I thought of the land of my mother's birth and for a moment considered whether the object of all my endeavours might not be called the 'Franklin'. But I, too, bore that name: the suggestion would be presumptuous.

I remembered an old precept of my father which, according to my mother, had saved his life in many a desperate situation: 'When in doubt, pass back the decision to your adversary; then make the best of his mistakes.'

I, too, am a practical man and so I felt able to put to Her Majesty that, greatly honoured though I was by her condescension, yet the choice of name should be hers.

She was almost childishly overjoyed at my response.

'Then you . . .' and she turned to Albert with a dazzling smile, 'then you must help me.'

The Prince, for once, had no ideas. Her Majesty was also silent for a few moments before she brought her hands together in a clap of joy.

'Professor,' she said, 'it was found necessary for you to experiment with your device upon the Jubila Plateau. You had to visit the great sub-continent; and what could provide a more fitting name? You have given us an Indian – a dark mystery which, if it is ever used, must be used for good.'

Thus my device became 'the Indians' – two Indians making one weapon – and as such I have thought of it for the rest of my life.

The Queen said she would summon me when necessary. It appeared that the audience was at an end. Then, as I started to back from the room, Her Majesty stopped me.

'It is a great gift that you have given to us and our peoples, Professor Huxtable,' she said. 'It is not clear how, if ever, we can reward you; though I know that reward counts for nothing. Yet if there ever comes a time when you, or your family, wish for an audience with the Queen, you have but to ask for it and to remind Her Majesty of her Indians.'

I thanked her, I thanked Prince Albert, and I bowed my way out, no doubt duly honoured. But I left the Castle with mixed feelings.

I was perturbed by the complexity of the great issues among which, I could already see, my device had disruptively arrived.

Yet I was also worried by something more intangible. Despite the emphasis which had been laid on great moral issues, despite the solemn tide of thought which had borne along our conversation, I could not help feeling that both Her Majesty and the Prince had failed to grasp the implications which my device held for the world. Perhaps this was natural; they had not seen the Jubila Plateau and its transformation.

Perhaps I misjudged them.

Maybe. But I wondered then, as I have wondered since, at the irony of life. Men had for centuries been calling for an end to war. Now I had given them the opportunity. And now, I feared, they were to fumble it.

6: The Crimean Disaster

It is the common sounds of life which for me have always summoned up the past in human detail. Yet when I think of the Crimea, of all its grievous losses and wasted opportunities, it is a silence that recalls the whole tragedy to my mind most vividly, the silence which engulfed the House of Commons as the country went to war.

Everyone had expected it since the day in February, six weeks previously, when the crowds had followed the first regiment of Guards from barracks to station through the streets of London, the first steps in a journey that was to take them to Southampton, to the borders of Asia – and many of them to a grave in the barren wastes of southern Russia.

At first it had seemed rather trifling. As though any sane man need have worried, in this age of enlightenment, as to who kept the keys of the Holy Places! And how incredible that so many were prepared to die – and so many others to encourage them – in the cause of a distant quarrel in an even more distant country! Yet the Russians had continued to assert their claims, even after what had seemed an amicable and honourable settlement. The patience of the Turks had been taxed beyond endurance, yet only after considerable discussion had they crossed the Danube and followed brilliant start with even more brilliant continuation. Then the Russians, totally destroying their enemies' navy, had redressed the balance. And, as a result, the fever for war mounted throughout Britain.

As passions waxed stronger, my thoughts turned to the Indians. For I had replaced those which had done their duty on the Jubila Plateau; and in Hanover Square and in Huxtable's Folly there now stood two silent shapes well suited to the cooling of all military ardour.

Yet it appeared that the significance of what I had done was still not fully appreciated. Perhaps the machinations of politics intervened: I do not know. But my suggestion to Her Majesty and to the Prince, couched in the most careful terms, was met by the reply that matters of this importance could not be considered until the final step had been taken and the country committed to war. Yet it was as a deterrent, not as the great leveller, that I had conceived my weapon!

Before February was over we had, with the French, sent an ultimatum to St. Petersburg; before mid-March the Baltic Fleet had sailed. Even so, hope held on, although when the Tsar saw no reason to answer the Allied note war was inevitable.

One would hardly have thought this so when, in the late afternoon of Monday, March 27th, I sat in the House, anxious to hear the news I had been informed was coming.

Below me the Chamber was unusually full, although few seemed to be listening to the speeches on the private Bills under discussion. Instead, an almost unseemly hubbub appeared to be the order of the day.

Then, exactly at five o'clock, Russell rose from his customary seat on the Ministerial bench and the murmuring was lowered. Called on by the Speaker, Mr. Charles Shaw Lefevre,* he announced that he had a message from the Crown.

*Charles Shaw-Lefevre (1794–1888), first elected Speaker in 1839, retired from the appointment three years after the outbreak of the Crimean War, being created Viscount Eversley.

To the immediate cry of 'Hats off!' Mr. Hume* and those other irrepressibles sitting next to him did not at first respond. But eventually even this ardent reformer and his disciples deigned to conform to the rest of the company.

Mr. Speaker then called on Russell in the accepted way to bring up the message, and as he did so the murmuring died out into a profound silence.

For nearly forty years the nation had been at peace. Now it was to be swept up in a desperate venture whose end no man could foretell. All, I reflected, could have been avoided by a judicious demonstration of the power locked within the Indians.

For once, it seemed, the House knew that it had reach a moment that history would remember. Mr. Speaker looked down at the paper in his hand and it appeared as though for an instant the whole concourse of members had been turned to stone. No sound broke the stillness and I shall always remember that scene, in which nothing moved but the shadows as the lights flickered in the passing currents of air.

'Victoria Regina, Her Majesty, thinks it proper to acquaint the House of Commons that the negotiations in which Her Majesty, in concert with her allies, has for some time past been engaged with His Majesty, the Emperor of all the Russias, have terminated,' proclaimed the Speaker, 'and that Her Majesty feels bound to afford active assistance to her ally the Sultan against unprovoked aggression.'

As the Speaker rolled out the words 'unprovoked aggression', I realized that for Britain, if not for the world,

*Joseph Hume (1777–1855), leader of the Radical Party for thirty years, who 'spoke longer and oftener and probably worse than any other private member.'

this might well be the last occasion on which they would ever be used. For the time had now surely come when my weapon would be utilized to demonstrate that a new era had arrived. My dear Tennyson was to be proven right – now at last we could 'ring out the thousand wars of old, Ring in the thousand years of peace.' It was a noble prospect; I could not but be moved as I sat there listening to the end of an age – fool that I was.

The Commons returned to its normal business. And the Gazette was soon ready with the Proclamation which was announced the following day, expressing Her Majesty's regret at 'the failure of her anxious and protracted endeavours to preserve for her people and for Europe the blessings of peace.'

She was still lamenting the failure when, less than a week later, I once again received the Royal summons. Once more, the Prince was present. Once more, I knew that we stood on the edge of great events. And this time when I arrived there was also the young Prince Albert Edward, not yet thirteen years of age. As he went obediently from the room, I could follow the train of Her Majesty's thought. 'He will be preserved from battle – for which I truly thank God,' she said. 'But he will,' and she sighed deeply, 'have other, and more *complicated* burdens to bear, Professor Huxtable.'

Indeed, this was to be so. I was to shape some of them.

Looking back across the years I wonder whether Her Majesty's faith had not already begun to fail her.

'Now that our troops are embarked on their great enterprise we must support their endeavours in every way,' she began. 'It is clear to us that our Indians form an important part of that support, and that they must be used in demonstration – so long, of course, as they can be used in moderation.'

At once I felt it necessary to ask myself how much Her Majesty knew of war. Moderation! I wondered, and indeed I almost inquired, how many limbs a man should have blown away before war became immoderate. Instead, I held my tongue, and merely reminded Her Majesty that we had discussed their use some years earlier.

She quickly sensed my feelings. 'You must not think, Professor Huxtable, that we are insensitive to what you have given us, nor that we do not intend to spare our troops whatever rigours of battle they *can* be spared. It is merely that . . .' For once Her Majesty seemed not only at a loss for words but almost embarrassed at the thought of using those which came.

'Her Majesty,' intervened the Prince, 'feels that even to demonstrate such a weapon without the greatest deliberation would be more than unwise; she feels that it would be wrong. We have, indeed, given great thought to the matter, and we have decided. But it is natural that even the wisest of mankind should hesitate when invoking the powers almost of the Almighty Himself. We shall be setting out, Professor Huxtable, along a path which will allow us neither to turn back nor to turn aside. Yet we are,' he continued almost in haste, 'confident that that path will lead us to the better ordering of the affairs of mankind.'

As he spoke he turned to the Queen, emphasizing his confidence with a smile, and I realized that in my efforts I had an ally.

'We have decided,' the Queen said, 'that you should take our Indians to the East. It will be necessary for you to consult Lord Hardinge. As you will know, when the Duke died two years ago he left, for his successor, the shorter version of your Jubila Report. So the new Commander-in-Chief will know at least a little of the reasons for your following our troops.

'We think it wrong,' she continued, 'that we should interfere unduly with the manner in which our officers carry out their duties, and we suggest that you should, on reaching the seat of war, consult with the Commander in the field as to the manner in which the Indians may best be demonstrated. We insist only that they should be used as a *warning* and not directly against the enemy; and also that all precautions are taken to ensure that while the warning may be as great as possible, the loss of life should be kept as small as possible. Indeed, we believe that the ideal method of utilizing the Indians would be for us to inform the enemy of its coming use, to suggest the evacuation of an area, and then to demonstrate the awful power which lies within our hands. We feel, Professor Huxtable, that this would be the only *civilized* method; we must ensure that we do not fall into the barbarian ways of those we fight.'

Thus once more was I left to thread my own way through the difficulties. A decade previously, the civilian authorities, the military, and the Company had shuffled the responsibility between themselves. Now it was I who was to bear the responsibility for Her Majesty and, I did not doubt, for whatever Cavalry nincompoop might be appointed Commander in the field. Even when my weapon finally brought peace to the world I did not doubt that there would be recriminations as to responsibility.

I did what I could to forestall the difficulties which I suspected would arise, asking Her Majesty whether it might not be possible to receive from her some note which might ensure the help of the authorities.

'An excellent idea,' she said.

She walked across to her desk, and as the Prince and I watched she wrote, on a single sheet of paper, the following words: 'We, Victoria Regina, request and require in the name of Her Majesty all those whom it may concern to allow the bearer, Mr. Franklin Huxtable, Professor of Natural Philosophy, to pass freely without let or hindrance; to afford him every assistance and protection of which he may stand in need; and to assist him in the military experiments with which he is concerned.'

As she signed it and handed it to me she said, 'We live in troubled times. If ever our subjects become in regular need of credentials when travelling abroad, this wording which Lord Malmesbury has devised will no doubt be followed.'

I thanked her and she and the Prince bade me adieu. Then I left, with high hopes and higher misgivings.

As I feared might be the case, Lord Hardinge was distant though courteous, a Commander-in-Chief aged sixty-eight who was but the first of those ancient Peninsular veterans with whom the management of military affairs was to be saddled in the months that followed. He was agreeable that a new weapon should be used against the Russians. But I could see that from my watered-down report he had gathered not the slightest idea of the power that was being made available. He was content, he said, with existing explosives – although, he added hastily, he had no wish to impede progress. And, like Her Majesty, he felt that details should be reserved for the Commander in the field. As yet, no Commander had been appointed, but troops were already on their way to the Black Sea, and it was suggested that I should follow with the others who would soon be sailing.

I explained how it was necessary for my second black

box to follow at a distance from the first, a matter which he could not understand. And his Lordship airily said that if I took one with my own baggage and left the second in charge of the Master-General of the Ordnance all would be well.

I could but hope that this would indeed be so, but there crossed my mind the idea of asking for the personal assistance of Colonel Swyre. By this time, however, he had established himself in his new military-diplomatic appointment; he was steadily becoming loaded with honours, and I thought that he would probably be considered, even if he did not so consider himself, too grand a person to help me. Yet he could have been master of my commissariat – with what results for the world I now hardly dare to consider. Instead, I satisfied my requirements with Dobbin, more than a servant and less than a colleague, who was to be in charge of my 'meteorological device'.

The weeks that followed my meeting with Lord Hardinge were packed tight with preparations. My wife found it difficult to understand why my work should take me east with Her Majesty's forces, yet greatly enjoyed the fact that she was brought to the fringe of some important secret. She at first wished to accompany me, as the wives of so many officers were doing, but I wisely dissuaded her. After a final embrace she stood on the quayside as, on the afternoon of Tuesday, April 25th, 1854, Dobbin and I were rowed out to the *Shooting Star* which lay in Plymouth Roads.

The first of my two black boxes, stoutly encased, had already been loaded. The second lay at Woolwich, a mere item in the multitude of stores for the campaign but an item which, I had by this time ensured, would soon be following me.

I will not trouble you with details of my voyage to the Black Sea, which began as Captain Fraser weighed anchor at three the following morning. We were a crowded vessel, with Hussars, numerous wives, and even more horses, the last being crowded below decks in a heat and stench which with the weather brought death to many.*

We started badly, being not twenty-four hours in the Channel before striking a gale which brought down the mizzen-top and the main-top gallant masts, so that the next morning the deck was strewn with wreckage. However, repairs were made and we sailed on without undue discomfort, arriving off Gibraltar early on the night of May 2nd, by the light of a moon which flooded the town and the huge bulk of the Rock rising ghost-like behind it.

Here I felt my first stab of anxiety: for among the messages which arrived from ashore was one which had come overland, sent to a Hussar by a brother officer. His field equipment, which was to follow, had by some inexplicable chance been dispatched with the Baltic Fleet, even though the military were, so far as all knew, making no preparations for a landing in high latitudes. I thought, for a moment, of the fate of my second black box, now separated by so many hundreds of miles from its partner lying snug in the hold below and well secured, as I had myself ensured, from the buffetings of the weather.

All I could do was to hope and to pray, as during the following weeks we sailed on to Malta, passed through yet another great storm, anchored off Greece,

*Many details of the *Shooting Star*'s voyage are given in *Journal Kept During the Russian War* (London, 1855), by Mrs. Duberly, an officer's wife who sailed in her.

overtook the *Maryanne* which had been sailing a week ahead of us with a detachment of the 8th Hussars, and then, at three on the afternoon of the 20th, caught our first sight of the minarets of Constantinople.

The Allied intention was, of course, to aid the Turks, already successfully opposing the enemy, and as a base for British and French forces the authorities had already chosen Varna. And at Varna we disembarked on June 1st, coming ashore on to a quay which, like the whole town and the Allied camp beyond it, was the epitome of confusion.

More than one ship stood off the coast, their masters making what arrangements they could for unloading their cargoes. When this had been contrived, by a combination of bribery, threats, and the co-operation of any friendly unit whose officers one could persuade – then, ah! then, one landed into the centre of a chaos the like of which I had never seen. Turks mingled with Greeks, and both with the ruddy-faced British infantrymen. Infantry intermingled with artillery and artillery with Hussars. All picked their way among pyramidal piles of shells and cannon-balls, already unloaded and now awaiting transport. There was, through this mass, a constant passage of horses – kicking, plunging, sometimes dripping with water from their landing and at times screaming with fear.

I was now grateful for my Scottish upbringing which had early brought me out into the world of men. Even so, I would have been lost without Dobbin.

That morning he attended me in my cabin wearing the most extraordinary uniform. Until then he had appeared soberly clad as my valet-cum-assistant, although I had noted him dropping hints that he was more than that. Now he appeared in half-boots, pantaloons and a

regimental tailcoat which must have been acquired from
an assortment of units. I gazed at him in astonishment,
trying to pick from the facings of his coat, the plume
in his shako or the braid decorations with which he
seemed to be liberally decked, some clue which would
betray imposture. I could light upon nothing. The complexity of Her Majesty's uniforms would have made it
impossible for a regimental historian, let alone a scientist, to deny that the figure before me served the Queen;
had they done so, Dobbin would no doubt have assured
them that he served one of her allies.

To me he merely smiled in his grim familiar way.
'Once an old soldier, sir, always an old soldier. No good
doing things by halves, sir.'

Our horses were brought off with Captain Fraser's
good offices; our belongings and my black box followed.
Then we were on our own. At least, we should have
been, but for Dobbin.

Before I could stop him he was clearing a way through
the milling crowd with a shout of 'Master of the
Ordnance! Make way for the Master of the Ordnance!'
He was quick to note three troopers who had become
separated from their units in the confusion, and these
were immediately commandeered to help. I found myself
caught up in the excitement and, shouting orders above
the din with the best of the Cavalry officers, quickly con-
voyed my precious black box and its escort through the
narrow streets of the town.

We were soon riding through the rolling country in
which lay the British camp, on our right hand the line
of the sea and on our left a scatter of villages, each with
its own assortment of storks' nests set perilously in the
tops of the surrounding trees.

Life at Varna has been too well chronicled for me to

describe it here. Most men are now aware of how the Allied forces were reinforced through the weeks, and how cholera kept pace with the reinforcements; of how the brave Turks held the Russians; and of how, before the British or French forces could be set in motion, the enemy retreated eastwards, leaving before us a vacuum into which there was no point in punching.

Long before this I had opened negotiations for use of the Indians. I use the phrase 'opened negotiations', but this is perhaps too grandiose a term for the events they describe. The officer who had arrived to command the forces was Lord Raglan; although he was only three years younger than Lord Hardinge, his handsome face, charming smile and courteous manner suggested vigour rather than decrepitude. Raglan had been one of the first to stand upon the breach at Badajoz, some forty years earlier. The right sleeve of his jacket hung empty from the loss he had suffered at Waterloo. If he refused to take the Indians with the seriousness which they deserved one must remember that he had, as token of their value, no more than the word of a man he had never before met and the acquiescence of Lord Hardinge which might, for all he knew, have been occasioned by nepotism, personal influence, or simply in response to favours given.

'I was informed of your presence, Professor,' he said as I stood in his headquarters tent, a small and modest affair, very different from the trappings of his French counterpart. 'However, I am not quite sure how you can assist us.'

I explained that the matter was one at the highest level and waited until he had, with some reluctance, motioned his aides-de-camp from the tent.

I then told him that it would be necessary to arrange

my mechanisms some miles distant from both the Russian and the Allied forces, that the Russian commander should be informed that the demonstration of an overwhelmingly powerful weapon was to take place, and that various precautions would have to be taken.

His Lordship was a kindly man, and I could see that he wished to humour me. It was also plain that he wished to thrust responsibility for such an irregular arrangement as far into the future as he could.

'We are not, Professor,' he said quite firmly, 'yet involved with the enemy. It is not certain that we shall be. I await orders from London – just as you, as you tell me, await the second half of your device. When both our expectations have been fulfilled, you must ask for me again. Meanwhile, I am glad that you should accompany our forces. You will have to fend for yourself, but I understand that you appear to be experienced enough to do so.'

I was not, of course, experienced in campaigning. Yet I had a certain mother-wit which, with Dobbin's able assistance, enabled me to obtain most of my requirements. I had procured an orderly and a servant, and I was now as well set up as any of those numerous civilians who had attached themselves to the Allied forces.

For many weeks Raglan waited for his orders, while I waited for news of my second black box and grew ever more anxious about its fate. The Commander-in-Chief was the first to receive satisfaction.

Some three hundred miles to the east of us, across the waters of the Black Sea, lay the Peninsula of the Crimea and the great port of Sebastopol in which the Russian fleet sheltered. It was decided in London that this Russian power be eliminated; if possible, the fleet should be destroyed – what a target for the Indians, I speculated – and that as a preparatory move the Allied forces should land on the Crimea itself.

Raglan and his staff, and indeed the majority of those few officers who knew of it, were sceptical about the enterprise. Little was known of the Russian land forces. Nothing was known of the enemy's fleet dispositions. Yet an army of men was to be ferried across this gigantic duck-pond, at the mercy of Russian attack, and then landed, possibly in the face of opposition, on a shore from which they would march to the walls of Sebastopol itself.

Sebastopol! What an opportunity for the Indians when my second black box arrived! For I was now informed that it had been dispatched on a transport due to arrive in not less than another two months.

Meanwhile, as Lord Raglan was good enough to inform me, I could embark for the Crimea with the rest of the troops and witness the excitement of action. On arrival of the second Indian I would confer with him once again.

So it was that early in September we returned through the hubbub of Varna. And what a sight it was as we breasted the hills above the town! The whole bay was dotted with vessels, both sail and steam; an armada of more than one hundred ships, on to which the first troops were already being embarked.

We had almost to fight our way through the town, and it was nearly dark before we were safely lodged below the decks of a steamer – one of those whose duty it was, in the absence of wind, to draw two loaded sailing-vessels on their journey to the enemy shore.

For nearly a week the embarkation continued, the transports being ordered into six echelons, one for each division. And on to them there poured infantry and artillery, horses and commissariat, until it did not seem possible that another load could be ferried out and then ordered below.

At last everything was ready. On the 7th, dawn broke from seaward in a cloudless sky. All was silent, all was still, and it was difficult to believe that no less than forty thousand men were lying below decks in the vessels around which not even a ripple moved.

Then, from the *Britannia*, Admiral Dundas's three-decker flagship, there came the sound of a gun whose report was thrown back to us from the surrounding hills. It was as though the sound had disturbed an antheap, and amid scurrying and the rattle of chains, the entire fleet slid slowly under way, protected on its flanks by sixteen men-o'-war, and moving now before a gentle breeze from the north.*

Our voyage lasted for six days – almost a week for three hundred miles! – and throughout it we were, according to the naval men, at the mercy of superior forces had the Russians chosen to strike.

We saw no enemy. And all was still calm as on the afternoon of the 13th there grew up on the horizon a grey shape from which emerged the cliffs extending either side of Eupatoria. On our right flank there sailed the vessels of the French fleet, and the whole armada now moved forward together.

A few miles offshore we hove to. So did the other vessels, dozen upon dozen of them, each intent upon its own business. On the transports, rising and falling with the swell, the men peered through the autumn twilight

*See *The Great War with Russia,* by W. H. Russell (Routledge, 1895); *The Invasion of the Crimea,* by A. W. Kinglake (Edinburgh and London, 1863–87); *The Russian War,* 1854: *Baltic and Black Sea Official Correspondence* (Navy Records Society, 1943); and contemporary magazines.

to the land which so many were never to leave. Between the two flagships the signals fluttered and then flickered, as the last arrangements for the landing were completed. Within each wooden wall the human company waited for the morrow, knowing only the part which it was ordered to play, obedient cogs in a military machine whose levers were soon to be pulled.

It was a fine starry night, its myriads of twinkling pin-points reflected in the waters. From the darkness of the shore a constant movement of lights showed where the people of Eupatoria had come to watch the invaders. At two a.m. the stillness was broken as a bright rocket flared into the sky from the French flagship. There came an answering trail of gold from Admiral Dundas, and the invasion fleet began to move in.

I had by this time learned sufficient to know one thing: that it would be unwise for me to be separated from my black box. I was determined to feel the heat of battle, but I knew that if I left my device on board the transports it might be returned to Varna at the whim of a captain's decision, sent back to the base at Scutari, or lost in the bottomless pit of inefficiency which the civilian suppliers and the military authorities had already combined to dig. I intended to go ashore with the troops at Old Shore Bay, but I intended that my black box should come with me.

To preserve the security of my device I felt it unwise to disembark with the first wave of troops. I was therefore still aboard the transport as, in the grey light of morning, the line of boats – a mere handful of the three hundred and fifty-seven which had been gathered for the operation – carried the assault infantry forward.

There was, almost miraculously, no opposition. Instead, the build-up proceeded smoothly, and soon after noon I stepped ashore through the surf, followed by Dobbin and four sailors who carried my box up the beach to above high-water mark.

Inland, pickets and forward troops had secured the ground commanding the beaches, while on these officers searched for their men and men for their officers; horses ranged at will, drenching all as they shook themselves after swimming the last few yards. There were camp fires, fuelled by the resources of foraging parties, staff officers riding about as resplendent as ever – and the confusion augmented by the constant arrival of more men, ferried ashore by relays of small craft.

By nightfall no less than twenty-six thousand infantrymen had been landed. But they lacked food and tents, and many must have lacked shot. Thank God the Russians were absent or I would have feared for the safety of my black box, which we brought to the shelter of a ruined farmhouse above the sands.

That night the sky inland was lit by the fires of burning villages where the enemy was destroying all shelter. And that night the weather broke, so that the following morning, what with the ground swell, the desperate need to bring in tents and the equal need to get artillery ashore, there reigned an even greater commotion.

But my story is of Her Majesty's Indians, so I need paint for you only in outline the pictures of those following days which rise so clearly before my eyes. I shall see for ever the extraordinary confusion of the beaches and, only forty-eight hours after the landing, walking along them as though in Piccadilly, three of Admiral Lyon's guests from the *Agamemnon* – Mr Charles Kinglake of *Eothen*, Layard of *Nineveh*, and a florid, bright-eyed man who looked more like a country squire than the editor who was to affect my life so greatly sixteen years later – Mr. John Thadeus Delane of *The Times*.

Days later I, an impartial observer, although one for ever informed by the cryptic comments of my companion, watched that epitome of magnificence and mismanagement, the British Army in the Crimea, advance inland across the rolling country, alight with prairie flowers, to the banks of the Buljanak, above which rose the heights of Alma.

Dobbin and I were among those who the following day joined Lord Raglan's little circle, well knowing that we should move to the best place for seeing battle. I heard the first shot, which fell short and bounded over us with a whizz, the Commander-in-Chief being in the most forward position, though Heaven knows why. And throughout that dreadful day we watched as from a grandstand, I soon learning how to distinguish the singing sound of the Minie bullets, so different from the round ball which whistles softly as it passes you.

Then, as you will know, we passed on towards Sebastopol, though not fast enough. And thus we came to invest that mighty town, basing ourselves on the little port of Balaklava and slowly ringing the Russian fortress with siege artillery.

Here, of course, was the ideal opportunity for demonstration of the Indians. And here, in the port to which I had safely brought my armament, I received news that in a matter of days the vessel bringing my long-awaited equipment would be standing off the shore.

When I tell you the name of the vessel which brought it, you may well gasp with surprise, since my story will explain a riddle which has puzzled men for many years. The message was brief and simple: 'Black box and equipment stowed on the *Prince*; expected Balaklava first week November.'

The *Prince*! That exemplar of the modern transport whose arrival was awaited with such expectations! Now at last I could confer again with Lord Raglan and organize that event which would end for ever those scenes of death and mutilation through which my horse had picked his way up the Alma heights.

The Commander-in-Chief was living as spartanly as before, with one small marquee for himself, a bell-tent for stores and a second one for an office, while his staff had each what they called a 'dog-kennel tent'.

The second Russian failure to force a way down to the port was but a day past and Raglan, whatever his other faults, was still deeply moved by the earlier massacre of the Light Brigade, for it was hardly less.

I was not well received.

'I have noticed you about the field,' said his lordship. 'You ride well for a civilian. But I trust you have not come to worry me about this device of yours; I have trouble enough as it is, what with Lucan and Cardigan and the bluster which Russell will no doubt whip into his account of the Cavalry's misfortunes.'

Russell! On more than one occasion I had been tempted to take William Howard Russell of *The Times* into my confidence, as there floated before my eyes the temptation of using the Press to support my aims. How different things would have turned out had I but conferred for an hour with that hard-headed reporter-turned-visionary! And what a queer twist of fate was to push us both into almost opposite camps less than two decades hence!

However, any thought of Russell was quickly driven from my head by Raglan's obdurate attitude.

I explained that if we were to sit down before Sebastopol for a winter, then there would be ideal conditions for a demonstration of the weapon which would show our enemy the futility of opposition. I received a rebuke for my pains.

'We are still glad to have you with us, Professor,' his lordship said stiffly, 'but it is not the duty of a civilian to talk to a soldier about war.'

It is always useless to argue with ignorance, so I drew from my pocket the sheet of paper which Her Majesty had written for me in London – a lifetime ago, it seemed – and handed it to the Commander-in-Chief without comment.

One wonders, at times, what foolishness military men may do in support of their oath of loyalty; but at least it makes them obedient. Raglan could not deny that signature.

'Very well,' he capitulated. 'But if it is Her Majesty's wish, it is suitable that the matter should be arranged through Her Majesty's cousin.' He called for an aide-de-camp and I knew that he was again to shuffle the matter off on to other shoulders.

'Present my compliments to the Duke of Cambridge,' he said, 'and inform His Royal Highness that there is something I would like to discuss with him at his early convenience.'

He then turned to me. 'I will tell him to make the necessary preparations. But before anything is finally done we must confer again. And now we must get on with the campaign.'

At this signal I thanked him and left to take up my new burdens.

I had watched the Duke of Cambridge at the Alma and I did not doubt his courage; only his wisdom. As commander of the 1st Division he had been the very essence of soldierly bearing; I could think of no one less likely to appreciate the possibilities of my weapon. Raglan, I suspected, thought the same. This was unfortunate enough. But there now commenced a series of unhappy events in which, were one a religious man, it would be possible to see the intervention of the Almighty.

I knew that it would be difficult to convince Cambridge that I had a weapon so terrible that it would end war for ever. Yet I believed it might be possible to play upon his natural curiosity. In many ways he was, as I had gathered from members of the staff, rather like a child. If he could only see my existing black box, if he could only stand before it and be told that it could spread destruction over an area many times that of Sebastopol – then might it not be possible to arouse his interest so that I could command my own terms for that demonstration?

This, indeed, appeared to be the solution, and from Raglan's headquarters I picked my way down the road to Balaklava, a road already so indistinguishable from the heights down which it wound, that the best route could be chosen only by using the markers provided by dead horses or dead men.

It was the evening of November 6th. The *Prince*, I was at once informed by Dobbin, was already off the Crimea, and would tomorrow be making for harbour. She was, as common gossip proclaimed, filled with the needs of life – winter clothing and stockings, boots, shoes, watch coats and woollens. She had also surgical instruments. And she had, also, packed somewhere below decks, my second black box.

This latter fact I now reported to Captain Dacres, the officer responsible for ordering into port those merchant ships whose captains wished to unload at the totally inadequate quays. It was a conversation I was to regret to the end of my days.

I wished only to inform him that part of the cargo on the *Prince* was of great importance; but I was incautious enough to say that this cargo represented the essential of an explosive device. I wished only to stress the measure of its worth. Instead, I aroused the good Captain's anxiety.

He could not, he said with some vigour, allow a powder ship into such a crowded harbour. To which I responded that my device did not consist of powder and was harmless. He would have none of it. He had already heard that scientific mechanisms designed to blast the Russian blockships from the mouth of Sebastopol might be included in the cargo of the *Prince*, and my words were enough to set his decision – with dire results.

'That part of the cargo of which you speak, Professor,' Dacres maintained, 'must be taken off in the roadstead. For me to allow more would endanger the harbour, a dereliction of duty.'

So I resigned myself to additional delay, wished him well, and returned up the path to the heights, accompanied, of course, by my black box and its retinue, and anxious to confront Cambridge with it as soon as possible.

Now our misfortunes began. There was delay in discovering the Duke's headquarters, delay in finding the Duke, and further delay before an appointment could be arranged. And by that time the Commander of the 1st Division had decided that illness and exhaustion justified a withdrawal from the seat of hostilities. He would take up his headquarters in the *Retribution*, one of Her Majesty's paddle frigates at anchor off the coast.

Thus it was almost a week before, in the dusk of

November 13th, we were rowed out to my appointment with the Duke; still with my black box, still optimistic, and perhaps now even confident, for from the shore there had been pointed out to me, more than a mile away, the sleek outline of the *Prince*. With her load and mine, I knew, we had the answer to all the problems that now confronted the authorities.

About one point I might have been anxious, had I but been able to disentangle it from the jungle of rumour and report which spread like the Crimean mud over all activities. For some ill will had already been created between the *Prince* and the port authorities. Dacres had indeed remembered our conversation. And when the transport had arrived in the roadstead on the 7th he had met her captain's request to unload with the reply: 'I have no authority to allow a powder ship to come in, although I certainly think she ought to be inside.'

Had I remained at Balaklava one more day; had I only kept Dobbin there to exercise his customary persuasion, I would no doubt have been able to smooth matters over, at least with the aid of Her Majesty's letter. Had the Duke been more readily accessible, matters would by this time have been completed. And had he not chosen to begin a period of sick leave on the *Retribution* I would not have been crossing to that ship on this lowering November afternoon.

In this enterprise as in all others, bad luck was always waiting in the slips, watching for any chance which fortune offered. This was one of them.

However, my reception was more cordial than I could have expected. The Duke was just thirty-five, knowledgable in the ways of the Army but not in those of war; indeed, until the Alma his experience of action had been limited to a confrontation with the Leeds rioters. He had, I could sense, been surprised by the slaughter of war and, for a while at least, he was amenable to suggestion.

I was quickly shown below decks, to the cabins which had been put at his disposal by officers who regarded the unexpected arrival of their royal guest as an honour rather than an inconvenience.

We exchanged only a few words and then, with the Duke's approval, I ordered Dobbin to bring in the weapon.

The Duke, I remember thinking, looked every inch a Hanoverian as he sat before my squat box. I could envisage him as a monarch in some rural German state, immensely pleased to have a new toy for inspection.

'So this is your weapon, Huxtable,' he said, sitting hands on knees. 'You must show it to me.'

I was reluctant to open it because I feared that Cambridge's hopes might be dashed; even the simplest muzzle-loaders would appear, to the uninitiated, a complicated affair compared with the Indian.

But Cambridge was persistent. The necessary implement was sent for. The Duke filled glasses for us both. Then, after the swinging lamps had been lit and the curtains drawn, I carefully removed four screws and lifted the lid.

The Duke peered in. 'Remarkable,' he said. 'Most remarkable. This must be your new powder ...' He stretched forth his hand, and for the only time in my life I restrained a member of the Royal Family, catching his wrist and warning him of great danger.

He understood – although, indeed, there was no danger – and began to smile.

'How simple,' he said. 'One pours this mixture down the muzzle of the instrument in your second box; one lights the fuse and stands clear. How ingenious! How magnificent! And can a whole company be destroyed by it?'

A muzzle! A company! I attempted to explain that my weapon worked on entirely different principles – though I was careful not to hint at them; that an immense explosion was engendered immediately the male and the female halves were brought into intimate contact – a description which delighted him. And I said in words as clear as I could that it was not companies but whole armies which might be destroyed by its power.

I saw immediately that I had made a mistake. It would have been better to have foregone honesty and to have let Cambridge ramble on. It was clear that he did not believe me. It was clear that he felt I had imposed on Her Majesty with some trickery, although that fact tickled his humour.

'To have cozen'd my dear cousin,' he exclaimed with an air not of wonder but of awe. 'Indeed, Professor, you are wasting your talents in this wilderness.'

I insisted – to such effect that, I feel sure, he believed I had been embroidering my story only with honest enthusiasm.

'Do not worry,' he went on. 'A company at a time will be enough.' He grew confiding. 'You see, Professor, there must be humanity and reason in all things. Now you talk of destroying whole armies. If this were possible, then where would lie the art of the military commander? You would destroy men by the regiment. But where then would be the chance for an ambitious subaltern to show his courage? You would make manoeuvre impossible, render useless the experience of sergeants who have spent a lifetime in learning the arts of war. In any case, sir, whatever we infantrymen might say, the Cavalry would not allow it.'

Here was an obstacle I had never expected to encounter – disbelief of gargantuan proportions; but Cambridge broke in upon my silence with a kindly hand on my shoulder.

'I repeat: do not worry. A company is enough. To-morrow you must tell me what you want and I will issue my instructions.'

There was nothing more to be done that night. I replaced the lid of the black box and called Dobbin, who supervised its removal. I bade Cambridge good night; and then retired to the cabin which Captain Drummond had put at my disposal.

As I went on deck before descending the afterstairway, the night was calm, almost ominously so. The shrouds hung motionless from the single mast of the *Retribution* and the seamen, sensitive as ever to the vagaries of Nature in all her moods, were commenting in undertones as they looked towards the great cliffs of the shore, only a few hundred yards away.

I slept soundly. But well before dawn I was awakened by a tug on the arm and found Dobbin standing by my bunk. Then I heard what I at first took to be the noise of the ship's paddles. It was, instead, the sound of the wind.

I dressed quickly and went on deck, moving with difficulty as the ship tugged at her three 140-fathom cables. For some while all I could see was the driven spray. The gale, for such it was quickly becoming, veered remarkably, and more than once a gust brought across half a mile the scream of terrified horses. For on shore, as we were later to learn, not a tent was left standing by dawn; waggons were overturned, tables sent flying and maddened animals by the score pulled their pegs from the sodden ground and galloped at will through the chaos.

With the coming of light the wind increased. Looking towards Balaklava, all that could be seen was a horizontal sheet of driving spume through whose gaps it was occasionally possible to glimpse a tossing vessel. Many of the merchant captains had tried to run for the safety of the harbour entrance. Their lot was better than those outside – those who, like the *Retribution*, lay at the mercy of the weather and of the iron-bound coast.*

Thank God Dobbin had ensured that the Indian was stoutly lashed between the forward stairs, or it would quickly have been pitched overboard. As it was, there loomed danger enough.

Through the drenching squalls it was possible to see that many of the transports riding at close quarters were tugging at their anchors. Before nine what we had feared took place: the *Rip Van Wynkle* tore loose and was carried past us. For a moment it seemed that she would foul us, and every man aboard, Drummond and the Duke included, stood by for action.

The transport cleared us, or we should certainly have gone too. What that would have meant was clear as the vessel was swept towards the coast. Minutes later, there was a thunder-crack and a vomit of debris as she split apart on the rocks.

Our own situation was desperate. At the first warning of danger, Drummond had got up all steam; and now, turned into the wind, with our cables stretched taut, we were holding our own. But at ten o'clock our

*See *Military Life of H.R.H. George, Duke of Cambridge,* by Colonel Willoughby Verner (John Murray, 1905), and the *Illustrated History of the War against Russia,* edited by E. H. Nolan (London, 1855–7).

rudder was swept away and it seemed that we too must be carried on to the cliffs.

Through all this turmoil, Cambridge remained remarkably calm, giving a hand where needed, speaking little and, though it may seem strange to say so, creating the impression that he was enjoying himself.

Then, as the *Retribution* rose high on the crest of a wave, he pointed through the driving sleet and rain. 'Perhaps you need not have asked my help, Professor. Nature herself may bring together your two black boxes.'

I followed his outstretched arm to where, only half a mile or so away, the *Prince* was, like us, steaming into the gale, apparently held on a single anchor, and in even greater danger of being torn free. I realized with consternation that if we both were torn adrift by the wind we might well lodge at the same place beneath the towering cliffs whose lower reaches were covered by a moving frieze of white breakers.

In the peril of the hour I had, I must admit, totally forgotten the *Prince*. Now the awful possibility was clear. It was not certain whether we were one mile or two from the centre of the port. It did not matter. Port and town, the whole British headquarters, would be dissolved if the *Prince* and the *Retribution* were pitched by the storm into lethal proximity. Chance, I realized, might equally have brought my black box to the Crimea in the *Rip Van Wynkle* whose beams had so nearly touched ours.

Of the implications Cambridge was, of course, in truly blissful ignorance, yet even without the apocalyptic danger from the Indians we were in peril enough. For we were now losing ground, and desperate measures were needed.

'Lighten by losing the upper-deck guns,' Drummond ordered, and a few moments later the men were at their dangerous work. High seas continually broke over the ship which canted this way and that, and great skill was needed to ensure that when the heavy monsters were loosed from their shackles they lurched into the sea and not across the slippery deck. Three had safely been delivered into the waves when the fourth, sent back on her tracks by an unexpected buffeting of the vessel, careered out of control across the deck, smashing bulkheads like matchboard, ripping loose metal fittings, lunging back and forth as though possessed with life. Eventually, by skill and luck, it was directed overboard – as were the rest of the upper-deck guns.

Thus lightened, we rode the waves more easily; and our attention wandered to the more desperate spectacle presented between our anchorage and the narrow entrance of the harbour.

Here more than one transport had already been wrenched from its moorings. And, as we watched, my eyes once more turned to the *Prince*, that new steam transport, larger than the rest, 2,700 tons and the pride of her makers. On her cargo there rested – in more ways than one, though I alone knew it – the fate of the British armies.

The previous evening, although I did not know it at the time, a Lieutenant Inglis of the Royal Engineers had been kindly sent aboard by Captain Dacres to supervise the disembarkation of my box, thought by him to be the apparatus on the *Prince* to be used for blowing up the ships blocking Sebastopol to Allied use.

Now the *Prince* was in dire trouble. Like the *Retribution* she had been steaming into the wind since the start of the hurricane. But unlike *Retribution* her safety had rested on only two anchors, and it was clear that one had already gone.

The ship seemed to be dragging, and as we saw a scurry of ant-like figures moving about her single mast I heard Drummond mutter: 'Desperate measures.' Desperate indeed, for the men, hanging on with difficulty against the gale, were attempting to cut away the mizzen-mast.

It was a delicate job. It took time, and before it was finished there was an abatement in the storm. Through the reek, the ship seemed to be holding her own, though her screw rose and fell from the water with every wave.

Then, with a roar which we could hear half a mile away, her mizzen-mast came tumbling down in a welter of spars and rigging. As it did so, the stern of the ship rose from the water, exposing her screw; and as this thrashed back into the waves it wrapped round itself the fallen ropes and cordage. At the same time it settled the fate of the Indians, so far as the Crimea was concerned.

For with all forward pressure stopped, the final cable parted with a report I can hear as I write. The great vessel lurched backwards towards the shore. In a few moments that seemed an age she was driven full tilt at the cliffs, which here rose to many hundreds of feet.

The *Prince* hit with a splintering crash, but for an instant it seemed that she and the one hundred and fifty souls on board might still be spared, for she had not broken. Then, as we watched, she was lifted almost clean from the sea by an abnormally high wave and dropped back on to the rocky fangs.

The vessel parted amidships, her back broken. In an instant the waves were topped with bales and packages and the flotsam that had once been men. Nothing could live in those seas.

And nothing, now, would give the Crimea the salvation of the Indians. For at the moment of impact, as the *Prince* had hit the rocks, there had come a blue-green flash which all those on the *Retribution* took to be but another flash of the lightning that had played about us intermittently all morning.

Only I knew that it was the Indian, harmlessly disintegrating.

Thus mortified, I knew not what to do. The storm abated. The wind died, though heavy seas continued. But my single box was as impotent as a new-born babe, and it was in the deepest dejection that I took it ashore later in the day with Dobbin's help. Cambridge consoled me, although I felt that he was greatly relieved that there would be long delay.

It was obvious that I must return to London and then sail back to the Crimea with a third box as replacement for the second. But what, meanwhile, was to happen to the first? I was loath to leave it in Balaklava, at the mercy of the Army's inefficiency, yet I felt I must. Without its counterpart it was, after all, safe enough. Its accidental destruction would produce merely a flash which would be frightening but harmless. Its significance would be known to none but myself. And I have sometimes wondered whether even today there does not still exist, forgotten and cobweb-covered in some military store, a black box whose contents no man will ever understand.

For I did not return to the Crimea. I was, in fact, lucky to leave it alive. I had been back in Balaklava but two days when I was seized with cramps whose import I well knew. Since the days at Varna, which now seemed so very far away, I had seen too many men die of cholera to be ignorant of the symptoms.

Yet I was fortunate. There were long weeks at Scutari, and more months before, aided by rough nursing, and encouraged by Dobbin, I again saw England – and learned that Amelia, months earlier, had presented me with Julie, a fair-haired daughter.

More like a match-stick than a man, I had survived. I had survived more than ever certain that my mission was to end the horrors which had been so clearly displayed in the Crimea. Thus I began preparing another Indian.

It was, such had been the delays occasioned by my illness, late summer before I could complete my work. And then, as I was preparing to set out again on what I now conceived to be my life's duty, there came the news so eagerly awaited by others: Sebastopol had fallen. The war, it was confidently believed, would be over before I arrived. My plans were cancelled. A great opportunity was lost.

However the Crimea was to have repercussions, and unexpected ones.

7 : The Nightingale, Lincoln, and Chlorister Affairs

In some ways the Crimean War thrust back the chances of my weapon being used. Much nonsense had been engendered at home among the civilians, secure in their profits and their piety, and the slaughter had thrown a new glamour on war – among those who had not witnessed it. Noble six hundred, indeed! Noble – undeniably and gloriously, but victims of gross mismanagement which my old friend Tennyson, now plump with his Laureateship, simply dubbed 'blunder'. I never again thought the same of him.

Now that Peel and Wellington were dead, only Her Majesty, Prince Albert and myself were aware of the Indians' truly apocalyptic power. The Prime Minister and the Commander-in-Chief had only the vaguer information in the castrated report that had been the inspiration of Prince Albert, and even that they considered – when they considered it at all – as information for their eyes alone. At lower levels still, as one sank to Under-Secretary rank, knowledge became mere rumour, unsubstantiated stories that a new weapon had years ago been the subject of extravagant claims. If rumour went too far, some superior person would be sure to point to an alleged confusion, and to claim that while there had been a plan to test such a weapon, it had been destroyed during one of those earthquakes which were known to ravage distant parts. The common people knew nothing, and the top people very little.

Whatever Colonel Swyre guessed, he remained dutifully silent. He had been lucky to remain apart from the Crimea, that graveyard of military reputations, and had continued to march stolidly up the ladder. He looked on me as the maker of his fortunes, and some months after my return from the East I was inveigled into speaking for him when he stood – unsuccessfully, I am glad to say – as a member for Parliament. I spoke on a public platform, as an acquaintance of some years' standing, although I naturally did not specify the details. I spoke of him, however, as a man to be relied upon in dangerous enterprises. At the time I had no idea of the rod I was making for my own back. I made the reference at random, drawing it from the air to illustrate my private thoughts. Chance brought it to my lips – although later I began to wonder if all was really chance or whether some pattern might not be imposed upon our lives.

It was from other quarters that there came, during the years which followed the end of the Crimea, the first threats to the security of my device. They were three in number and of increasing danger.

Some months after the conclusion of the war there came once more a summons from the Queen. Once more I found myself driving up that curving High Street and past the sentries into the Castle.

Both Her Majesty and the Prince were agreeable, consoling me on the misfortune to the Indians, and assuring me of their confidence that I was in no way to blame for the miserable fiasco.

'We are doubly grieved,' said the Queen, 'since a demonstration of your device would have shortened the months of suffering which our soldiers had to endure, and would also have shown that the people of our small island have a leadership not only in military ardour but in scientific ingenuity. However . . .'

Some inner qualm made me fear what was coming. Surely Her Majesty's regret, I asked myself, could not be qualified. I was wrong.

'However,' she continued, 'we must remember that we lie always within the hand of God. However much we regret events, Professor Huxtable, we must remember that it was He who sent the tempest and He who brought our plans to nought. It may be that in His omniscience He saw that the time was not propitious for the use of such power. It may be that we were presumptuous, and that He thus decided to strike the weapon from our hands.'

At Her Majesty's words I felt even more profoundly depressed. Nevertheless, I could but acquiesce – and note that there would be other opportunities.

'Indeed,' said the Prince, 'it is likely that this will be so. And it is certain aspects of such possibilities that Her Majesty and I felt we should discuss with you.'

He took down from the shelf behind him one of the volumes illustrating the contents of the Great Exhibition which had been his pride and joy.

'You will be well aware,' he said, 'of the inventions, of the ingenious contrivances which were exhibited in Hyde Park. Many are already being made in more than one country. This,' he continued, 'is but another example of that development of which, I am certain, all men of science are cognisant. I speak of the international character not only of the laws of nature but of their applicability to man's needs.'

He looked up from the book, and as he spoke on I was astonished by his knowledge.

'It is only a few years past that the electric locomotive engine was produced – by a gentleman in the United States. Foucault, whose gyroscope is such an ingenious device, is of course a Frenchman. The duplex telegraph system comes from Austria, while this extraordinary aniline dye' – and he turned to the Queen – 'of which we have recently seen samples, comes from the Englishman Perkin.

'We live in an age of stirring invention, Professor Huxtable, an age in which we see more clearly every day that knowledge knows no national boundaries, that ideas have the ability of the intrepid balloonists who sail across frontiers from one country to the next with a speed which the governors of the world may applaud or deplore, but which they would be unwise to ignore.'

I agreed with all this, of course, but could hardly see its relevance.

'Thus,' continued the Prince, 'we cannot ignore the possibility that other men may light upon your secret – other men in other countries.'

Possible? Of course; but how absurd to imagine that the same train of thought would really be followed by another for so long, through so many devious twists and turns. The coincidences would be too great – as though one might set a chimpanzee to a piano and find it, by chance, hitting the notes of a Bach fugue!

'The possibilities are remote in the extreme,' I said, 'but it would no doubt be wise to consider them.'

'We feel in like manner,' said Her Majesty. 'That such a device might one day come into the hands of those of ill intent is almost too dreadful to contemplate. It is unlikely that even the most evil of men would wish to use it in battle; but they might consider its utility as a deterrent; and we are not easily deterred, Professor Huxtable.'

She did not wish to alarm her soldiers who might in a remote extremity have to suffer from such a weapon, Her Majesty went on. 'We do feel, however, that you should consult with those who might be able to limit its effects.'

I nearly remarked that my experiences had given me little cause to believe that the effects could be limited. But I held my tongue, as Her Majesty now continued.

'We have therefore suggested, Professor, that Miss Nightingale should call upon you. We do not think it right that she, a woman, should be burdened with the full knowledge of what your device would accomplish. We know that we can rely upon your discretion, and your ability to aid her without revealing what it would be most unwise to reveal.'

I realized that once again it was I who had to take the decisions. But I thanked Her Majesty, said I would do my best, and assured her that I would be honoured to help Miss Nightingale whenever she wished to call upon me.

'I imagine,' Her Majesty replied, 'that it will be soon.' Indeed, it was soon.

I must admit to some trepidation as, two days later, I awaited in my study the arrival – only fifteen hours after her letter – of this formidable woman. She came. So far as I was concerned, she conquered.

At Scutari I had heard of her nightly rounds with the lamp; I expected to encounter a woman whose whole being exuded the substance of command. Not so. Although the figure before me exhibited no positive beauty, Miss Nightingale was yet of a prepossessing countenance and manner. It is true that her chin, so prominent at the base of her pear-shaped face that it looked like the growth on a fruit, spoke of firmness and resolution;

it is true that her eyes conveyed a steadiness which in a man might betoken expert marksmanship. Yet these features were submerged in an obvious gentleness of character, and subordinated in the smile which not infrequently passed across her face. Rarely have I seen a more equable combination of humanity and grave earnestness. In a busy life one is accustomed to meeting, occasionally, the great man; here was that rarer thing, a great woman.

She had barely been seated when I found myself subjected to the full force of what has been called 'the Nightingale power'.

'As you are aware, Professor,' she began, 'we are hopeful of lessening the future sufferings of our troops by forethought and wise management. Her Majesty has told me that there is a future possibility – remote, I gather, but of an order which should be considered in our plans – that a weapon greatly more destructive than any now known, might in some war to come be used against our troops; that – for reasons which are quite unknown to me but of which I am certain I would disapprove – no reference must be made to this weapon by me, even to my closest collaborators and advisers. And that in spite of this hampering difficulty, I might, with help from you, be able so to guide matters that the sufferings of our soldiers would be kept to the minimum.'

She looked at me most amiably.

'Professor, I am at your service.'

I had feared just this. Even the Queen and Prince Albert, I realized, did not fully comprehend, or perhaps did not even fully believe, my report of the Jubila experiment. They too looked on the Indian as merely a more efficient explosive. My doubts were confirmed by Miss

Nightingale's next words.

'It is above all necessary,' she said, 'that we should know what order of casualties would be produced by each projectile. Would there be tens or perhaps even hundreds?'

Poor woman! How could I possibly begin to explain!

'Miss Nightingale,' I said, 'the casualties would naturally depend on the circumstances. But the devastation produced would be so great, the area affected of so many acres, that the casualties would be numbered in many, many thousands.'

I immediately saw that something was deeply troubling her.

'Professor Huxtable,' she said, as though determined to confide in me, 'I have come to you on the orders of the Queen. But the Commander-in-Chief also knows of my visit.'

I thought of Cambridge, now hoisted into the military saddle by the chances of fate and the disingenuousness of Palmerston. I thought of him as I had last seen him, commiserating with me as I followed my black box from the *Retribution* into the jolly-boat, and saying how 'useful it would have been to have dealt with the enemy a whole company at a time.'

'He warned me,' Miss Nightingale continued, 'that you would give me an account of your weapon which would, as he described it, be apocalyptic. He said that he had long suspected that it was just a more powerful powder.* And he added –' she looked at me as though I had been deliberately prevaricating, '– he added that

*'I do not think it will be as effective as is expected,' Admiral Leahy, President Roosevelt's Chief-of-Staff, told King George VI shortly after the test of the atomic bomb in 1945. 'It sounds like a professor's dream to me.'

130

when he was appointed Commander-in-Chief he found a paper which justified his suspicions.'

I thought – and now how disparagingly – of Prince Albert's ingenious scheme by which the successors to Peel and Wellington were to have only a discreetly edited version of my Jubila Report. I was now being hoist on my own caution.

'I am sorry, Miss Nightingale,' I said, 'but I must ask you to consider how much weight you would give to the Duke's military ability, or to his ability to assess the potentialities of science.'

I saw what was almost a smile cross her face. But she would not be disloyal and said merely, 'Please continue, Professor.'

I continued.

'But,' she at last said, 'if destruction is to be so widespread how will it be possible to discriminate? Surely large numbers of non-combatants – possibly even civilians – might be killed?'

I had to admit that this might indeed be so.

'In that case, this weapon will not be used,' Miss Nightingale said with assurance. 'Since I am permitted to know no details, I cannot speculate on its complexity. But it is clear that it is a weapon which could only be made by a civilized nation. Such a nation might be prepared to demonstrate it; no civilized nation would use it in battle when the chance of killing civilians, let alone medical staff, might be great indeed.

'However, we must assume that such a weapon might at last fall into the hands of a non-Christian nation. So we must, as Her Majesty says, be prepared.'

She opened the large flat exercise book that she had been carrying.

'What *sort* of injuries?' Miss Nightingale then wanted

to know. Would burns, amputation of limbs, or other effects, predominate?

My mind went back to the horses on the Jubila Plateau. I said that burns would be certain and numerous. But how was it possible for me to describe the transmutation into natural elements which would be brought about within close proximity to the weapon?

I explained that it would be necessary for me to consider certain matters and to make careful calculations. Perhaps the very mystery with which the weapon was shrouded invoked her woman's curiosity. But I felt that she would not readily let the subject rest.

So indeed it was. Over the years Miss Nightingale visited me often, dining with us to the intense enjoyment of Amelia, and of my growing daughter Julie, who was always allowed in to shake hands with the great lady before being sent back to bed. At times I was unable to appreciate the subtleties with which she invested the possible use of my device. Thus during the Mutiny it seemed clear to me that all opposition might have been easily removed, but my tentative suggestion to Her Majesty was brusquely turned down.

Miss Nightingale sympathized with the Queen. 'To use such a weapon at all may be a crime, Professor Huxtable,' she said. 'To use it against coloured people would be a mistake.'

With the outbreak of the American Civil War – she helped from afar and the Secretary of the United States Christian Communion said that her 'influence, and our indebtedness, to you, can never be known' – Miss Nightingale's interest in my weapon appeared to abate.

I was satisfied that the secret was safe. But now, and directly emerging from Miss Nightingale's activities, there arose a more serious threat of disclosure.

I had visited her in the Burlington Hotel where she had set up her headquarters, so cluttered with Blue Books that it appeared more work-room than rest-room. We had spoken of America and as I rose to go she rested a hand on my arm.

'To us here below, the fight of brother against brother is the hardest of all,' she said. 'Whatever the ends, one must wonder at the means.'

I said, as I had said before, that new weapons now had the power to banish war for ever.

'I wonder,' she said. 'I wonder, Professor.'

I bade her good-bye. And I thought no more of the matter until, on the evening of June 5th, I attended a meeting of the Society of Arts presided over by Prince Albert, by this time Prince Consort, whose brain-child the Society had been. I listened intently to a discourse outlining the proposed Exhibition of 1862; and I was afterwards one of the select few with whom the Prince spoke.

As though reminded of something by our meeting he said, most unexpectedly, that he had been discussing me with Miss Nightingale; and he asked me to call upon him the following day. The arrangements were quickly made with his equerry.

When I called upon His Royal Highness the next day, I thought that he looked tired – as, indeed, did many of us forced to remain in the capital throughout the heat of that cloudless summer. Even his study, spacious and airy though its proportions were, carried a hint of oppression. I would have been happy had the side-tables, so heavily laden with volumes, been less multi-tudinous, had the walls been less closely covered with portraits. Even the trees of the Park, vaguely seen across Constitution Hill, looked parched in the sunlight.

As usual, His Royal Highness came quickly to business.

'During the last two decades,' he said, 'we have tended to see your device in a constantly changing light. Thus we asked Miss Nightingale to seek your advice on the assumption that wars would still continue.

'She tells me you are still convinced that even a threat of your weapon would be enough to stop war?'

I agreed that this was so.

'And thus,' said the Prince, 'that anyone who had witnessed the test on the Jubila Plateau would not dare to proceed with hostilities?'

Again I agreed.

'Thus,' he went on, 'an accurate account of such devastation would, no doubt, be sufficient to do the same?'

Here I felt it necessary to qualify my agreement.

'That,' I pointed out, 'would depend on the circumstances of the phrase "proceed with hostilities". As a threat, a mere description might suffice in the case of a nation which stood on the verge of war. But if battle had begun, if passions had been roused – then, I fear, Sir, nothing less than a demonstration in the field would suffice.'

'In this case,' he replied, almost thinking aloud, 'such a course would be quite impossible.'

He turned to me again and said bluntly, 'War has already started; war is being waged against the legal government of the United States of America; yet a demonstration is clearly impossible. Words must suffice.'

He smiled as he saw the apprehension cross my face.

'I know that we are neutral,' he said. 'Her Majesty has proclaimed us so and so we shall remain. Yet our very neutrality is our strength; and it should be stated that it lies within our power not merely to ask for peace but to plead for it.'

You will know how His Royal Highness intervened in the *Trent** affair; you will know how his urbane amendments to the Prime Minister's note of protest almost certainly prevented the outbreak of war between Britain and the Union. Yet at the time of which I write even I, well informed of events though I was, suspected little of the extent to which the Prince Consort would exert himself in support of legally constituted governments.

'We have,' he went on, 'the moral power of the unimplicated neutral down the years. But we have something else which is more than mere power, Professor Huxtable. We have your deterrent.'

He continued. And as he painted the picture of a new world living peacefully within the shadow of the Indians, I could not but admire his breadth of vision. But there were difficulties, and not merely constitutional ones.

'The situation must be handled with extreme care,' the Prince Consort continued. 'There is much to be said for my handling it alone.'

He looked at me intently. 'Alone, that is, with the exception of your help.'

So I was now to be embroiled once more. If only they would leave me at my job, as I left them at theirs!

'All I need,' the Prince continued, 'is your aid in so

*In November 1861 the British steamer *Trent* was intercepted by a U.S. vessel and Mason and Slidell, two supporters of the Southern States on a diplomatic mission to England, were removed from it by the U.S. authorities. Lincoln – helped by the tactful intervention of Prince Albert – finally ordered the release of the captured men.

describing our device to Mr. Lincoln that he will be cognisant of its omnipotence in the field.'

And so, for a week or more, I attended the Palace almost daily. His Royal Highness began by describing the Indians almost in the terms of the Jubila Plateau experiment.

This was all very well; I felt that it was too much. The Americans certainly lack our background. But there is little doubt that they are quick to note straws in the wind, persistent in pursuit of knowledge, skilful in overcoming opposition. I looked at the Prince's draft and saw how one aspect of the physical processes involved might be suggested by one phrase, how the manner in which one started might be hinted at by another. As we sat side by side at his long desk facing the window, I struck my pencil through word after word, meeting his protests with explanation, convincing him of what was necessary.

This was only the beginning. Day by day his description grew shorter.

'Here, then,' said the Prince at last, 'we have the nub of the matter.'

There now came, he went on, the more difficult problem – of explaining that the appearance of this new power within man's armoury meant that war was no longer viable as a solution to the problems arising between nations.

'And,' the Prince added, 'I must so weave my words that my natural feelings do not infringe neutrality. I shall start by repeating the words of the first public address I made in this country.'*

He stopped in his pacings back and forth, turned to

*Given before the Society for the Extinction of the Slave Trade, June 1st 1840.

me, and declaimed rather than spoke: 'I deeply regret that the benevolent and persevering exertion of England to abolish that atrocious traffic in human beings, at once the desolation of Africa and the blackest stain upon civilized Europe, has not as yet led to any satisfactory conclusion. I sincerely trust that this great country will not relax in its efforts until it has finally and for ever put an end to a state of things so repugnant to the spirit of Christianity and to the best feelings of our nature.'

He resumed his pacing, adding to me with a sideways glance: 'That will show Mr. President the spirit of our legal neutrality.'

He stopped again. 'I will then go on, Professor, with some form of the words I have used more than once elsewhere: that we are living at a period of the most wonderful transition, one which tends rapidly to accomplish that great end to which all history points – I mean, of course, the realization of the unity of mankind.'*

For a moment he held out his right hand towards me, its fingers half-clenched – as though, I thought, he might be holding an invisible cricket ball.

'All mankind, working together for one end,' he said. 'Professor Huxtable, your device has not only made that possible; it has made it inevitable. We, with the Americans, must make the world one. But first they must end their fratricidal conflict.'

He returned to his desk. I saw that I was no longer needed. And I left the Palace wondering what the outcome would be.

It was autumn before I knew, before I once again met the Prince, on a morning when the Palace sailed in a

* Quoted in *Prince Albert's Golden Precepts*.

sea of fog and when he handed me, without a word, the reply he had received from the United States.

As I read Lincoln's letter I was at first surprised, then shocked. It ran:

Your Royal Highness,

I am honoured that you see fit to write to me, and with my whole heart I subscribe to your wish that the conflict which now engulfs our States could be ended. I agree, also, with your verdict on the awfulness of hostilities.

You reinforce your argument with the statement that there exists, in the arsenal of Britain, a weapon so overwhelming that a revelation of its power would for ever outlaw war. And you suggest that we – a Britain and an America which had settled its internal conflict – might enforce a peace that would enfold the globe. It is a noble thought.

Yet experience teaches us that it is unwise for men to threaten either one another, or nations, unless they are prepared to implement their threats. Thus, although you yourself do not appear to contemplate it, your letter implies the use, against men and women, of a weapon which would appear inevitably to strike non-combatant and combatant alike; the innocent with the guilty. To imagine less is to delude oneself of the reality of power.

Your intent is Peace, and to this intent, even were the Union less hard-pressed than it is today, I would say 'Amen'. I believe, although men should not be certain in such matters, that your sympathies lie with us, the elected Government. I speculate, for I can do no more, as to the willingness of Jefferson Davis to ignore the differences which now divide us, and to join freely in a greater Union whose indisputable power would demand the peace of the world. Yet, to speak with truth, I feel – perhaps I even hope – that Davis would decline. For we know, because our conscience leaves us in no doubt, that while men are born free they are yet born with the burden of choice – the choice between good and evil; and I cannot but believe that the weapon of manifold destruction which you describe, whatever the ends to which it is put, must harbour within itself the seeds of evil.

To those of you in the Old World who look on us as allies in man's march towards better things, I say this: Do not despair. We shall fight on. The Union will survive. A society of good men ready to die will conquer in the end, despite all calamity, over those who, with their equal bravery, are willing to die for less noble ends. And in God's good time, when the fighting is done, we shall be proud that we saw it to be right, whatever the cost, to follow to its end the road we see ahead.

And so, commending Her Majesty, Your Royal Highness and the Prince Royal to the blessing and the protection of Almighty God, I remain your Good Friend

ABRAHAM LINCOLN

I handed back the letter and I noticed that the Prince's hand was shaking as he took it from me. The fatal illness was already upon him and I am sure that that alone was responsible for the crumpling of spirit which the rebuff appeared to have produced.

'I wonder, Professor Huxtable,' he said speculatively. 'I wonder. The seeds of evil! Can that be all you have sown? Can it be possible that there are curtains hiding the deepest secrets that can be lifted only at extreme penalty? Are we approaching not the millennium but a nightmare?'

This, of course, was a sign of that approaching calamity which was to take him from Her Majesty's side at the height of his power, and reduce to two the number of those certain of the omnipotence of the Indians – Her Majesty and myself.

Yet the third, and fatal, threat to security was but a few years away. Even today I can recall only with distaste what a modern newspaper would describe as the Chlorister Affair.

*

The small seed from which the trouble grew had been planted more than twenty years earlier, in the spacious study of Sir Archibald Chlorister at Jubila. How often had I wondered at my rash promise to keep an eye on his son!

Charles Chlorister might have become almost a member of the family, I almost his uncle. Yet some inner caution warned me against becoming too closely involved with the affairs of the young man, who had trodden a somewhat turbulent path from public school to university, and then – for I had kept my part of the bargain – through the portals of Her Majesty's Foreign Office.

At the time of which I write, Charles Chlorister was twenty-three. He was a tall youth, round-faced, and of an appearance which to myself I described as 'curly'. It was not only that his rich brown hair curled into his extravagant side-whiskers and that his silky moustache appeared to do the same. The flower which he contrived to wear in his button-hole throughout the year was invariably convoluted. His hands and his fingers, plump though delicate, seemed to be for ever on the move, sinuously pressing round a chair-arm, a glass, or a pack of cards. The two rings which ornamented his left hand tended to emphasize the effect. Even when he moved, he did not walk so much as sway.

All this was in keeping with his mode of life – and with his extravagance. From India there came an allowance which in my day at Cambridge would have kept a score of men and even half a score of undergraduates. Yet from Oxford, where Charles had pursued a career punctured with disturbances and threats, representations had more than once to be made to India. The money was always forthcoming. And by the first months of 1863 Charles Chlorister was, in his own inimitable way, assisting Her Majesty's Secretary of State for Foreign Affairs.

My knowledge of events came from numerous sources, but it will be best if I recount, in purely chronological fashion, the happenings which were to have such grave repercussions – and which might have had still worse.

Chlorister suffered from two somewhat complementary weaknesses. One was for gambling: he was a man who would wager a thousand pounds on the turn of a card without thought of where, in the event of loss, the thousand pounds was to come from. The second weakness was an over-weening personal ambition, founded not on hard work, but on the firm belief that whatever the best man in any sphere might achieve, Charles Chlorister could achieve more. On entry into government service his doubt was not whether he would ever attain the

141

Secretaryship of State; the only undetermined factor was 'when'.

It was perhaps inevitable that he should become a member of that select circle whose activities revolved around one man: that young man who nine years before had obediently left the room before I discussed with Her Majesty the impact of the Indians on the Crimea – Albert Edward, Prince of Wales, Duke of Cornwall, Lord of the Isles.

I gave Chlorister what warnings I could – not against the Prince, since I felt that the Press was too quick to latch upon those peccadilloes which are but the failings of our human species – but against the financial morass into which he might easily stumble.

Chlorister took little heed of what I said. For a while, moreover, it appeared that the expensive manner of life into which he had thrown himself might be truly possible. For in India Sir Archibald died – as his son irreverently put it, 'making, beyond his years, a last shake at the pagoda tree.'

The blow fell in the early spring of 1864. Sir Archibald had indeed lived truly to that ideal of service which he had paraded in his effort to prevent me from demonstrating my device. He had made huge sums, but he had spent huge sums – largely on the welfare of those whom he had virtually ruled. The inheritance of Charles Chlorister, 2nd Baronet, was no fortune, but a load of debt.

The climax came in early summer.

I myself had once known the house concerned and can still see that long room with its double windows opening on the gardens. Coming through them there was the scent of wistaria; outside, the flitter of the bats high above the lawns, the light of the full moon, so refulgent but outshone by the lamps above the green baize table.

His Royal Highness was sitting at the centre and, ranged either side and opposite him, those gentlemen of means, or of business, who enjoyed such pastimes.

The stakes that night were high enough to tempt Charles Chlorister into a belief that he might jump the debts to come. Chance decreed otherwise. When the players eventually rose Chlorister walked into the garden. Behind him, unobserved, there walked another figure.

His Royal Highness's talent for divining the complexities of human nature was remarkable. He had correctly sensed what was to happen; and it was a Royal command that now cut sharply across the silence.

'No, Chlorister – no.'

There had always been some weakness in the boy's character; perhaps it would have been better had he now raised the courage to disobey. I do not write of the moral issue – merely of the results which flowed from his actions. He lowered the revolver which he had pointed at his head, and turned to the Prince who now emerged from the shadows.

The next afternoon, when Chlorister visited me to discuss what he described as a personal matter, he was still only semi-coherent about the details of what had followed. I doubt if he would have confided in me at all had he not feared I might hear of the occurrence through other channels. As it was, he explained how the Prince had dissuaded him from suicide; had promised to settle the losses which the young man had so rashly incurred that night, and had in fact done so, discreetly, that very morning.

Chlorister, at heart an honest if weak vessel, was still full of what he considered to be regal magnanimity. I, perhaps harshly, attributed the royal action to a wish to avoid scandal. Whatever the reason, Chlorister's name had been saved and he was now enthusiastic for the future, sparkling with that scatter of bright phrases of which Amelia was so permanently suspicious.

It was with some doubts of Amelia's reactions that I asked Chlorister to stay to tea. He sat with an almost convivial elegance, his back to the windows looking out across the square, his conversation entrancing Amelia against her better judgment. And I can still see Julie, almost ten and looking with her long fair hair like the original of the Reverend Dodgson's Alice, running into the room – unconsciously the *dea ex machina* of that fateful day.

Chlorister patted her head affectionately, smiled at her, teased her, remarked that she was looking particularly beautiful.

Julie smiled back. 'You are looking wonderfully happy today,' she said. 'Why are you so happy?'

'A very great gentleman has been extremely kind to me,' he replied. 'In fact, he has given me a new life.'

'That is very, very nice of him,' said Julie gaily. 'Now *you* must do something for *him*.'

Chlorister looked across at me with the most engaging of smiles. 'Now I wonder if that would be possible,' he said slowly.

For a moment I could almost see the idea worrying around his mind. Then I dismissed the matter from my head. Not so young Chlorister.

Less than a week later it became necessary for his Minister to consult certain instructions given by Lord John Russell during the Crimean War. The only annotated copy was believed to be that retained among Prince Albert's papers. Chlorister was chosen as the junior official sent to search for it among the vaults of

Windsor. And it thus came about that the Prince of Wales, visiting the Castle while Her Majesty was at Balmoral, was one evening suddenly confronted by a slightly dishevelled Chlorister who emerged, rather like a devil from a pantomime trap-door, from one of the castle's subterranean corridors.

Both men were surprised, but it was Chlorister, taking an unusual liberty, who spoke first, frankly and in explanation.

'I have been looking at the Prince Consort's papers, Your Royal Highness,' he said.

'Indeed,' replied the Prince of Wales, wondering what business the Foreign Office had with his father's personal papers. Through his mind there welled up, as he told me later, a great filial feeling. He had always admired his father; he had always known so little of what lay inside the outer shell. And since the Prince Consort's death, only three years earlier, the mystery of the force which had driven him still remained. The Prince of Wales was therefore emotionally primed to respond when Chlorister, acting impulsively as was his custom, wishing only to return hard cash with good will, said: 'Allow me to show you, Sir.'

He indicated the stairs he had just ascended, led the way down, pushed open a stout door at their foot, and stepped back to allow His Royal Highness to precede him.

From an alcove he relit a lamp still warm from its earlier use. Then he led down a maze of passages, through rooms in which, even then, there lay the accumulating discards of many reigns, past alcoves stuffed with State presents which had not found favour, and the purely personal trophies of half a dozen monarchs.*

* Information obtained from a private source.

Making a turn round one of the giant stone pillars supporting the ceiling, Chlorister came to a series of long shelves lining a wall.

Stacked on the shelves in tall piles, there rested a multitude of documents. Below each pile, chalked on the deal, there shone a line of dates – 1860, 1859, 1858, back to the year of the Queen's marriage.

The Prince sat down on one of the rough wooden chairs, gazing at his family past. How many riddles of his own life, he wondered, could not be answered from those piles of yellowing paper?

'A little higher,' he said to Chlorister, indicating the lamp.

As Chlorister raised it slightly, the Prince looked along the shelves towards the year of his birth. He stretched out his hand for half a dozen papers and sat back in his chair. At first he read almost casually. Then the top of a document caught his interest. He leaned up and drew the lamp nearer. A slight whistle escaped from his lips, and as Chlorister instinctively bent forward towards him, he held up his left hand, forbidding nearer approach.

What Chlorister did not know, and never was to know, was the nature of that document – Prince Albert's copy of the Jubila Report.

His Royal Highness was seized by the words I had written. He was carried on from line to line. Only when he had digested the substance of my sentences did the awful truth suddenly illuminate his position.

He turned to his companion and his words were not a statement but an accusation.

'These papers are not personal documents, Chlorister. They are State papers.'

Thus was Chlorister confounded by his inexperience.

Thus did the Prince walk into a distressing situation; for he appreciated, even though he deplored, the Royal prerogative that insisted that the letter as well as the spirit of the constitution must be obeyed; that the Prince of Wales must carry out his duties ignorant of the secrets contained in the red Cabinet dispatch boxes.

Chlorister, as ignorant of the situation as he was innocent of guile, waved the lamp towards the end of the shelf as he smilingly said: 'But naturally, Sir!'

There were the red boxes, thrown in disarray as they had been emptied of their contents years earlier.

For a moment there was silence.

'You have placed me in an impossible situation,' said the Prince in a voice as restrained as he could make it and as firm as was necessary. 'You have done so, I am certain, through ignorance. You should forget your indiscretion and the events of the last hour.'

The following day, when Chlorister confided the story to me, he was still perturbed. He had reason enough, for by this time further debts were coming home to roost. Only now did he admit their scale. And only now did I feel my inability to help.

I did what I could, yet I feared it was not enough. Two days later I found that this was so. The young man had been found in his rooms with his brains blown out – perhaps an inevitable epilogue to a progress that not even a prince could stop. There were, however, to be repercussions far beyond Chlorister's life and death. For his chance visit to the Windsor archives was but one link in a lengthening chain of events.

His Royal Highness had been married in the March of 1863 to H.R.H. Princess Alexandra of Denmark. Towards the end of that year there arose, above the waters of the North Sea, a cloud no bigger than a man's hand.

It surrounded the Duchy of Schleswig – and about the rights or wrongs of the matter I am no more competent to speak than I am to decide on the obscurities of Mr. Whistler.

But about the miniature war that followed, passions ran high; Her Majesty feeling that neutrality should be observed, Palmerston and Russell not so certain, and the Prince of Wales openly solicitous for his wife's invaded country.* In the summer of 1864 a tenuous armistice was debated by a Conference in London. And it was just at this juncture, with Palmerston and Russell urging the Danish cause, and the rest of the Cabinet supporting Her Majesty's ingrained neutrality, that the wretched Chlorister made his own contribution to affairs.

Shortly after his death there arrived at Hanover Square one morning a communication from His Royal Highness the Prince of Wales. He asked me to attend on him, at a particular day and hour. He added a noncommittal compliment. But the reason for his request was still a mystery as I drove to Marlborough House.

The Prince was less plump than I had imagined, more of a man. I could not help liking him, and not only because, I realized, he had actually read some of my papers.

He came quickly to business. 'Professor Huxtable,' he asked, 'was the affair of the Jubila Plateau carried out at the request of Her Majesty and my father, or would you regard it as a matter of State?'

I was quick enough to see two things immediately. One was that the document which had so intrigued His Royal Highness at Windsor a few days earlier must

*See *King Edward VII, A Biography,* by Sir Sidney Lee (Macmillan, 1925).

have been the Prince Consort's copy of my report. The other was that there existed no clear and honest answer to the question.

'It could,' I said, 'be considered purely as a matter between Her Majesty and myself . . .'

I was about to qualify my judgment, but His Royal Highness gave me no opportunity.

'In that case,' he said – I could see that I had taken a weight off his shoulders – 'in that case, Professor Huxtable, I am able to do what I believe to be right without fear of unconstitutional dabbling.'

I wondered. But believing it wrong for a physicist to correct a prince, I remained silent as His Royal Highness turned to me in the most friendly way. 'I would like you,' he said, 'to accompany me on a visit to Her Majesty, who as you will know, has recently returned from Balmoral. I wish to have at hand what I might call my personal scientific adviser.'

I had not seen Her Majesty for many years – indeed, few of her subjects had; and as we were ushered into her presence the following day, I realized that the changes caused by her bereavement were different from those I had been led to expect.

After the end of the Crimean War she had still been a young woman; now she was looking across the plateau of middle age. Yet the widow's peak of her bonnet pointed down towards a face not merely older but of a different nature; and if her black draperies were those to which we had become accustomed, they yet seemed to clothe a different person. Something new seemed to have grown out of her – something more restrained, more commanding, more pathetic yet more regal. I knew what people were saying, how they deplored her retirement, how they felt that she should take the air with the rest of the world. Perhaps so. Yet I could see that she had grown from a woman into a queen.

She had, as I learned later, been given only the briefest warning that her son was to be accompanied by myself, but if she felt surprise she ably concealed it.

'I have brought Professor Huxtable with me,' His Royal Highness began, when the preliminary courtesies were over.

The Queen raised her head only slightly, glanced at me with a kindly look, and turned to the Prince. 'So I see,' she said.

'Professor Huxtable has already been involved in high affairs of State,' said the Prince, as though pleading a cause.

'Professor Huxtable,' said the Queen, inclining her head most graciously towards me, 'has already served our country. I do not doubt that he would be willing to do so again . . .'

I heard so far. Then, as Her Majesty continued, I realized that she had retained her ability to conceal, in the tail of her sentences, her genuine meaning.

' . . . to do so again in whatever way we should direct.'

The gentle emphasis on that 'we', so subtle yet so sure, was the sign of a master-hand.

I knew, as I heard her words, that I had been drawn into an embarrassing entanglement. Suddenly, as though a veil had been drawn away, I saw the two generations preparing for a confrontation.

His Royal Highness had also sensed something of the awareness, almost greater than one should expect from any human, which suffused Her Majesty's intelligence. But he was now embarked on his enterprise and could not draw back.

'In the present dispute between the Kingdom of Denmark and the Kingdom of Prussia' – I noted how provocatively he hung on that word 'Prussia' – 'Your Majesty naturally bears down on the side of peace.'

I watched a slow and cautious nod, as though the oracle were admitting that with this proposition it would be impossible to disagree.

The Prince cleared his throat, knowing that the crisis was at hand. 'Yet with peace there must be justice. Justice rests, as always, on power. And power, Your Majesty, rests within your own hands.'

So far, all I could discern was the gentle nodding head, the kindly figure, the not-so-elderly mother graciously acquiescent to a son quite naturally pleading his wife's cause.

The castle was very silent. I could hear the Queen's rather heavy breathing, and I do not think that it was entirely my imagination, so uncalled-for in a scientist, which heard the ticking of that very clock which I had listened to in that same room so many years before.

'It rests with Your Majesty,' the Prince continued. 'But a just peace, providing Denmark with defence against an invader, could be imposed by a demonstration of Professor Huxtable's device, that device which was demonstrated on the Jubila Plateau more than two decades ago.'

No phrase of mine can convey the feelings which surged through me at His Royal Highness's words. No phrase can describe the change which I now witnessed in the short figure before me.

In a moment Her Majesty was transformed from a mother into a Queen.

'Has Professor Huxtable...?' There was amazement in her tone.

'Professor Huxtable knew nothing of the matter I was to raise,' intervened the Prince.

'Then has Colonel Swyre . . .?'

Her Majesty could see by my consternation that I was at as great a loss as she herself was. She turned to me with great dignity. 'Perhaps you would be good enough to leave us, Professor Huxtable.'

I was glad to bow my way out, to take a seat in the ante-room, and to reflect on the picture which I had seen for a moment as I left – the picture of a Royal Highness shifting uncomfortably from one foot to another, embarrassed and awkward, diminished to the stature of a schoolboy caught red-handed.

For what must have been almost a quarter of an hour I heard no sound from the room beyond. Her Majesty was no doubt talking firmly, quietly, and with all the authority of Victoria, by the Grace of God Queen of the United Kingdom of Great Britain and Ireland, Defender of the Faith.

Eventually the door opened and the Prince of Wales emerged. I rose. He walked up to me. He shrugged his shoulders with a despondent air of resignation. He said:

'I am so very sorry, Professor . . .' And before he could go further the Queen herself appeared at the open doorway and summoned me.

Two things became clear as Her Majesty began to speak: that I now had the friendship of a Queen; and that some aura of disenchantment hung over the Indians and their use in the great purpose for which I had conceived them. Perhaps it was Her Majesty's views on God's intervention in the Crimea. Perhaps it was Lincoln's rebuff. Yet I could not brush off an uncomfortable feeling that when it came to the point of demonstration other factors made themselves felt – what Her Majesty described as the moral issue and that other hobby-horse of hers, the balance of European power.

For a scientist it was all most confusing. It was to become far more so six years later.

For historians, the year 1870 signifies the defeat of France and the resurrection of the German Empire. For me, the significant events of that year marked a watershed in the history of the Indians; the first took place on the evening of Friday, July 15th.

As you will know, the Prince of Wales made a habit of conferring in private with many public men. The dinner party was the occasion, and on the evening of July 15th such a dinner party was held at Marlborough House. Among those present were the Duke of Cambridge, still Commander-in-Chief, although many wondered why; Sir Robert Morier, that able diplomat recently arrived from Darmstadt; and, among others, Delane, commander of *The Times*, the John Thadeus whose almost rustic figure I had seen on the beach of the Crimea sixteen years previously, a man of infinite resource whose network of information channels was even more closely dug than had been supposed.

It was late in the evening when a message was brought in to Delane. The news was grave. His message was from Paris and informed him of the declaration given by the French Government to the Corps Legislatif. Its accuracy was undoubted and its import undeniable. The French were marching to war.

His Royal Highness gave vent to an exclamation of mingled regret and anger. All bemoaned what was regarded as the failure of British attempts at mediation.

'This war,' said Sir Robert, 'could have been prevented if for twenty-four hours the British people could have been furnished with a backbone. It is too late now.'*

Cambridge knew better.

By this time Cambridge always knew better. Little more than fifty years old, he appeared to have aged backwards, so that in each succeeding decade his military ideal seemed to be placed a further ten years in the past. If in the Crimea he had been wedded to the state of the art at Waterloo, he was now back to the turn of the 18th century, regretting the gradual abandonment of those traditional army usages which by the year 1870 had no relevance at all to contemporary problems.

It was natural, therefore, that Cambridge should now mutteringly complain. What, he asked, would have been the use of a backbone without an Army, something which the country no longer had?

Here the Prince of Wales intervened. More than once since the Chlorister affair of six years previously he had tentatively raised with the Commander-in-Chief – 'Uncle George', as he was affectionately known throughout their mutually long lives – the question of what he called 'a superior weapon'. Yet the two men for ever spoke at cross-purposes. The Prince had perused the Prince Consort's full-length Jubila Report only by accident, knew of no other, and believed that Cambridge relied on hearsay. On the other hand, Cambridge, ignorant of the Prince's illicit knowledge, spoke with what he believed to be higher wisdom – although in fact his only written information came from my expurgated version. Here, of course, existed a fruitful source of misunderstanding – and one which the Prince, with the memory of Her

*See *Memoirs and Letters of Sir Robert Morier*, by Lady Wester-Wemyss (Edward Arnold, 1911).

Majesty's reprimands no doubt still tingling in his ears, was fearful of dispersing.

Thus on the few occasions when the Prince had dropped hints to Cambridge, he had been quickly rebuffed. The Commander-in-Chief knew all there was to know about new weapons; he had actually seen, with his own eyes, such a new weapon which might have been used in the Crimea. And it was no good for the Heir Apparent to hint at something monstrous. This device, he would confidentially be told, could deal with men no more than one company at a time – a possibility which of itself was by this time repugnant to the Commander-in-Chief's hardening mental arteries.

Thus by 1870 the Prince of Wales had grown dispirited by his special knowledge. And on this summer evening it was almost with resignation that he turned to Cambridge. Delane told me later that he was not at first sure of the words, since they were muttered rather than uttered. Later events proved him to have been correct.

'We have more than a backbone,' said the Prince. 'We have the ultimate deterrent.'

Delane looked questioningly, but the phrase appeared to have caused embarrassment. Cambridge expostulated. Morier failed to see any significance in the remark, and the Prince of Wales skilfully turned what must have been a dangerous corner in the conversation.

However, after his guests had left, a number of possibilities began to speed through the Royal brain. The most potentially useful, the Prince felt, would be the impartial revelation of Britain's power – perhaps on an island such as Heligoland which could be specially cleared for the occasion. This, he felt, might even at this late date avert the calamity of hostilities and suggest, if no more, that the two powers negotiate beneath the shadow of Britain's omnipotence.

A pretty idea – particularly for one ignorant of the response which Lincoln had already given to a comparable proposal.

Yet when it came to the point of telegraphing to Her Majesty at Osborne, filial obedience came uppermost. The Queen had forbidden her son ever again to raise with her the question of the Indians; her son now obeyed. Even so, ingenuity was to equal obedience, as I was to learn the following morning.

It was shortly before noon on Saturday that a messenger arrived at Hanover Square with a note from the Prime Minister. It was imperative, he said, that Professor Huxtable should attend upon him immediately. A Cabinet was being called at noon and he could only speculate as to its duration, but he greatly wished me to be on hand. I therefore changed for the occasion, Dobbin perceiving the need almost with the arrival of the message, and drove speedily round to Downing Street.

It was almost four in the afternoon before there was a bustle beyond the ante-room where I was waiting, and I realized that the members of the Cabinet were at last dispersing. A few moments later I was alone with Gladstone.

He was shorter, more square, more resolute, than I had expected, somehow almost middle-class, as though his merchant background showed through the covering of Eton and Christ Church. Yet from the moment that I received his blunt stare I knew that I was in the presence of a man more overpowering in intellect, more unswerving in principle, than any I had met. In a long life, no person has made upon me a greater impact in shorter time. Here was a man different not only in quality but almost in kind from Prince Albert and Peel, from the Prince of Wales and Cambridge, even from Wellington – from all those into whose orbits the Indians had drawn me. Here, I knew, was either formidable friend or obdurate opponent.

He came to the point immediately.

'Six hours ago,' he said, 'I was paid a visit by the Prince of Wales. He came strictly incognito. He said he wished to preserve the constitutional proprieties; he said, also, that it was within your power to preserve the peace of the world – even at this late hour.'

Gladstone had suggested that His Royal Highness should first consult Her Majesty.

'He seemed strangely reluctant to do so,' the Prime Minister continued. 'In fact, our brief exchange was contingent on my preserving the utmost secrecy about his visit – except to yourself.'

He pushed a two-page document across the desk towards me, and I immediately saw that it was the emasculated version of my Jubila Report.

'It concerns this, no doubt,' said the Prime Minister, 'although I fail to see anything of revolutionary import in a weapon described in your own words here only as being "of considerable power".'

He looked at me for a moment with the innocence of Cambridge and of Miss Nightingale and those others who had been shielded from the full implications of the Indians.

'I know integrity when I see it, Professor, and I can scent wisdom. Both were in the cast of the Prince of Wales's countenance and in his speech. There is something which has been kept from me.'

He looked at me and I at him.

'You must be honest,' he said.

I would, indeed, have found it difficult not to be honest to such a man. My leanings were all for utmost disclosure. I rose and walked slowly to the centre of the room and faced Gladstone as he remained at his desk, his eyes watching my every move as though I might have an infernal device in each pocket.

Then I began. I explained how my weapon could be made at small cost. I explained how it could eliminate from this world all that existed within a circle miles across; that there was no conceivable defence against it; and that castles and cities, troops and civilians, all that breathed and lived as well as the very substances of the material world, could be, as proved at Jubila, evaporated by its use.

Here the Prime Minister interrupted me for the first time.

'How did the Almighty speak to you and give you His secret?' he asked.

For a moment I thought of Dalton.

'God comes to us in different fashions,' he went on, and I realized in time that we spoke on separate planes.

I did not know the answer to his question and I could only deal with the issue by reference to the progress of science. I did so, telling Gladstone all with extreme frankness and emphasizing, at every stage, that my one object was the elimination of war.

It was clear, when I had finished, that I had made at least this point.

'We are in agreement on the evil of war,' the Prime Minister said. 'I have already written, and I will no doubt write again, that war has a peculiar quality in that it is most susceptible of being decked out in gaudy trappings, and of fascinating the imagination of those whose proud and angry passions it inflames. I know, quite as well as you, that on this very count it is a perilous delusion to teach that war is a cure for moral evil, in any other sense than as the sister tribulations are.'*

So far, so good. I could see that in this respect Gladstone was a man after my own heart. I was thus doubly unprepared for the shock he now administered.

'However, Professor Huxtable,' he went on, 'it appears to me that you have failed to carry your thoughts far enough. It is no solution to remove one evil by the imposition of a greater. You will talk, of course, only of threats . . .' He held up his hand to stop me as I was about to intervene.

'No, Professor, you are unacquainted with the realities of power. Deterrents deter only so long as they remain credible. Any attempt to impose our will by means of your weapon would be mere sophism were we not prepared to use it. Moreover, it would in that case fail to deter.'

As he rose from his desk and came towards me I could sense a tremor of anger in his voice.

'The use of this weapon, Professor Huxtable, would be not an act of war, but terrorism. It would be quite indiscriminate and it would therefore be both intolerable and indefensible. The mere consideration of such things makes it quite clear that when the Almighty put such power into your hands He was merely testing that special quality of *homo sapiens* with which we have been specially endowed, and which is denigrated so ignobly by Mr. Darwin and Professor Huxley.'

As I listened to Gladstone in that very room where I

*See *Gleanings of Past Years,* by W. E. Gladstone (John Murray, 1879).

160

had once listened to Peel and Wellington I felt sick at heart.

'If your device proves anything, Professor Huxtable,' the Prime Minister concluded, as though hammering the last nail into the Indians' coffin, 'it proves that we should close the doors of the temple of Janus for ever more; but one cannot start on that operation by opening them wide.'

For the moment I was beaten. There was no point in arguing against the master once he had got into his stride. All I could do was to attempt a retreat in good order.

Of one point I was fearful. With a Prime Minister of such disposition – supported by the Commander-in-Chief, no doubt, although for different reasons – it seemed essential that news of the Indians should be kept as confidential as ever. Were their existence to be revealed now, they would be damned for ever from the highest quarters.

'No, sir,' said the Prime Minister in answer to my inquiry. 'Our conversation will remain secret to our two selves. I am against murder. I am therefore against the spread of any knowledge which might bring it about.'

*

My discussion with Gladstone was but the first consequence of that fateful dinner party in Marlborough House on the evening of July 15th. I believed the incident was finished with Gladstone's blunt decision. So, no doubt, did the Prince of Wales when the Prime Minister told him of this in whatever discreet words he chose to send. All three of us had reckoned without John Thadeus Delane, an omission which more than one man of affairs had learned to regret over the years.

It was on the Tuesday after my meeting with the Prime Minister that I received a summons to appear at Marlborough House. It was written, as my summons six years earlier had been written, in the Prince's own sloping hand, and the short words suggested that this, too, was to be something different from a social occasion.

I was left in no doubt from the moment that the door closed behind me and I found myself facing the bright light from the windows that looked out across the Park. Between these and myself stood the massive figure of His Royal Highness, not so much silhouetted against the light as tending to blot it out.

He looked tired. I noticed that his hand fluttered slightly as he nervously tapped with his finger-tips a few sheets of paper on the desk before him. My slight knowledge of physiology suggested that here was a man tensed to breaking-point.

'Professor Huxtable,' he began – and for a moment even I, for whom Germany was a spiritual home, could hardly comprehend him through the thickness of his accent – 'Professor Huxtable, you have been talking.'

I looked at him, I hope, with some rigidity, Heir Apparent though he was.

'I was sent for,' I said as dispassionately as I could, 'by the Prime Minister.'

'Not Gladstone,' he burst out impatiently. 'I am not speaking of Gladstone. I refrain from commenting on the Prime Minister's action or lack of it. That would probably be unconstitutional; everything seems to be so nowadays.' He had been walking back and forth as he spoke but he now stopped and stabbed a finger at me.

'Why – did – you – speak – to – Delane?'

Luckily I kept my wits about me.

'I assume you mean the editor of *The Times*, Sir,' I

said. 'I first saw him some sixteen years ago when he landed in the Crimea from Admiral Lyons' *Agamemnon* with Mr. Layard and Mr. Kinglake. I have seen him, at a distance, a few times since. We have never spoken.'

For what seemed an hour but can scarcely have been a minute, the Prince stood motionless. I thought for one terrible moment that he was about to have a fit. Then his hand slowly dropped.

'I am sorry,' he said. 'Truly sorry. Your innocence betrays itself. But when I describe the events of the last few hours you will understand my feelings.'

He drew a magnificent silk handkerchief from his pocket, wiped his forehead, sat down, cleared his throat and became confidential.

'Yesterday evening,' he began, 'I attended the Rifle Brigade's annual dinner at Willis's Rooms. Afterwards, while returning home, I chanced to call . . .' And he mentioned one of London's most fashionable houses.

As His Royal Highness continued, I could picture the scene – one of these late evening gatherings which, since Her Majesty's retirement almost a decade ago, had become more fashionable. The lights shone, indeed, on fair women and brave men, and if there was an enemy on the horizon preparing for battle, it was the shape of Delane, invited as always, confident as always, for ever in the right place at the right time to ask the right question, unostentatiously making his way through the throng till he neared the Prince's side.

They stood chatting for a moment until, whether by chance or the practised manoeuvrings of Delane I do not know, the two men found themselves surrounded by an even larger screen of space than that which normally isolated the Prince.

'A matter of some moment, Sir,' said Delane, looking

straight at His Royal Highness. 'Are you to press for a demonstration of the ultimate deterrent?'

It says much for His Royal Highness's phlegmatic calm that no change was noted in his countenance. He was shocked – as he repeated now, almost as though Royalty itself had been assaulted – 'deeply, deeply shocked.' Yet he took it well.

'Mr. Delane,' he said, 'I would be obliged if you would call on me tomorrow morning; we can then discuss this further.'

So far, so good.

'I did not wish to prevaricate,' said His Royal Highness, turning to me with an almost man-to-man air. 'As you know, Huxtable, these things can be arranged among gentlemen. The correct word of advice, the discreet confidence – that is all that is needed. That was how I believed the affair might be arranged.'

'You felt, Sir,' Delane had said without delay the following morning, 'that we might discuss, in greater detail, the matter of the ultimate deterrent.'

Now, only a few hours later, the Prince turned to me. 'You must remember, Huxtable,' he said, 'that I believed Delane's information to be of the most slender kind. He might have heard my unguarded comment to Cambridge. He might have speculated on the existence of a new weapon. I believed that he could *know* nothing.' And, believing that, the Prince decided it might be permissible to tell a little.

'Delane,' he said, 'it is best that I should speak to you quite freely. I can do so only in confidence. I must have your word that nothing I tell you will go, in any shape or form, beyond the confines of this room in which we sit.'

Delane's reply had been startling, his action more so.

'I thank you, Sir, for your offer of confidence,' he

said. 'But there are times when the editor of a great newspaper can be embarrassed by confidences. He holds himself responsible for what he prints to the people of England. Thus there are times, Sir, when he can be not merely embarrassed but iron-bound by confidences. Indeed, Sir, I think the time for confidences is past. It is necessary that the implications of this, Sir, should be discussed not only by the people of England, but by the peoples of the world.'

Delane pulled a document from his pocket and handed it to the Prince.

'What he handed me, Huxtable,' said the Prince, pushing out his words from between almost closed lips, 'was this.'

I took the document from his hands. I did not recognize the writing. But I saw that it was headed 'Report of an Experiment on the Jubila Plateau . . .'

It was quite clear that the writer had copied it direct from one of the five full reports which I had so carefully prepared in my own hand more than a quarter of a century earlier.

'Even for Delane,' said the Prince, 'something of a coup.'

A coup indeed! Greater even than that momentous event of 1845 when *The Times* had announced the coming repeal of the Corn Laws, a decision known only to the Prime Minister and two others; greater than the announcement, which was to come in but a week's time, of the draft treaty mortgaging the future of Belgium – a scrap of paper drawn up in the greatest secrecy between France and Germany.*

*See *Delane of 'The Times'*, by Sir Edward Cook (Constable, 1915), and *John Thadeus Delane,* by Arthur Irwin Dasent (Murray, 1908).

To this day I do not know how Delane gained access to a copy of the full Jubila Report. Yet on that bright summer day of 1870 it was not so much the mechanism of his success with which we were concerned as the prospect that the Indians might be revealed to the world – not carefully and with circumspection, but with all the trappings of horrific detail which I had felt bound by duty to include in my report.

'It is essential, my dear Huxtable,' the Prince went on, 'that Delane should be persuaded not to publish. For Her Majesty, for the Government – even, in the circumstances, for myself – a revelation in the columns of *The Times* would be little less than a tragedy.'

I agreed. It was one thing for the Prime Minister, supported by the Queen, by the Cabinet, and by the country, to usher in a new age with the help of my weapon. It was quite another to have the weapon's existence dragged into the light of day in the columns of a daily newspaper – and, as I was sure would be the case in these circumstances, subsequently condemned with all the force of Mr. Gladstone's oratory.

'Sir,' I said, 'we must not let the history of the world be guided by newspaper editors.'

'Exactly, my dear Huxtable,' said the Prince, laying his hand on my sleeve. 'I, as you may know, am leaving for Denmark on Friday. You are the man who must make Delane change his mind.'

At first I was appalled at the prospect – then honoured. For His Royal Highness pointed out that, in any case, constitutional etiquette prevented his own intervention; ignorance of the details would prevent Gladstone from making more than a gesture. 'Only you,' he said, 'have all the material, all the arguments, at your finger-tips. Only you, Huxtable, can guide the course of events.'

I saw that there was no time to be lost. And it was from Marlborough House that I thereupon wrote a note to Delane. He, too, was a man who did not tarry; almost by return an appointment was made.

Thus it was only a few hours after I had arrived in such perplexity to see His Royal Highness that I found myself, in even greater perplexity, outside Delane's rooms at Sergeant's Inn.

'*The* Professor Huxtable,' he said as I was shown in, 'and just in time to dot the i's and cross the t's of my thoughts.'

He stretched back to his desk, picked up a sheaf of papers and handed them to me.

'As you may realize, Professor, there are times when we begin our leading article with the most important item of our news,' he said. 'This is one of them.'

He motioned me to a chair, and watched as I turned the sheets.

The British Government [I read] has the power, by use of a scientific device tested almost thirty years ago, to wipe out all life within any chosen fifty square miles of the globe. This device can be made at little cost; against it there is no possible defence; and it is of such a nature that all within many miles of the detonation are exposed to a heat as intense as that of the sun itself. Within this circle, all life shrivels and dies, translated as it were to its natural elements. Beyond, there is a blast beside which the repercussion from our heaviest artillery would be but a spring breeze; and there may well be a multiplicity of after-effects of which we have, as yet, no knowledge. Thus it is now possible totally to destroy all living creatures within the bounds not only of the largest army in the world but of the largest city. Our readers may feel disbelief. To succour that disbelief would be to raise false hope. The evidence is incontrovertible, the facts known to us beyond all possibility of mistake.

The site chosen for this experiment – for once the military embraces such perversions of natural science it becomes necessary to use scientific terms – was the Jubila Plateau of India, an area on the fringe of Her Majesty's realm, free of inhabitants and distant from populous parts. It may well be asked how such a development could have been shielded from human knowledge. Indeed, this would have been impossible but for two facts. One was the immense care taken by the authorities – and we speak here not only of the military authorities and those in Britain on whose orders they acted, but also of the East India Company, then still clinging to a power from which it has since, and most happily, been separated. The second fact, which combined with human ingenuity to hide from the world all knowledge of what had taken place, is a momentous one. There was, indeed, no need to dissimulate; the effects of this new weapon were so vast, its destruction so widespread, that it was possible to claim, to those who witnessed its effects at long range, that natural causes alone had been at work. It is unusual for a government, or a newspaper, to talk of the weapons which lie within a nation's armoury, and it is unusual for either to describe, before its use, any new engine of destruction whose sudden deployment before an enemy might gain by surprise. Yet there comes a time when the customary conventions should be pushed aside by the weight of more significant events, when the accepted balance and counter-balance of military advantage should be ignored and when the interests of a nation should be submerged in the interests of the world. We believe that such a time is now upon us: that we face the greatest moral issue of our time.

This issue is one of which the people of our country have so far been kept ignorant by a conspiracy: a conspiracy – and we use the word after careful thought – of governments and princes, of science and of the military. It is a conspiracy which in the public interest we believe it our duty to reveal. For we stand, although the nation is unaware of the fact, upon a watershed of history; unless due care is taken we shall cross it blindfold and march on to a destination which is hidden from our gaze.

We believe that this new weapon could bring to armaments and war, to the relationships between civilized states and even to the future of the race, an entirely new dimension. It will be claimed that its possession could make our confident nation the arbiter of the world. This may well be so, although it is significant that there has been no hint of such use throughout the last three decades. The Crimean tragedy went unresolved by it. The mutineers in that vast sub-continent where it was experimentally detonated continued, too long, in their progress of pillage and rapine. There is no suggestion that it might have been invoked to end the fratricidal conflict which has set back the progress of the American States a whole generation of men. Thus it would seem that we have shrunk from such arbitration – as well we might. For with thought it becomes clear that the threat of such a weapon against an army in the field is but the first of possibilities open to a country intent upon arbitration – or upon conquest. Indiscriminate destruction of military combatants and military non-combatants alike might well be but the first step on a ladder leading to the depths. It is useless for its proponents – and they will no doubt make their voices heard – to claim that the maximum precautions would be taken. It is useless for them to protest – though they would do so with sincerity – that such a weapon would not be used against civilians. War corrupts, and such total war would corrupt totally, bringing this most testing of human occupations to the level of the butcher's yard. It is, moreover, irrelevant to protest that Britain, and Britain alone, is ever likely to have this device which summons up the biggest battalions of all. This is of course true. But the most significant of the new weapon's characteristics is that its destructiveness raises man to that level of ultimate arbiter which all Christian peoples – and many others – feel has so far, and rightly, rested elsewhere.

We believe that great danger lies in the secrecy which has shrouded this development. It is our complaint that the authorities – and whether those most involved are parliamentary, military or regal we do not at this moment inquire – have so far forfeited by their silence the trust not only of the British public but of the human race. There must be open discussion – which in the context of

170

today's unhappy circumstances might restrain the two powers who each appear to claim the hegemony of Europe. In a different field there has been sufficient, perhaps more than sufficient, open discussion about the revolutionary theories which were sprung upon the world by Mr. Charles Darwin a decade ago. Yet this scientist who would trace us back to the trees dealt only with the distant past of the human race. Those who have brought this new weapon to the world have faced us with the future; to restrict debate upon its implications would be a policy not only of cowardice but of mortal crime.

We do not attempt to decide in these columns whether the use of such a weapon would ever be justified. But we believe that the subject must be debated among the rulers of the world, among its peoples – and among its scientists, too, for it is they who have brought to us this discovery against which man's descent from the trees, if descent there were, is almost a minor event. The facts of this momentous step – we will not prejudice the issue by writing 'step forward' – must be brought into the light and honestly examined. Then man must ask himself whether he can truly see, as Pope had it,

> with equal eye, as God of all
> A hero perish, or a sparrow fall,
> Atoms or systems into ruin hurled
> And now a bubble burst and now a world.

If not, he might well be advised to replace the ultimate deterrent in the Pandora's box where it has lain so long.

I looked up as I read the final paragraph. I saw that Delane's eyes were still fixed upon me.

But I had become used to concealing my thoughts. I remained unrevealing as my mind began to grapple with the problem. How, indeed, to dissuade Delane? The task seemed impossible; I knew it was essential.

He spoke as I considered the matter, and as I turned back to the earlier paragraphs of the leader, ostensibly because of their interest, in fact to give myself time.

'I have had from the Prime Minister what he calls a "Notice",' he said. 'This tells me that while there is nothing in the law of the country to prevent me from publishing this material, it would yet be against the national interest and I might therefore find myself arraigned under some obscure rule or regulation.'

Delane smiled grimly. 'It is not a good thing to threaten *The Times*, Professor Huxtable. It is not expedient. And in this case I realize that the interest is but political; neither national nor scientific.'

There was, I felt, just the hint of a question in his voice, and his uncertainty gave me the opening I required. I saw that ignorance of the scientific world was his weakness.

'You are not, of course, a man of science, Mr. Delane?' I began. He shook his head as he replied: 'A mere editor.'

I spoke with what I hoped would sound like the wisdom of the years. 'For that reason you are unaware that the consequences of publication would be appalling,' I said.

'Open discussion,' he said. 'An honest appraisal of what might or might not be achieved under shadow of the awful power that Britain could wield.'

I shook my head. 'Mr. Delane,' I said, 'it is clear that

you are ignorant of the situation. You do not appear to realize that publication of this –' I pointed rather disparagingly towards the sheets in my lap ' – will for all practical purposes give this weapon to the nations of the world.'

His response was as fierce as I had expected. 'There is no scientific or technical information involved,' he protested. 'Indeed, I have exercised the most scrupulous care in omitting from my material anything which could in any way assist enemies or potential enemies.'

As I began to reply to him, my conscience hid its head. I still believed that only I could make my weapon, that only I would ever be likely to have such capability. What I said was the opposite.

'I imagine, Mr. Delane,' I said, 'that the phrase "physical constants" means nothing to you?'

He shook his head, and I was relieved for the confirmation of his ignorance.

'I will not attempt to explain them,' I went on. 'But all rests on whether certain physical constants are plus or minus; the revelation that this weapon has been successfully exploded will be a clear signpost to the fact that they are more, not less, than zero. I am afraid you do not realize, Mr. Delane, that for practical purposes the most important secret about this weapon is that it works.'

I could see that he was impressed. Encouraged, I went on, greatly daring.

'You surely do not believe that use of such a weapon would have been withheld in the Crimea, or during the Mutiny, without good reason? No, no, Mr. Delane, this is a unique weapon which remains unique only so long as its existence is unrevealed. After that' – I held up my hands in despair – 'proliferation.'

And I went on to paint a picture of how, within months of any such revelation as he proposed, a score of scientists would be busy in every civilized country in the world. They would require time, of course, but not all that time.

'Within a few years,' I warned, 'the merest Continental Grand Duchy might well have at its disposal such power as would devastate the whole of London.'

'I see,' he said. 'This does indeed shed a new light on the matter.'

He glanced at his watch. 'I am already overdue at Printing House Square. Perhaps you would be good enough to await my return.' He called to his man to attend to my requirements and left with a courteous word.

You may imagine my feelings as I waited in his rooms, my senses taking in the fragrance from the flowers outside the open window, my mind fearful of hoping.

The birds were announcing the first streaks of dawn as Delane returned. He looked careworn and tired, and I imagined that it was not merely the work of the day's news that made him so.

'I find my position difficult in view of Gladstone's threatening note,' he said, ' – an incitement to revelation if ever there were one. However, you have convinced me. To twist the old Duke's memory, I will admit that were I to publish I would be damned.'

So I had won! I congratulated Delane on his wise judgment, said that Gladstone would erase from his memory and his records all mention of my weapon, and trusted that Delane would do the same.

For a moment he looked uncomfortable. He was, after all, a man of transparent honesty.

'To be truthful, Huxtable,' he said, 'I did drop a

phrase to Russell before sending him off to Berlin. But I am glad to say that his vanity prevented the idea from taking root.'

And he explained how as he had bade his correspondent farewell and God speed, he had made one comment: 'It will be a long and bloody war, Russell – unless it is halted in its tracks by the ultimate deterrent.'

He had then had second thoughts, deciding on the instant that even William Howard Russell should not be given too much knowledge. 'I do not mean a military deterrent, of course' he had quickly added. 'I mean the deterrent not of physical but of moral force.'

'I need not have been anxious,' said Delane, now smiling. 'Russell has the confidence one needs for war. "Mr Delane," he replied, "I know you speak of moral force. Had there been a military deterrent I would have reported it." '

Once again, I breathed more freely. I rose to leave.

It was now that Delane turned to me with that frank, open and almost bucolic look which masked such a complex knowledge of events. He stared me straight in the eye as he asked: 'Professor Huxtable, how long do you really think that you, or Britain for that matter, can retain this secret of the natural laws? And, perhaps more important, Huxtable, in an age of increasing democracy, who will eventually control such power?'

As I walked back through the fresh morning towards where I would find my good wife awaiting whatever explanation I could contrive for her, I began to wonder. I began to feel a slight tremor; partly of conscience, since I had always thought it wrong to put any limitation upon knowledge; partly a disconcerting tremor of doubt about the inevitable goodness of the world. I had always thought that I alone would discover how to unlock the gate, and that in my hands only right would be done. Yet what if the spectre I had raised before Delane was not the nightmare but the reality? What then would happen when my weapon was eventually used? I began to wonder at the possibility of absolute power being used for absolute evil. It was an unnerving sensation, like a cold finger being pressed down the spine; an altogether disagreeable sensation.

However, by the time I reached home I had comforted myself away from these unpleasant speculations. The affair of Delane, I reflected, was now closed.

*

It was less than a year later that I received a gentlemen's card through the post, together with the urgent request for an appointment on matters which were claimed to be of great moment. The name on the card was that of Archibald Forbes. I remembered it from the accounts of war which I had read in the popular papers, but even then I did not connect my correspondent with the affairs of the previous summer.

Three days later Forbes was shown into my study. He was a large and somewhat coarse-looking man, but I soon measured his intellectual alertness and decided that he was not to be trifled with. He came quickly to the point.

'Professor Huxtable,' he said, 'I have come about the affair of the Jubila Plateau – thirty years ago, but still of interest to the world, I think you will agree.'

Indeed, no one could agree more warmly. I concealed my shock, and by the use of considerable mental dexterity drew his story from him before he drew mine.

Both Russell of *The Times* and Forbes of the *Daily*

News had ridden to the war the previous summer. Both had witnessed the debacle of Sedan, and had followed the Prussian columns as they surged across France to encircle Paris. And both had been present when Wilhelm I, King of Prussia, had been transformed, as by a magic wand wielded by a nation, into the Emperor of all the Germanies.

'The date was January 18th,' said Forbes. 'The inauguration of an Emperor does not come every day, even to men in my profession, and I naturally rode to Versailles, having dressed myself for the occasion. Russell, Deputy-Constable of the Tower, had of course decked himself out in full uniform – silver epaulettes, cock-feathered hat, and all manner of gorgeous colours.'

They made their way through the Place de la Cour Royale, filled with Brandenburgers and Pomeranians, Mecklenburgers and Hanoverians, all spurred and booted, all reflecting with burnished metal and polished leather, the thin light of the wintry morning sun.*

As Forbes spoke I could almost hear the stamp of armed men in Hanover Square.

The two correspondents strode up the curving steps past helmeted sentries, catching through high windows a glimpse of the open country which led towards the lines investing the capital. Eventually, after what seemed like leagues but was only yards, they came to the Hall of Mirrors.

The long gallery had been metamorphosed. In the centre, behind a temporary altar, were draped the regimental Colours. On either side, the scene was a blaze of light, of gilding, of mirrors.

'Exactly at noon,' Forbes went on, 'there came a roll

*See contemporary newspaper reports from Russell and Forbes.

of drums from the courtyard below and the boom of a distant gun. Then there came up to us the strains of a chorale chanted by the troops of massed regimental bands. As the sounds rose and fell, almost tribal in their primitive significance, Wilhelm I appeared, dressed in the uniform of a German general, bearing his helmet in his hand.

'He stalked up the long Gallery, not hurrying; reached the centre, bowed to the clergy, halted, turned to stand in line and then, a hand to the point of his heavy white moustache, regarded the scene.'

On the King's right stood the Crown Prince in the uniform of a Field Marshal. Yet it was another figure which caught the eye – a figure stalwart and square, in full cuirassier uniform, and leaning on a great sword. No expression showed on his countenance. No man stood within a yard of him.

'It was,' said Forbes, 'as though Bismarck felt he was more than a king.'

To Forbes the service which followed was but a series of flashes seen against a background – a priest's black figure, Bismarck's hand upon the pommel of his sword, a streak of light down the glittering line of decorations in the Gallery, the Emperor's gloved hand caressing the silky curl of his moustache.

The service finished, Wilhelm proclaimed the re-establishment of the German Empire. The Grand Duke of Baden stepped forward with a shout of 'Long Live the German Emperor'. As he did so the assembled company broke into a tempest of cheering, waving helmets and swords, stamping with booted feet on the polished floor. Below, the sound of massed bands swelled up into the climax of the German Anthem, and simultaneously there was heard, faintly distant, the roll of French cannon from Mont Valérien.

Russell, regarding the scene objectively, from outside this brotherhood of race, murmured under his breath: 'Only the ultimate deterrent could have prevented this.'

Forbes, standing but a few feet behind, heard the words escape his colleague.

'I followed him out in silence,' he said, 'but once we were clear of the hubbub he spoke to me in terms which we were later to use in our dispatches: "What a prospect for the closing years of this wicked and bloody old century! What a legacy to the future! No faith in Treaties; mitrailleuses and rifled cannon, military service, iron-clad fleets – the preparations for the millennium."

'I was glad he carried on like this,' said Forbes confidently, 'for I knew that Russell was rich in experience of war and I knew that this ultimate deterrent he mentioned must be something more important than rifled cannon or the spectre of fire-bombs dropped from balloons with which the French were experimenting.'

As Forbes sat there in my study that summer's morning I thought for the moment that Delane must have deceived me – or perhaps himself. Yet this was not the case.

'I tackled Russell,' said Forbes, 'trying to tempt him with the argument that nothing whatsoever could have deterred Bismarck.'

Russell disagreed. 'Moral force,' he said. 'Moral force – that is the ultimate deterrent, greater than guns, more powerful than an army on the move. The trouble is that most of us are too cowardly to exercise it.'

Forbes looked at me and shook his head slowly. 'I

am a realist, Professor Huxtable. I am sorry that Russell, who has known me long enough, should have thought otherwise. I let the matter drop. But I was sure that if William Howard Russell talked of an ultimate deterrent, then some such weapon there must surely be.'

My spirits now sank to my boots. Yet I was still unable to see how our curtain of secrecy could have been pierced.

'Tell me, Mr. Forbes,' I said in the most engaging manner I could muster, 'what did you do next?' Astonishingly, the fellow was so sure of himself that he told me.

'We newspaper men,' he said, 'keep as close a record as we can of our rivals' comings and goings. Now if Russell had exceptional information, it was quite likely to have been provided by his editor. And an inspection of our material showed that John Thadeus Delane had been closeted for an extraordinarily long time at one crucial period with – Professor Franklin Huxtable.

'There were a number of cuttings dealing with yourself,' he continued. 'I perused them carefully – and there was one that interested me greatly. I learned, Professor, that more than a decade ago you suggested, on a public platform, that you had been involved in a dangerous, if not a desperate, enterprise.'

He looked at me in anticipation. I admit that I had no remembrance of such an occasion. 'It was,' he said slowly, 'when you spoke in favour of a Parliamentary candidate – General Swyre.'

The name came as a hammer-blow, as I remembered that evening with Swyre – 'a man to be relied upon in dangerous enterprises.' However, there were compensations if Forbes had followed his trail to Swyre. Rich with honours, he had become in his seventies a man fuddled with age, confused with the memory of things past and with regrets for earlier times. He was apt to ramble, I had heard, and in his ramblings India would be confused with Waterloo and the Afghan troubles become intermingled with the battle of Vittoria. His trouble was not that old men forgot but that they remembered all wrong.

'I naturally traced General Swyre without difficulty,' Forbes went on. 'He is advancing in years, as you will appreciate, but he told me of your expedition to Jubila. He told me that you were employed on the testing of a new weapon of war; that the military authorities – even he himself – knew little of this; and that some story of a meteor or an earthquake, he was not sure which, was spread to account for the destruction caused.'

He looked at me intently, and I found it difficult to know whether the suspicion was more apparent in his gaze or in his voice.

But his honesty had undone him! Thank Heaven for that 'meteorite'. Thank Heaven for all the care which I had taken in concocting my story for Amelia.

At heart I did not like it. But I well knew that the dangers of Forbes spreading the story of the Indians across the pages of a popular paper would be even more damaging than the worst that Delane could do. In the vulgar mind the poor scientists would so easily be seen as adding to the horrors of war rather than wiping them out for ever. And so, once again, I was forced to lie.

I congratulated Forbes upon his perspicacity, upon his initiative, upon his wisdom in coming to see me. But I was sorry to tell him that Russell's 'ultimate deterrent' meant in fact what Russell himself had said – the moral deterrent.

"There is," I said, 'a broken link in the chain of events

181

which you have traced back. It comes between Russell and my interview with Delane.'

I got up and rested my hand on his shoulder in what I hoped was a fatherly way. 'My dear Forbes,' I went on, 'I did indeed see Delane to discuss a very important matter, and you were correct in tracing it back to my association with Swyre, and to our expedition to Jubila. Both in India almost three decades ago, and in Delane's study last year, I quite possibly did use the word "deterrent"; it is also possible that this word was dropped by Delane to Russell and that it lingered in your colleague's mind, so that he used it to describe the moral opprobrium of which he spoke. But I am afraid our "deterrent" had nothing to do with war, although over the years, and with advancing age, it is understandable that poor Swyre's memory should become confused.'

By this time I was warming to my lies. 'I imagine,' I said, 'that you have no great acquaintance with the mysteries of meteorology?'

Forbes admitted that he was as innocent as a babe of more than the most rudimentary facts.

'Ah!' I replied, 'that would explain much. You see, the deterrent with which poor Swyre and I were concerned was to be a deterrent against the vagaries of meteorological conditions in general and of the monsoons in particular – a matter in which Delane had become interested for its possible effects upon agriculture.

'Meteorites, those uninvited visitors from outer space, play a great part in the government of climate; and at certain seasons of the year, and in certain latitudes, meteorites may be observed in abundance.'

None of this Forbes could deny, since it was no more than the truth.

'I had done more than study them,' I went on. 'I had

produced a device – you might almost call it an artillery device – by which I believed it would be possible so to affect the meteorites in the upper atmosphere, that we should not only deter their entry into our atmosphere but also control their effect on the weather.'

I was able to support my story with evidence which I knew would impress Forbes of the *Daily News*.

'I assume you know Glaisher who helped set up your own paper's daily weather report some years ago,' I continued.* 'He has recently been making weather observations from balloons. My work was not only very different but a quarter of a century earlier.'

I now became confidential. 'All men, particularly young ones, make mistakes, and I was young at the time. My device was complicated. It was also potentially dangerous, and for this latter reason, apart from any other, we felt it necessary to ensure secrecy – and you will know how the superstitious natives are affected if they believe one is tampering with the weather.'

But it was not only, I reluctantly admitted, that my theories were wrong. 'I had chosen the locality for my experiments almost too well. We were treated to an earthquake as well as to the descent of a meteorite greatly beyond normal size – though not, alas, before I had discovered the uselessness of my work.'

Delane had been in the chair at *The Times* for but a few months. 'He was interested, as he had remained interested over the years; and our conversation last summer, as he was about to send Russell off to the wars, is the sole cause of your misunderstanding.

'My theories came to nought; much as yours, I am sorry to say, have been following a will-o'-the-wisp.'

*James Glaisher (1809–1903). The *Daily News* weather service began in 1849.

When he had left, I wondered. However, it was not long before my fears were put to rest. Forbes wrote, as he was to write more than once, on the future of warfare. I scanned his articles with the greatest care. They contained nothing more than speculation as to the normal advances in shot and shell. I had successfully deceived him.

*

A footnote to these events was written shortly afterwards. Gladstone, as well as His Royal Highness, had been relieved, the previous year, at Delane's decision not to publish and, tactfully without involving the heir to the throne, had mentioned my services to the Queen. Thus, more than a year after I had sat with Delane in Sergeant's Inn, I was invited, together with Amelia and our daughter, to visit Her Majesty at Balmoral.

The Queen was kindness itself – and discretion, letting it be known that I was being honoured for some past service of scientific tuition to the Prince Consort. This, as she said, avoided public comment and also explained how it was that she was thus receiving me in her private residence. 'It is,' she said, 'as he would have *wished*.'

So much still rested on that 'he'. Wherever Her Majesty moved, the spirit of the Prince Consort marched ahead, a shadow for ever attached to her and one which cast itself over all she approached. Thus 'a favourite drive of hers still' was the comment of John Brown, a rough man, but with more philosophical content than many give him credit for, when he took us one memorable day up the length of Glen Muick. We passed 'The Hut', or Alt-na-guithasach, where Her Majesty and the Prince Consort had first stayed together on their visit to the Cairngorms more than twenty years previously, and Glassalt Shiel, only two years old – 'the first *widow's house*, not built by him or hallowed by his memory', as Her Majesty was to describe it.

As we descended the Glen, Brown pointed out the peaks and viewpoints to Amelia and my much excited daughter. And as we were within a few miles of Ballater, he stopped the horses and described how Her Majesty would still stop at this same bend of the road before looking back for a final glimpse towards Alt-na-guithasach.

I still remember that drive. And I remember a September evening as Her Majesty sat at the window of an elaborately tartan-hung room, looking north across the Dee.

'As we have written elsewhere,' she said, 'this world is not, thank God, our permanent home, Professor. But we would hesitate to send from it any living creature unless we believed that it was *really* necessary. You will claim that the invention of explosives long ago made the difference between just and unjust killing a difficult one to determine. In one respect this may be *so*. Yet in others, which we find it impossible to *explain*, but which we *feel*, we believe our Indians are very *different*.'

Perhaps. In fact, for a moment later that evening, as I looked out to the shape of Lochnagar, black against the stars, and to the surrounding hills I had known so well as a boy, I half wondered if the Queen was right. I wondered at the random chances which over the years had crossed together the paths of Her Majesty and myself; of old Sir Archibald, his son, and the Prince of Wales; of Delane and Forbes and Swyre who between them had so nearly burst open the secret of the Indians.

And I wondered what fate still held in store.

When you consider my faith in the Indians, you will find it difficult to understand how I should ever have doubted them. Yet two incidents temporarily disturbed me – though years before preparations were started for the expedition from which I am now returning.

The first occurred a few years after my visit to Balmoral. Amelia and I had driven down to visit the Hookers at Kew, Joseph at this time overjoyed with his Presidency of the Royal. We passed as usual through the ivy-covered brick portico into the long passage at the end of which lay the Director's two simple book-lined studies.* As usual, the great man was busy, a Director in his shirt-sleeves as I called him. However, contrary to normal practice, Lady Hooker followed the exchange of greetings by leading Amelia and Julie into the gardens, an indication that my friend had business to discuss with me.

Before him, almost filling the broad south window, stood a table piled with papers ranged like sentries round his microscope. To his right, there stretched an improvised desk which ran almost the length of the room, bearing correspondence and books, coloured prints or rare plants, a pot of multi-coloured flowers, and less important-looking horticultural specimens.

As the Director walked to the desk, I could see that he was deeply puzzled, a state of affairs not customary with Joseph Dalton Hooker.

*See *Life and Letters of Sir Joseph Dalton Hooker*, by Leonard Huxley (John Murray, 1918).

'These come,' he said, handing me a shoot, 'from an area I believe you once visited.'

I sensed, by some instinct, what was coming next. '... from the edge of the Jubila Plateau.'

At first, to my untrained eye, the limp plant in my hand looked much like any other. Then, as I examined it more closely, I could see that from the centre of some buds small leaves were shooting. Elsewhere, buds appeared to be sprouting from the stems, malformed and appearing where buds had no right to be.

'It is almost,' said Hooker, 'as though the laws of life had been strangely disturbed. There have been examples of other species. All come from the same area.'

I felt that some remark was expected from me – as though I, because I had visited the district more than a third of a century before, had some responsibility for these curious botanical abortions that had been sent halfway round the world. All I could muster was the solitary comment that it was very odd.

'Exceedingly odd,' said Hooker, 'but –' and he looked back at me over his spectacles as he replaced the plant '– exceedingly interesting.'

I thought no more of the incident until, some while afterwards, I was attending a meeting of the Anthropological Institute. My host was a member of the Alpine Club and it was natural that he should introduce me to Colonel Godwin-Austen, that fearless surveyor after whom the world's second highest peak has been named. It was equally natural that we should sit together.

The paper read that evening dealt with those weapons of prehistoric man about which natives still retain superstitious fears. During the subsequent session of question and answer, Godwin-Austen had risen, a military paradigm among scientific men, and had spoken of how a

187

native had claimed of these prehistoric weapons that 'such stones fall with the lightning'.*

As he sat down he half-muttered to himself: 'If that were true, then Jubila would be thick with them.'

I looked surprised, and my companion explained to Godwin-Austen that many years ago I had visited the area in a scientific capacity.

'How interesting,' commented Godwin-Austen, his words as much as the circumstances echoing Hooker. 'How very interesting.'

At the conclusion of the meeting he drew me aside. 'I did not realize that you had visited the Jubila area, Professor,' he said. 'You must be one of the very few men of science to have done so.'

I agreed that this was true – and began to wonder at the security of the great secret, for it was clear that the Colonel had something to say. I thought it wise to take suitable action, and I deftly explained how my meteorological inquiries had been brought to nought by natural events.

Our conversation was somewhat desultory, somewhat guarded. It was clear that he was hesitant as the little eddies of guests drifted round us.

'I visited the Jubila area myself only a few years ago,' he said drawing me into a relatively quiet corner of the salon. 'The natives still talk of the earthquake and, as they call it, "the great lightnings" of about that time. Tell me . . .'

He looked about him, and if a man of Godwin-Austen's bearing could look conspiratorial he would have looked so at that moment.

*At a meeting of The Anthropological Institute held on May 9th, 1876, with Colonel Lane-Fox in the chair.

'Tell me, Professor, was there anything curious about the inhabitants?'

I felt that 'curious', spoken in such a way, was a singularly unscientific word.

'I refer,' he went on, 'to the "monsters". Do not mistake me. I am as well acquainted with the deformities of goitre as most men. I mean something of a different order, Professor – men with many limbs, or none. Men who do not see because they have no eyes, and the occasional man of the most astounding proportions.'

They were mainly, he continued, of a certain tribe. He named it, and across thirty years I remembered that it was they who had dwelt beyond the far side of the plateau, miles downwind from the site of the explosion.

The 'monsters' were small in numbers, it appeared, and of those who survived to manhood many were killed by their fellows. It was, as he put it, 'not his subject', and this – combined, I felt, with an indisposition to arouse disbelief – had induced him to keep the matter within the pages of his private diaries.

Remembering Tom Thumb, I speculated on whether it might not be possible to bring one or more of these people to England, perhaps even as an exhibition for Her Majesty who had always evinced great interest in natural phenomena.

Godwin-Austen looked down at me for a moment, as from a great height.

'You must remember that you have not seen them, Professor Huxtable,' he said with a tone in his voice which I could not comprehend. 'They would not be suitable – for Her Majesty or for any other civilized being.'

It was, of course, the purest coincidence; yet for some months the matter continued to irk me. For a while I thought of heredity, and there came into my mind an idea that Darwin's great theory might be carried out in practice by particular factors of inheritance; by atomic components passed on by some strange means from one generation to the next. If this were true, then it might be possible that my transmutation of the elements could affect both plant and human life to come – as though some unknown god's breath had blown through the substance of nature itself. I soon realized that, on sound scientific principles alone, the idea was such fantasy that I could dismiss it. Afterwards, I must admit, I slept more easily.

These doubts, if I may call them such, arose some years before a transformation in the status of the Indians led to the climax of my later life.

The first hint of these things to come arrived one morning when I found waiting for me on my breakfast table a more than usually large number of letters. I put on one side a long, officially postmarked envelope at whose contents I could not guess. When I had attended to the matters of Tom, Dick and Harry I would see if this contained something of importance or merely an invitation to one of those official functions which make such demands on both the stomach and the patience.

I had not finished my perusal of the post when a card was sent in to me.

I looked at the paste-board with some surprise. It was not the name itself which occasioned me to wonder, for who had not heard of Hiram Maxim? Fashionable society had taken to visiting his Hatton Garden factory to press the trigger of his new gun almost as an after-dinner excitement, and many had begun to wonder whether the rapid-firer had been designed for the army or for the gratification of young men with time on their hands and no worthwhile method of employing it.* But I was by no means prepared for a call from this thrustful American who had taken a part of the technical world by storm.

I had never before seen Maxim, and must admit to an intense curiosity as he was shown into my study.

The man who stood before me was of middle height, broad, and with a firm rectangular face. His hair was thick, grey, and cropped short so that it stood from his head like an expanse of shorn stubble. He wore a luxuriant moustache and a fierce beard. Yet it was his eyes on which my attention was focused – black yet almost luminous eyes which shone out from his face with a burning intensity, as though trying to light up the dark corners of the world. I was reminded of Swyre in his happier and younger days.

He held out his hand in an informal gesture and I shook it before motioning him to a seat.

"You will have heard that I was coming, Professor,' he said, 'and I thought I would waste no time.'

'I am sorry . . .' I began, and I then remembered the envelope which still lay, unopened, on my breakfast-table. With a word of apology, I sent for it.

'My dear Huxtable,' I read a few moments later, 'however concentrated are your energies on a purely scientific life, you will have heard of Mr. Hiram Maxim.' I glanced at the signature and saw that my correspondent was Wolseley, a regimental officer in the Crimea, but now in high command at the War Office, a man of modern ideas and one with whom I had kept contact. His letter continued :

You may also know that he has designed a new

*See *My Life*, by Sir Hiram Maxim (Methuen, 1915).

type of gun which, should it realize his high hopes, will revolutionize warfare. I was discussing this some few days past with the Commander-in-Chief. The Duke of Cambridge rarely favours new ideas but he mentioned, in a somewhat mysterious manner, a weapon which he claims you have available. He appeared critical of its usefulness, but in the national interest I felt it wise to make certain inquiries. I later mentioned this to the Prince of Wales who has such a devoted interest in all military affairs, and who, like myself, was much impressed with Mr. Maxim's device. He was reluctant to say more than the minimum. However, it appears clear to me that I should be lacking in duty did I not ensure that supplies of your weapon were available should they be needed.

I fully appreciate that you are likely to be involved in scientific affairs. But it occurred to me that the fertility of your scientific mind might well be combined with Mr. Maxim's technical experience. I have suggested that he should call upon you.

I put down the letter and regarded my visitor with very mixed feelings. I was both astonished and shocked to realize that Maxim had thus, almost by accident, been brought into the Queen's business. But perhaps, I thought, this might at last offer the chance of presenting my weapon to the world. How often, I reflected, had I followed the progress of the minor conflicts which had marred the last few decades, wishing only that the use of my weapon would end such senseless slaughter.

'Tell me,' I said to Maxim, and not revealing that I knew how little he knew, 'tell me what you have in mind.'

'Well, Professor," he said, 'I don't rightly know. Perhaps I had better start at the starting-point.

'Your Commander-in-Chief, your Prince of Wales and your Duke of Edinburgh have all inspected my new gun – in fact, for the last week or so the place has been more like a salon than a workshop.* Then Wolseley asked me to call on him. He swore me to secrecy, praised my quick-firer, said you British had an even more formidable weapon, hinted at manufacture and proposed that I should call upon Professor Franklin Huxtable.'

He put his hands on his knees and looked at me foursquare. 'So, Professor, here I am.'

I could not help liking the man. And I reflected that now, unexpectedly, official interest in my device was stirring with a new impulse. I reflected that I would be totally wrong to rebuff my visitor.

I wondered whether the Queen or the Prime Minister were aware of the development. I thought not; supply of weapons was, after all, purely a military matter, and in aiding Wolseley I would merely be aiding his Minister – a very constitutional action. I quickly saw, moreover, that I would be able to keep the matter within my own hands. I had learned much since that day when I had watched Skindling use his Civil Servant's guile!

'Mr. Maxim,' I said, 'Lord Wolseley must set up a small private committee.'

Thus, in my own study, on the spur of the moment, was born what I later named the Indian Committee.

Mr. Maxim was agreeable. I decided that I should write to Wolseley, and after the minimum of delay I found myself one morning quietly chatting with his lordship in his Whitehall office, and awaiting Captain Berkeley who was to act as our secretary.

*See *My Life,* by Sir Hiram Maxim.

'Berkeley will provide the link through which you will be able to request advice,' said Wolseley, 'and he will be responsible for ensuring that any spread of knowledge is kept strictly within the necessary limits.'

I shook hands with a pleasantly smiling, immensely tall Hussar, a young man more full of courage than of wisdom.

'There will be yourself and Maxim,' said Wolseley. 'Maxim wishes one of his business partners to attend, and if you would like to bring in a colleague you are, of course, quite at liberty to do so. I want only to ensure results.'

It was with the greatest difficulty that I refrained from telling him that there already existed, in my Hanover Square house, a small case in which there still rested the male half of the Indian I had prepared on my return from the Crimea, ready for all eventualities; and that in Huxtable's Folly, remote in the Vale of Pewsey, there still rested a female half, only awaiting the opportunity to fulfil her destiny.

I could have told Wolseley all. But had he learned the true power of the Indians he might have sought permission from high levels, a move which in the circumstances I was anxious to avoid; and had he learned that his bright new plan involved a weapon which had stood idle for three decades, he might well have dropped it as an antiquity. Thus I kept silent.

Berkeley and I traversed the dark cavernous corridors which must bring despondency to a soldier's mind, and I was shown into a small quiet room to find Maxim awaiting me. Beside him sat a tall, somewhat angular man with a smooth pear-shaped face, a short trimmed beard and a manner so over-courteous that it affronted me.

'Meet my colleague, Basil Zaharoff,' said Maxim.

'I am honoured,' he said, and as he took my hand I felt that he would bow over it. 'I am honoured to meet a man of science who carries within his brain a design for what has, I have heard it said, been called "the ultimate weapon".'

Then, as we seated ourselves, he added, '. . . although, of course, there is no such thing.'

As I pointed out without more ado, we were gathered together to discuss a weapon so considerable in its impact that it would – and here I was forced to remember that none of those present had an inkling of its power – make war unthinkable.

Zaharoff's reaction was disturbing.

'My dear Huxtable,' he said, seating himself more comfortably in his chair, looking out of the window, across Whitehall and into a distance which only he could comprehend, 'you need have no fear. The self-deception of man is unlimited. There is always an ultimate weapon. There is always another."

For a moment I was at a loss. It would be fatal to reveal, especially at this stage, exactly the quality of weapon which we were discussing. Yet anything less seemed unlikely to puncture his arrogant confidence.

'I am afraid, Mr. Zaharoff,' I said with as much stiffness as I could muster, 'that we are embarked here on production of a weapon which is different not merely in quality but also in kind.'

If I expected to ruffle, let alone convince, him I was to be disappointed.

He nodded. 'I know. I know. It is always the same. Indeed it must be so to keep the wheels turning. But when it comes to matters in the field, to the practical methods of killing men! Ah, then! –' he held up his hands as though he was blessing a Christian gathering

'– then, my dear Huxtable, we find that we have merely trodden one rung up the ladder to find that the ladder has sunk below us to the necessary degree.'

He reached across the table and I felt his hand on my arm. 'Do not fear. As long as other men do so we shall be ready to serve them.'

Zaharoff really meant 'serve'. Other men might provide food and drink, clothes or carriages. To Zaharoff these were no more essential to life than arms for war, and of these he regarded himself as the universal provider. Had one queried the morality of his trade he would have regarded himself like an honest baker whose provision of the staff of life was being questioned. Had he believed that I really thought it possible to stop all war – had he believed that, he might have laughed out loud, for such a thing was beyond his comprehension.

I had no right to complain. I had, of my own free will, entered into the industrial world of such men where standards were not the same as in the world I knew. However, our collaboration nearly came to a sudden end that first morning, after I had given a careful though impressive account of what might be achieved by the Indians. I was brusquely interrupted by Zaharoff.

"A fine idea, no doubt, but we must be careful not to look fools.'*

*Basil Zaharoff was in good company. 'This is the biggest fool thing we have ever done,' Admiral Leahy, President Roosevelt's Chief of Staff, told President Truman of the atomic weapon. 'The bomb will never go off and I speak as an expert in explosives.' (*Command Decisions*, U.S. Department of the Army, Office of the Chief of Military History, 1960.) As late as March 1945, Lord Cherwell, Churchill's scientific adviser, commented: 'No one can be sure it will go off – there's many a slip 'twixt cup and lip. Think what fools the Americans will look if the bomb does not work, now that they have spent 1,600,000,000 dollars.' (Quoted in *The Birth of the Bomb*, by Ronald Clark, Phoenix, 1961.)

As I stared at him in some surprise he added: 'The thing will never go off.' Nevertheless he worked on without complaint, industrially happy if scientifically sceptical.

I soon decided to ensure that science was not overwhelmed by industry. I had admirable means of doing so – if Maxim could play Basil Zaharoff, I had Ludwig Mond up my sleeve.

Amelia, Julie and I had stayed more than once with the Monds at Winnington Park. He and I would spend the early evening in his study, discussing the marvellous complexities of the chemical and physical worlds. Then, after dinner, the man of science would dissolve into the human being. With his fine bass voice Mond would join in the Mendelssohn quartets; he would need no coaxing to give the company Schumann's 'Two Grenadiers' – and on more than one occasion I watched the great man standing before the huge fireplace of the Hall's main chamber singing the student songs of his Heidelberg days.*

Mond was happy to join the Indian Committee. And whenever doubts arose as to the course which should be taken he, a man of science like myself, would take the correct view, whatever opinion might be held by Messrs. Maxim and Zaharoff; and Captain Berkeley, as suspicious of commerce as are most military men, would cast the Secretary's decisive vote in our favour.

It was Zaharoff who first saw the dangers of our open presence together in the club where, except for Berkeley, we lunched after our weekly meetings. In fact he did not appear too anxious to be seen in public at all, claiming that no one should know that he was in Europe, let alone

*See *Recollections of Dr Ludwig Mond*, by L. M. Richter (Spottiswoode, 1910).

England. For myself, I doubt if anyone cared, although the man may one day become famous because of the Indian Committee.

However, Zaharoff had a point. We had taken our coffee to a corner of the library to talk in comfort and security, when he stared down the long room from our alcove and said slowly:

'Gentlemen, we must have a reason.'

As we looked at him inquiringly, he continued: 'Here is Dr. Mond, one of the greatest chemists of our age. Here is Mr. Maxim, whose gun will one day be equipping the armies of the world – or at least the armies of Britain and her Allies. Here is Professor Huxtable, that quietly able physicist of whom wise men know little but must suspect much. And here am I – an ironmaster, gentlemen, concerned with the future of cold steel.'

He gave a long rumbling chuckle.

'Now what, gentlemen, could we be so earnestly discussing? What could we be talking about when we are seen here, as undoubtedly we shall be seen, in about a week's time, and in about a week's time after that? We can talk here as securely as if we sat on four chairs in the middle of Hyde Park, but we must surely be noticed by observant eyes.'*

'We might,' said Maxim, turning to Mond, 'be discussing some new and revolutionary development of your industrial processes.'

'We might indeed,' agreed Mond, with a smile spreading across his face, 'and Mr. Maxim and Mr. Zaharoff might be pouring their money into it – on the easiest of

*When members of the British Maud Committee were drawing up a blueprint for the atomic bomb in 1940, before America's entry into the war, they took care not to be seen together too frequently in the Athenaeum.

terms, of course – while Professor Huxtable was giving me the benefit of his highly technical knowledge. Gentlemen, what a dream! What opportunities you are offering me! How grateful I am!'

For the first time in my experience Mond allowed himself to wink: 'I must certainly see that my friends get a hint of what is afoot.'

More than once during the next few months I heard vague questions as to what he might be up to next; and one evening I was congratulated in all innocence by an acquaintance who said how gratified I must be, now that I was advising the great Ludwig Mond! Thus our work continued and at times we were even able to speak, within the earshot of others, of our Indian scheme – so that men began wondering what use Dr. Mond was to make of the produce from that great sub-continent! And all the time we could talk securely, in our corner of the Club, of events which were to change the history of the world!

I speculated on the public discussion there would have been had the existence of the Indians been known – and the bother which would have been raised about their manufacture on a commercial scale. But there was no public discussion. And more than once I wondered how the eventual use of the weapon would be received. For I had no doubt that it would one day be used; we were not, after all, wasting our time.

Or, to be more accurate, I was not wasting my time.

Maxim produced, in his works at Hatton Garden, the metal containers which were the successors to the elementary black boxes I had taken to India. A small company which was provided by Zaharoff, and to which we gave a harmless name, produced the necessary material in Cornwall and sent it to Mond's works in Cheshire.

Here it was processed and dispatched in small quantities to me by rail, packed in stout boxes and labelled, to disarm suspicion, 'Industrial Alloys'.

The other members of the Indian Committee, to whom I had revealed none of the essential, believed that at this stage I had only to fill the containers and fuse them, a process which I reserved to myself. In fact, the material coming south by rail had to be further refined by my electro-magnetic process before its potentials were realized. And, since I had the two halves of an Indian already prepared, standing waiting in Wiltshire and Hanover Square, why should I worry with more? The fine powdery material which I stored conveniently in sacks in my cellar was harmless enough; the secret of how to transform it remained, as it still remains, within my brain alone.

On one occasion I began to wonder if Mond might have stumbled upon my secret. We were talking after dinner in his Regent's Park home, 'The Poplars', and he had settled me down in one of the two comfortable armchairs which I always found in his laboratory, as grotesquely out of place in that galaxy of chemical apparatus as two elephants in a steel-works.

'I have been thinking,' he said. 'The other members of the Indian Committee are quite content with your promise of a large explosion; but you must have discovered some way of releasing in a minimum of time a maximum of energy.'

'In a way, that is so,' I agreed.

'And in that case,' he continued, turning round to face me, 'it must be possible to utilize this immense release of energy for industrial purposes.'

I thought of the troops, running from their tents at Jubila with their shouts of 'earthquake' – miles away from the explosion. I thought of the heat which must have been generated to melt those solid rocks of the plateau. I thought of the elemental forces involved and for a moment I almost laughed outright at Mond's suggestion.

'That,' I said, 'will never be possible. The methods I have devised can be directed for use in a bomb, but never in a boiler.'

'And yet .. .' He persisted, and I found it difficult to convince him. Even had I been willing to reveal all the cards in my hand – which I was not – he would still have remained unconvinced. A crazy belief that should men wish to harness such energy they would be able to do so, made even such a man totally impervious to argument.

'In this,' he concluded, 'you are the expert. Yet something within tells me that you are wrong. I may not live to see it, but I believe that my son, or my son's son, will do so. Indeed, one of them may even be foster-father to such a development.'*

I saw little of either Zaharoff or Maxim for many, many months, and met Mond only occasionally in the course of business. It was therefore with some surprise that I opened a letter one morning and found it to contain a message from Captain Berkeley.

'Lord Wolseley asks,' this said, 'whether you would call upon him at your earliest convenience regarding an important development concerning the Indian Committee.'

I attended upon Wolseley the following morning, won-

*Mond's grandson, the 2nd Lord Melchett, Vice-Chairman of I.C.I., played a significant part in encouraging and supporting nuclear research in 1940, when plans for a nuclear weapon were being prepared by the Maud Committee.

dering whether a turning-point in the affairs of the Indians might at last be arriving. This was so.

He came briskly to the point.

'We have decided,' he said, 'to detonate a pair of the Indians, Professor.'

I looked out through the windows from the cool of the room to the heat of the pavements, shimmering in the summer sun. I thought of all my efforts, all my expectations. The words tumbled my thoughts into disarray like an unexpected delivery from disaster in the mountains.

'We have,' he went on, 'a small war in Africa – in fact, it might at this stage be classed a series of tribal engagements rather than war; but it will, without doubt, grow into that unless it is quenched at source. It is an ideal situation for a demonstration.'

For a moment he must have seen disappointment on my face. I had not expected my weapon to be frittered away in the Dark Continent, so distant from those places where its real importance might be assessed.

I made my point reasonably, not protesting.

'No doubt,' agreed Wolseley confidently, as though I had little knowledge of affairs, 'but you must remember that the eyes of the world are upon us. A small war it may be. Yet if it can be settled sharply, decisively, moreover in a way which will be totally new ...' He brought his fist down and I thought what a determined little figure he looked.

But a question arose. 'I assume,' I said, 'that the other members of the Indian Committee know of this?'

'They know, or will know,' he said. 'I do not think that Mond has yet been informed.' He turned to me and for a moment I wondered whether he was master in his own house.

'Politics,' he said cryptically, 'enter into most things, and you must agree that this is a splendid opportunity for us all.'

I wondered how the Prime Minister would react. I knew, though Wolseley presumably did not, how resolute Gladstone had been in his veto a decade or so previously. Then I realized that at this stage the whole matter was, of course, confined to the War Office.

How odd, I thought at the time – and as I have often thought since – that we should have argued high policy at higher levels for more years than I cared to remember, and that now the decision to unleash my weapon was being taken almost casually, without apparent need for any decision in those distinguished circles where I had previously been moving. Even now I am intrigued by the fact that once the existence of the Indians had been, so to speak, properly regularized, personal responsibility ceased; and by the fact that once the machinery had been set in motion, as it had by Wolselsey's casual suggestion to Maxim and my more determined suggestion of a Committee, then no hand was available to halt it.

All these thoughts passed through my mind as I thanked Wolseley and said I would make the necessary arrangements. Yet I walked out into the glare of Whitehall discomfited at my victory. After all these years I had achieved my aim; yet in some perverse way the victory had already begun to evaporate.

I concluded that the reason for my misgiving lay in the doubts I had previously felt following my meetings with Hooker and Godwin-Austen. I needed time for thought, and I decided that there was no better place than Cambridge – the environment in which I had laid the foundations of my success and where I had walked and talked with Dalton. I had lectured there frequently over the years, had kept touch with university life, and knew many of the undergraduates who were now up. It would be a pleasant excursion. It was also to be one which strangely resolved my doubts.

Two days later I was perambulating those very Backs where more than five decades earlier I had spoken with the man whose brain had laid the foundations of the atomic theory. I sat on the same seat. I looked down across the years. And it was here that, as I ruminated on the past, I saw coming towards me the figure of Arthur Benson, one of the brightest stars in the contemporary Cambridge firmament. Though more interested in the humanities than the sciences, he was of an inquiring mind, and I had more than once met his father at those social gatherings graced by Churchmen climbing the ladder of ecclesiastical preferment. He acknowledged me and I broke away from my thoughts to ask after the health of his father, by this time the Most Reverend Father in God, by Divine Providence Lord Archbishop of Canterbury.

Divine Providence, I later felt, must have sent his son my way that morning. He sat down beside me, flushed with undergraduate enthusiasms, and before long my private consideration of the Indians was overwhelmed by his plans for overcoming the problems of the world, conceived in the simple manner usual among men of that age.

I do not know which of us first raised the subject of Africa, but I suspect it was myself – a subject with which my young companion was unexpectedly familiar.

'My father was discussing this very problem with Ran-

204

dall Davidson,'* he said. I thought of Davidson, the former Archbishop's resident chaplain, and I could imagine the many subjects on which his views would be very different from Benson's.

'There really could be a Pax Britannica had we but the will and the power to enforce the peace,' the young man went on, turning to me as though he were a poet declaiming to the multitude. 'There would be a period of conquest rather than conciliation. But then – Britain could expand into the Mother of the Free. She would be set to conquer but to conquer with a purpose. Wider still and wider would her bounds be set. God who made her mighty would make her mightier yet.'

He broke off for a moment in his ardour. 'Oh, if only I had music to which I could set those words I could start a crusade with them.'

True enough. But that would come later. First things first – and as I became fired by this lad, young enough to be my grandson, my foolish qualifications were swept away. I must have been getting old to worry about Delane's hypothetical spectre of the secret spreading, about my own fears that a physical device could affect the development of living organisms.

I felt reassured and I returned to London comforted, all doubts resolved.† There followed the usual seemingly

*Baron Davidson of Lambeth (1848–1930), Archbishop of Canterbury, who protested against the use by British troops of poison gas, and against air reprisals, during the First World War.

†An author's note in *The Professor*, by A. C. Benson, 100 copies of which were privately printed in 1895, describes the professor of the poem 'whose work it is to pry into the deepest and holiest secrets of existence ... a man for whom life has parted with its reticence, and death with its mystery ... he lighted upon a guarded treasure, but he fumbled strangely with the lock; God help him to turn the key.'

interminable delays; then, having given my family but the vaguest idea of what work took me abroad, I sailed from England.

This time there was to be no confusion. I sailed with one shining metal canister, the charge so adjusted that with its companion it would eliminate life over a smaller radius than the Jubila weapon, thus making the demonstration more manageable – but still spreading destruction over a number of square miles.

A day's voyage behind me, guarded by Dobbin in another of Her Majesty's vessels, came the second half of the Indian.

As Smeaton's light on the red rocks of Eddystone faded into the haze behind, I felt that all my life had been but a preparation for the events that lay ahead.

10: To a Small War in Africa

Her Majesty's gunboat anchored off the Dark Continent shortly before dawn. How fitting, I thought. My device had been tested in Asia; it had been wasted in Europe during the Crimean campaign; now its power was to be revealed to the world from a third continent. How Pliny was to be justified – indeed, 'always something new out of Africa'.

In the growing light, the chief town of the Colony began to appear, stretching along the shores of a land-locked bay. On one side lay a high and luxuriantly wooded promontory dotted with the bright roofs of houses; on the other, the lower land with its poorer dwellings, running out into shallows from which coloured navigation lights indicated the difficult entrance. Inside the harbour bar a forest of masts showed where some scores of smaller ships were moored; outside lay the larger vessels, and here in the roadstead we hove to, the chains rattling out with startling suddenness as the anchor splashed down to disturb the oily morning calm of the waters.

Minutes later a tug could be seen making for our vessel. It carried a uniformed crew and it came from the Governor, whose message announced that his own carriage was awaiting me. How different, I thought, from the bungled business of the Crimea!

There was hardly a white man stirring as we clattered through the streets twenty minutes later, up a broad road flanked with tropical palms and on towards a commanding hill outside the town where stood the Residency.

Before leaving England I had made discreet inquiries and had learned much about the Governor. It was said that he held a profound belief in all that had happened before the Reform Bill, and that he owed as much to a pretty and considerably younger wife as he owed to good luck. I browsed over what I had heard as the carriage rolled through the gates and as for the first time in my life I found myself being saluted by Her Majesty's troops.

It was common, I later learned, for the Governor to be up at any early hour, and he was waiting to welcome me. In stature, he was shorter than I had expected, somewhat barrel-shaped, with long arms that gave a simian appearance as he moved; he was clad in an untidily old-fashioned uniform whose ribbons spoke of service in days long past. His knobbly hand almost embraced me. I was bustled inside the house amid a rumble of orders to those who stood around, hanging on his words. I was accommodated, breakfasted, bowed over, looked at with quizzical eye – all amid a rattle of small talk presided over by this man whose speech, spotted rugosity of countenance and brusque bluntness all indicated his early upbringing in the remote Scottish Highlands from which he had come south with great ambition and even greater energy.

It was some while later, but still only the hour for civilized waking, when he took me by the arm with a grip that was almost painful and half propelled me into his study. He dismissed the servants, closed the heavy doors and, looking at me from under bushy eyebrows that were as luxuriant as his decorations, came to the business in hand.

'I understand from London, Professor Huxtable,' he

began, 'that you have a weapon whose astonishing power will dissuade the tribes from launching a major campaign.'

I modestly admitted that this was so.

He stared at me fiercely, for what seemed a long while. 'I hope you are right,' he said at last. 'There has been enough bloodshed during these last few months. I hope so . . . but . . .'

He gazed at me again, more benignly but as though I were a boy at school.

'You must realize, Professor, that our enemy is more than a tribe of untutored natives. They may call them that in London. They may be right. Their customs are appalling. But you must realize that they are brave men. If they were not, my task would be easier.'

I bowed, and he suddenly decided to take me into his confidence.

'Professor Huxtable,' he said, 'I find it difficult fully to understand the import of my instructions. But it appears, if the guarded information is not deliberately misleading, that you have touched a spring which can release the power almost of God.'

He sighed with the resignation of an old man – although he must have been only a few years older than I – who realized that knowledge had slipped past him and that he would never catch up.

'All Scotsmen,' he added, 'all Scotsmen recognize and seize the moment when history thrusts greatness upon them. You are to have the best that we can offer, sir. You are to have Colonel Burton-Brown as Commander of . . .'

For a moment he flurried among his papers and was forced to drape himself with a pair of enormous gold-rimmed spectacles.

'As Commander . . .' he came up with it triumphantly, '. . . of Force Indian.'

For a moment his face reflected the wisdom of Whitehall. 'What an admirable phrase,' he said. 'Here in Africa the Indians are still but insignificant in the community, a small, civilizing, but most beneficent force. How correct of the authorities to think of such a telling phrase.'

He repeated it, as pleased with them as he was with himself. 'How correct! How very, very correct!'

I thanked him and we emerged, passing the guards stationed outside. Now we were no longer alone. Now the Governor was again cushioned among a drove of servants, both black and white, who swarmed wherever he went like bees round an ancient honey-pot – but bees who flew as required, wherever the slightest wish of the master commanded, almost without orders, as though by a warning from his slow brain creaking into action they could anticipate his desires.

Later that day, the Colonel rode up to the Residency. I was handed over to his care, with the Governor's blessing and with the promise that whatever we required would be provided.

Even I had heard of Burton-Brown. Twenty years previously he had been the darling of fashionable London, his thick and fiercely spiked black moustache the subject of many a cartoonist. But he had been too unconventional for Society to hold. He had achieved fame, if not notoriety, in one desperately brave but quite irregular exploit beyond the frontiers of India. Then he had returned to regimental soldiering and had made Hobday's Horse into one of the Army's most redoubtable Lancer regiments.

As I came to know Burton-Brown during the days that followed, I compared him with another simpler yet

similar figure – one who was in some ways his predeces-
sor. But whereas Swyre was a man self-tailored to the
trade of war, it seemed that war had been created to
satisfy the particular qualities of Burton-Brown. I realized how experience had strengthened him, so that while
the old daring still flashed out there now lay beneath it a
determined rock-steadiness that would have continued
on a tightrope, above an abyss. Burton-Brown was a
man entirely without bravado; indeed, he had no need of
it. He assumed that where he led others followed; he was
always right.

It was this quality combined of daring and resolution
which had enabled him to make Hobday's Horse a by-
word in military circles; one commander-in-chief had
said of the regiment that 'one could always ask and it
would always be given.' It had served in many lands and
for the last few months, as I was soon to learn, had been
making a series of forays deep into enemy country, dis-
appearing for weeks at a time, supporting isolated
groups of settlers, and then returning across the Blue
Fish River.

Burton-Brown had been seconded from the regiment
for his special duties only a few days before. Under his
second-in-command, Major Chamberlain, the regiment's
lancers had disappeared once more into the blue distances of the interior. Their commander was left, as he
must have regarded it, to chaperone a professor almost
as old as the Governor, with little knowledge of war
and no experience of life in the field.

Yet even from the first he took his task in good part.
What is more, and to my mingled relief and surprise,
Burton-Brown accepted Dobbin and Dobbin accepted
Burton-Brown. The ship carrying the second half of the
Indian had arrived on schedule the day after my arrival

and Burton-Brown and I had ridden down to the quay-side.

The crated canister had already been unloaded and now lay on the cobbles. Sitting at each corner of the crate was a native bearer. Standing a few yards off, watching with the air of a hen guarding her chicks, stood Dobbin, slightly shrunken now in his old age, still ramrod-straight, dressed as soberly as myself and by this time carrying an air almost of authority.

'Ready to move when ordered, sir,' he said. 'I understand that the first case has been moved to the Residency.'

'An old soldier,' said Burton-Brown, more as statement than question.

'Some time ago, sir,' said Dobbin cautiously.

For a moment question and answer shot between them. Then the match was over. Perhaps each had recognized in the other that strong strain of the unorthodox which flowed through both; whatever the reason, there bubbled up a strong mutual respect that was to ease my task.

Later that day Burton-Brown introduced me to the Garrison, while Dobbin was conducting the second half of the Indian to its quarters. Then he led me into the large office which had been put at his disposal, a room from whose shaded windows one looked west towards a blue haze of foot-hills.

'It will be best if you know our problem at once," he said, leading me to a large wall-map.

'There is no trouble south of the Blue Fish River' – and he pointed to a straggling line which ran eastwards from the interior and reached the coast after much devious winding.

'As you will see, this is not difficult to control. The

natives are good men on the land, and the land itself is equally good. North of the Blue Fish River the country changes.'

Even I, accustomed to reading equations more readily than maps, was able to see what he meant. North of the Blue Fish River the country had not yet been properly surveyed, but there was no mistaking the meaning of the numerous *hachures*, thick through bad printing, and the brown layers of colour which made it difficult for the layman to understand the terrain with accuracy.

'Until recently,' said Burton-Brown, 'we have controlled the area by good will and good luck. Now the good will has expired with a change of chieftainships and the good luck appears to have run out. You will remember Burke's Column. We have no wish to repeat that disaster. From our reconnaissance in strength – and those by Hobday's Horse are, I must admit, only the most successful of a number – it seems that the chieftains are preparing for full-scale war.'

He regarded me keenly. 'It is just possible, Professor, that the weapon you are to demonstrate might dissuade them. Possible, but unlikely,' he added.

'You must tell me,' he continued, leading me back to a huge table in the middle of the room, a table cluttered with maps, rulers, compasses and coloured pins, 'you must tell me all you want. But first tell me how many men your weapon could kill.'

Colonel Burton-Brown sat down facing me. I drew forward one of the maps and looked at the scale. He assented to my marking it. I picked up a pair of compasses and drew a circle in open country.

'All within such an area,' I said. 'It is a small model, mainly for demonstration purposes; but it will utterly destroy everyone and everything within a radius of 3,000 yards.'

Colonel Burton-Brown continued to look at me. He said nothing. Not a muscle in his face moved, nor was there in the eyes that slight tremor of the irises by which men are apt to betray their doubts. I found the experience unnerving, and for a moment it seemed that he might be looking into my skull and seeing there the clearly written evidence of all that I had experienced since my fateful discovery.

'I believe you,' he said eventually. 'You must tell me more.'

I could not, of course, tell him very much more. He wanted to know the weight of the device, how it should be transported, whether it could suffer rough handling without disaster, how much delay could be produced between setting of the mechanism and the detonation.

I explained that I had one small load of ancillary equipment – the track which I had now so adapted that it could be laid with speed, by unskilled labour; and that my two canisters must be kept apart a minimum distance of four hundred yards, the safety limit which I had settled.

'But Professor,' he exclaimed, 'in the case of ambush, in the case of the column being forced to laager unexpectedly, this will be . . .' He threw up his hands in military despair.

He insisted that it was surely possible for a charge and a fuse – for so he naively considered the device – to be brought together so long as they lacked physical contact.

I explained, as well as I could, that the problem could not be considered in those terms. I thought of that moment on the approach to Jubila, where head and tail had almost met. 'If armies could fly,' I pointed out, 'military men would have to think totally differently, in terms of three dimensions. You will have to think differently when my device has been demonstrated.'

He rose from the table and began to stride back and forth, talking half to me and half to himself.

'The weapon itself sounds simple enough. But it is, from my point of view, a weapon four hundred yards long. We shall be vulnerable. We shall need two companies, and scouts, and artillery.

'We must penetrate far enough to be sure that our demonstration will be properly seen. We must be sure of an audience, but at this stage it is not essential to kill.'

He turned to me suddenly. 'Does altitude affect your weapon, Professor?'

He seemed reassured to learn that the weapon would work perfectly at any altitude, and he called me over to the wall-map once again.

'Here we have just the place,' he said.

He pointed to a little knot of contour-lines and hill-shading a few miles north of the Blue Fish River.

'The Baluba Basin,' he explained. 'Originally, I am told, a volcanic crater, and certainly an admirable site for our purpose. An approach from the Blue Fish River will be feasible – and since the place is normally avoided by the natives we should have no difficulty in laying your device.'

I raised a question on his expression 'normally avoided'.

'That is right,' he replied. 'The Baluba Basin is considered by the natives as the home of bad spirits. But there are legends concerning it which we shall be able to use for our own ends. M'Bambi will see to that.'

To this day I wonder exactly what Burton-Brown

meant when he used the word 'our'. For I felt again, as I had felt with Wolseley in the War Office some weeks previously, that a new and less open method of controlling public events was now in operation. The old machinery of Cabinet and War Office and officials still worked, of course, but beside it there worked another machine, invisible but perhaps more powerful, its levers in the firm hands of men who preferred not to enter public life – and who, indeed, had no need to do so.

I said nothing, but merely listened as Burton-Brown explained all I wanted to know.

As our column moved off three days later, one of my canisters was strapped up as an inconspicuous load at the head of the column, and the second was a load under Dobbin's charge at the tail. Between them, on my special instructions, there was placed a small squad of carefully chosen men; they knew nothing of the reason for their orders. But in the event of unexpected happenings they were at all costs to prevent the animal carrying my second canister from reaching the head of the column.

We started on our enterprise in the cool of the morning – two companies of infantry, a gun-team with a solitary field-piece and its attendant ammunition-limber, and an escort of cavalry. It was a column, I understood, of unconventional make-up; but then our task was unconventional, and as we marched inland, along a track whose course followed a gravelly riverbed, I knew that none other had enjoyed a mission such as ours.

We rested in the heat of the day and then continued our journey across country that rose gradually, so that by evening we could look back along the river valley far beneath, across the minor spurs we had crossed, to a horizon beyond which there shimmered the darker blue of the Indian Ocean.

As we set out on the second day's march, the country into which we were moving became more formidable. For we now dropped steadily down from bush into forest, a tangle of huge trees which rose high above the plants fringing the track. The road had now ended, our pace was slower, and at more than one point the men had to prepare the way for the field-piece.

We travelled all day, at first beneath creepers festooned from the overhanging branches, past green depths from which there came the flitter of innumerable birds and the incessant chatter of the monkeys who eyed us fearlessly and with curiosity. By afternoon we had traversed the forest belt. Before us lay the Blue Fish River. That night we laagered by it, and with more care than on the first night. I heard the men being numbered off for sentry duty, the strict instructions as to lights.

After we had dined in the long mess-tent Burton-Brown invited me to his quarters so that we could discuss the details of the coming day's work; for a few hours' march would now take us to the Baluba Basin, whose ragged summit ridge had been pointed out to me among the hills ahead.

I still could not understand how the natives could be induced to watch the demonstration.

'You will soon know,' Burton-Brown assured me, as his orderly adjusted the swinging oil-lamp and then left us.

We had been poring over the map on the camp table for some twenty minutes when I noticed a shadow on the canvas. From outside the tent-flap a trooper called out, 'A native says he must see you, sir. He claims he has urgent business.'

Burton-Brown turned to me silently with a quizzical

look, called out his assent and waited as a tall figure entered the tent.

The man before us must have been some inches over six feet. He was of a lighter colour than most of the natives I had so far seen, and there was some other difference about him I could not place. I sought back through my early anthropological knowledge, failed to find what I was seeking, and decided only that there was something in the man's air of authority, in his confidence, which marked him off from those natives I had seen during the last few days.

Our visitor inclined the top half of his body in a half-bow, a graceful movement which sent the rays from the oil-lamp rippling over his almost naked body.

'M'Bambi,' he announced, 'has come.'

Burton-Brown turned to me. 'He belongs, as you will judge from his colour,' he said, 'to a distant territory in the north. But he came south with great knowledge; he has been accepted; more than once' – and here I thought he smiled slightly – 'he has told his people of what the white men wish. He is now believed. At times, he is also obeyed.'

The man bowed again. 'That is so,' he said simply.

'It is true, is it not, M'Bambi,' said the Colonel, 'that the Baluba Basin is shunned?'

He was answered by an assenting bow.

'And it is true, is it not, that many generations ago men spoke of a great coming, of a magic transformation which would alter, for all time, the future of the peoples of this country; and that the transformation would be seen on the floor of Baluba?'

Once again the man inclined his head.

'We have come,' said Burton-Brown, 'and we bring with us the White Queen's Magic. Two hours after two dawns the transformation will take place. You must tell the leaders of the tribes that this transformation must be witnessed. But it must be witnessed at a great distance. All who are too close to the Magic will die; all who look towards it will be blinded.' He spelt out the figures I had given him.

I was much impressed. So was M'Bambi, though I saw that he now wished to speak with Burton-Brown and was embarrassed by my presence.

The Colonel turned to me with a confiding sweep of his arm.

'We have here,' he said, 'the Keeper of the White Queen's Magic. You may speak freely – Captain Ferguson.'

It would be untrue to say that the face of the figure before me altered. But just as the same coloured parts in a kalaeidoscope may produce different patterns, so did the same features of the man now produce a different shape, as though my vision had altered as it can alter when one gazes too long at a chequerboard of black and white.

M'Bambi was still more than six foot. He was still shining with what I took to be his natural brown glow. But now beneath the mask I could sense if not see the real man – although, I realized, I might for ever have remained in ignorance.

For a few moments the two officers spoke together. Burton-Brown explaining what he knew of our mission, M'Bambi – for as such I will always think of him – asking such questions as were necessary.

At one point the Colonel turned to me. 'We can decide, then, on seven-fifteen as the time for the demonstration?' he asked. I agreed, and he turned back to his companion to emphasize, once again, the two most important facts: the necessary safe distance, and the time of seven-fifteen on the morning after next.

Burton-Brown went to the tent-flap and called the trooper. M'Bambi bowed yet again. 'Give the man a meal,' the trooper was told, 'then let him go.' The tall figure bowed himself out.

'In only a few years,' said Burton-Brown, returning to the table, 'he has acquired an astonishing reputation. His ability, and his bravery, are the equal of Sir Richard Burton's. If it comes to war we shall have four columns advancing on the natives; he will be a fifth column with the enemy.'

It was time for me to go. I bade Burton-Brown good night and stepped outside, from the light of the lamp into what at first seemed to be velvet tropical darkness. My own tent was but a score of steps away but before I reached it my eyes had become accustomed to the night.

I looked up at the black canopy sprinkled with millions of stars, some visibly quivering as their light came through the immeasurable distances of space, some almost glowing in their intensity, and the Southern Cross itself shining like a candelabrum of golden lamps. Near by, the fireflies floated like sparks among the bushes. A night-jar skimmed overhead with its shrill whirring note, and from the distance there came the bark of a prowling jackal among the thorns. All else was still. For a moment, as the insignificance of man was pressed in upon me by surrounding nature, I wondered how history would judge me, the bearer of a new power to this silent continent.

As I wondered, the extraordinarily apposite words of Browning passed through my mind.

Here and here did England help me: how
    can I help England? – say,
Whoso turns as I, this evening, turn to God
    to praise and pray,
While Jove's planet rises yonder, silent over
    Africa.

I opened the flaps of my tent-door, well knowing that
we were on the eve of great events.

11 : The Baluba Basin

I was awakened at first light by the slow paling of the canvas which surrounded me, by the arrival of Dobbin, and by the sounds of the troops breaking camp.

We crossed the Blue Fish River shortly afterwards. Even to my untutored eye our dispositions were very different from those of the preceding days. To left and right, as well as ahead, scouts circled constantly, for ever alert for sight or sound of an enemy. The troops themselves were in different marching order and I realized that there was now the constant danger of attack.

We had been riding for less than an hour when a fold of the country brought our objective into view once again. Now that we were nearer I could see how the grassy sea through which we rode gave out as the country rose. At first there were merely clumps of bush, then the bush gave out to stunted scrub, and the scrub to stones. Our surroundings had been open and park-like; now, as we went higher, they acquired the freedom of the barren Scottish mountains I had known in my youth.

The rays of the sun, reflected up by the rocks, struck at us with increasing heat, but this was tempered by a breeze. We were by now some thousands of feet up, and on three sides the ground dropped steadily away. I reined in my horse and looked around.

Far away, beyond the more open country, the forests stretched for mile upon mile; beyond them, more distant and obscured by a faint haze, there were the foothills of other territories, while beyond them again, appearing like a mirage, hanging in the air above a cordon of faint clouds, were dark outlines, insubstantial yet commanding, which I knew were the mountains of the interior.

Immediately before us lay the outer slopes of the Baluba Basin and up these the column now made its way.

At first the ground rose gently, then more steeply, but never with an inclination which caused difficulty, for three or four miles. It ended in a ridge every detail of which was picked out against the blue sky.

We rode on, saying little, going more slowly as the slope steepened. A few hundred yards from the crest ahead the column was halted.

'Now you will see the site for your demonstration,' said Burton-Brown. He remained beside me as our horses picked their way up the slope. Then, a few yards from the crest, he drew back slightly, as though wishing to see my expression.

My mount struggled up the last few feet of scrabbly rock. I drew level with, and then over-topped, the rugged crest which had obscured our view northwards for so long, and looked down into the Baluba Basin.

Before me, the long ridge on which we stood dropped steeply downwards in a glacis of boulders and scree, descending some hundreds of feet to the crater floor. East and west it continued in similar form, broken in places by narrow gullies and by broader breaches where rockfalls had been transformed over the centuries into tracks used by animals. Thus we stood, as it were, at the top of a broken parapet, a parapet which stretched for some two miles in either direction and whose extremities curved out and away from us, forming a crescent whose horns stretched forward some hundreds of yards.

This was not all. Before us, some four miles to the north, its rocky buttresses glistening so sharply in the sun that I felt I might stretch out and touch them, there ran a counterpart to the ridge, dropping in height in like fashion, just failing to meet it both east and west, so that the huge arena on to which we looked down had both natural entrance and natural exit.

And what an arena! While the tangle of rocks and scree falling to its floor was even more barren of vegetation than the slopes up which we had ridden, it was an almost fertile landscape which lay below us, covered in most places with thick savannah grass which waved in the morning breeze. Only in the centre of the great oval plain was the ground-cover lacking; there, about a mile and a half away, the grass gave way to a surface of sand and pebbles. There, within full view of the whole circumference of God's grandstand, was the place to prepare Her Majesty's Indians.

Natives in their thousands would be able to line the twin ridges; all would be more than the necessary distance from the Indians if they were properly placed in the centre of the arena. Further thousands would be able, if they wished, to watch from the steep slopes which rose from the crater floor to the ridges. And if any were rash enough to approach closer to the weapon, then they too would play their own parts in the demonstration.

A few moments later Burton-Brown was ordering up the troops carrying the first of the Indians; others were prospecting the easiest way down the slopes to the crater floors. The men, who had of course been told no more than was absolutely necessary, now began to make their way down-hill, supervising with much rude comment what appeared to them to be hardly a weapon of war.

It was a good hour before the first loads had been taken from the horses, the lengths of track butted up to one another, and the first of my canisters erected at its northern end.

Only then did the signaller with the heliograph flash his message up to the men waiting on the ridge. And now I could see the animal bearing my second canister – preceded by the special escort. The final load was brought without hitch to the southern end of the track.

The men were ordered back. And with only Burton-Brown beside me I now attended to the mechanism. In the new and improved specimen, the business of bringing the two halves together had been simplified. One canister remained stationary; only one moved – but at double the speed of the Jubila model – and thus the chances of mechanical impediment were halved.

We could hear the faint voices of the men on the ridge, and an occasional flurry of stones as a horse stumbled up the steeper portion of the slope; yet I felt as though Burton-Brown and I were alone in all Africa. I looked round again at the huge oval amphitheatre of slopes and found it difficult to realize that within twenty-four hours all would be thick with the figures of natives. At either end of the crater, where the cliffs were less high, one could see nothing between the grass and, many miles away, the blue of distant hills. All was still except for an occasional spreuw whistling overhead, intent on its flight, and the wind brushing the grass into waves as though it were corn in a Scottish field at harvest-time.

I bent down and again confirmed the setting of the timing device.

'At seven fifteen,' I said.

'At seven fifteen,' repeated the Colonel.

I checked that the tracks ran true, ensured that the wheels of the trolleys moved freely on the rails.

'All is now ready, Colonel,' I said. 'We have but to wait for the Indians to do their duty.'

In an excess of care I suggested that we should lead our horses back across the crater floor, half fearful lest the reverberation of their hooves should disturb the mechanism.

It was hot work up the slope and I was glad when we reached the troops awaiting us on the ridge. It was already nearly midday. If M'Bambi had done his work, the first of the natives would within a few hours be gathering, anxious to see what the future held for their people.

That night, back in camp, Burton-Brown called the officers and myself into his tent and in a small ceremony we drank to the success of what was now formally called a new artillery weapon – although I was careful to stress, when asked to say a few words, that 'weapon', rather than 'artillery weapon' in any conventional sense of the phrase, would be a better description.

Only a few hours later, while it was still dark, our horses splashed back across the shallows of the river as we rode to a vantage-point from which to estimate both the extent of the native gathering and then their reaction to the demonstration.

This time we were a smaller body of men, a company of infantry, a mere handful of scouts, and the field-piece which the Colonel insisted on retaining as military insurance.

Well before dawn we had ensconced ourselves on our hillock; below, the rest of the column stood to. Impatiently we awaited the first slash of colour on the eastern horizon, and as impatiently the strengthening light through which the outline of the Baluba ridge slowly became visible. Our vantage-point was nearer than I had hoped for, and a wide segment of the slopes leading up to it was within our sight.

Only I knew what we were awaiting. At least, I was confident of that until I found Dobbin pressing a pair of field-glasses into my hands and heard him whisper: 'Well, sir. Soon we shall see.' How much, I wondered, did he really know?

All was still covered in the half-light – until with an almost startling suddenness the sun's rays hit the upper hillside in front of us. The ridge itself was first illuminated. Below it, all became clear as a long horizontal line travelled quickly downhill and the rising sun rolled back the darkness.

Within a few moments all the upper slopes of the Baluba Basin were in bright sunlight, clearly visible.

On them there moved no living thing.

The Colonel put down his glasses, grunted as though in disbelief, and raised them again. As he lowered them once more, he called back and down over his shoulder.

'Mr. Martin. Telescope forward.'

There was a delay as the lieutenant shouted to the gunners and a man came up with the instrument. A few seconds later the Colonel was straddled flat on the ground, the telescope propped on a rock. He gazed through it for a full five minutes, shifting his position slightly so that he could scan different portions of the ground. Then, without a word, he handed it to me.

At first I had some difficulty in sighting the instrument; but soon there could be no doubt. I handed back the telescope as Burton-Brown said: 'Not a native – not a living soul on a good two-thirds of the southern ridge. Our luck seems to be out today, Professor.'

For more than one reason it was difficult to believe that this was the case. Although we had seen none of the enemy on the previous day's trek, the scouts were sure that we had been observed from a distance. It seemed certain that the natives would be inquisitive about our activities on the crater floor. And even if M'Bambi had failed to do his job, the lack of activity was still inexplicable.

We would have to go nearer.

We went down to the men below and after a few moments the column moved on. For a while our objective lay out of sight, then it began to rise before us again. Once more we stopped to scan the ridge through the telescope; and once more we were unrewarded. The whole landscape was still and silent, as though swept clean by a hand which had wiped all life from it.

We halted once again. And now Burton-Brown showed his disappointment. 'No enemy, Professor. No point in a demonstration.'

As I explained, it was essential to know what had happened.

For what, I speculated, if M'Bambi had done his work too well? If the Indians had been tampered with? I realized with dismay that those two canisters might even now be on the shoulders of native bearers, travelling to some end far beyond our scientific investigation.

'It is essential, Colonel,' I urged, 'that we should know what is happening.'

Colonel Burton-Brown looked back at the Blue Fish River, now a thin silver streak in the distance. During our previous advance into enemy territory we had been protected by all the fire-power of Indian Force, but even then I had noticed the great care which he had taken in the disposition of his men.

228

Now we were fewer in numbers, more vulnerable. Now the enemy might be aware of our presence. And now even I could see, as I considered the lie of the land, that any further advance would render us powerless if an enemy wished to cut off the retreat of such a small party.

'Somewhere out there,' said Burton-Brown, waving his hand towards the rolling country which stretched on each side of the crater into the green depths of Africa, 'somewhere out there, Hobday's Horse is at work. But they would be of little help to us if . . .'

He turned in his saddle to scan the route we had come, and I could almost watch his mind working out the chances of a fighting retreat towards the river.

He began to explain the situation, so that I should be left in no doubt of the dangers – those dangers which might perturb a civilian but were to him but the common coin of life.

'That is the situation, Professor,' he concluded, 'I am completely at your service.'

I repeated that it was essential to know what was happening to my canisters and there was no tremor in his voice as he called back to the men, 'Let the column proceed.'

His phrase tinkled a bell. I thought back to that day decades earlier when we had been passing through the last village on the approach to the Jubila Plateau. I remembered Colonel Swyre's peremptory order after we had been stopped by the soothsayer. And as Burton-Brown's outriders recognized the signals and pricked their horses forward again I remembered the soothsayer's nodding acquiescence – and his words.

We continued to move forward slowly and cautiously across long stretches of boiler-plate rocks, grey and purplish-brown. At places there were small outcrops where the bare bones of the earth thrust through their covering. A solitary warrior might, it is true, have concealed himself behind such natural cairns. All were innocent of men. There were still no natives to be seen.

I could now sense a tenseness among the men. The distant riders on our flanks, for ever circling, for ever watching for any indication of an enemy, seemed to move with a new alertness. Behind us the men marched in silence. The gun-team, watchful of its charge, eased this forward over the rougher patches of the trail with a heave in the right direction, a quick shoulder to the wheel; but they did so, I noticed, without the curses which had previously accompanied such minor difficulties.

We moved on in silence for another twenty minutes. Through the glasses it was now possible to scan every detail of the slopes leading to the crest of the ridge. It was clear that the southern of the two great parapets was empty of the enemy.

Another twenty minutes brought us to within a hundred yards of the crest. Here, below the skyline, Burton-Brown halted the column with raised hand. There were a few quick orders and the troops, carrying out a drill which was second nature, formed themselves into a defensive laager.

Burton-Brown and I moved to the ridge. This time we went forward cautiously, crawling up the last few feet before looking over into the crater. Had we expected a startling scene, we should have been disappointed.

Below us, and but a score of feet lower down it seemed, there boiled a sea of white cloud. At places, this momentarily reached up into great castles which changed shape, forming and reforming as we watched. With these exceptions it lay as flat as a carpet, a huge unbroken layer stretching to the northern ridge whose higher pinnacles rose above it like disembodied towers from another world.

We watched the scene in silence for a full five minutes. From behind us there came only the occasional sharp sound of a horse pawing the ground, the chink of metal as one of the gunners went about his duty, or the long scrabble as one of the men pulled his forty-pound haversack into a more convenient position.

Then I became aware of an unusual sound. From below there drifted up to us a continuous heavy hum as though an immense swarm of bees was at work. As the sound grew, the cloud-sea began to change. With the strengthening of the sun, great columns of mist rose and dispersed into shimmering curtains, and through them the light produced a myriad of iridescent rainbows. At places, through the gaps in the cloud-sea, the floor of the crater became visible. The humming became louder, rhythmically rising and falling. Now I could feel the warmth of the sun on my face. As it grew in intensity the sounds beat upon our ears. The last of the white billows below us began to dissolve, and within a few more seconds we were gazing down on to the crystal-clear floor of the Basin.

The whole vast arena was alive with natives.

There they moved, pin-sharp in the morning light, hundred upon hundred of them leaping like human marionettes, raising in gesticulating hands their cow-hide shields or their long assegais, forming into circles which dissolved into larger groups and then again reformed. As they danced, they chanted and sang so that there rose up to us a huge cacophony, mounting and falling swelling and diminishing, so that I was reminded of the multitude of bird-voices I had heard from the cliffs of Ailsa Crag as a boy.

Near the foot of the slopes that led down from the two ridges the natives were smaller in numbers. But towards the centre of the arena they crowded more thickly together – except in the very centre, where about my two canisters and the track linking them they formed an oval ring a mere score of yards away from the Indians.

As Burton-Brown lowered his glasses he muttered the name of M'Bambi. 'And so,' he said, 'he did his job too well.'

This had not been the case. Later we were to learn how the chieftains had received the news of the white man's plans; they were, as the Governor had warned, brave men, and they had decided to overcome their fears of the crater floor by casting the requisite spells and diverting the new magic to their own purposes. They had listened to M'Bambi's advice, they had killed him in a particularly repulsive way, and they had ordered a great gathering – at which the chiefs, on the floor of the Baluba Basin would, two hours after sunrise, subvert the White Queen's Magic.

We knew nothing of this as we watched the scene below us and, looking at our watches, realized that it was already seven o'clock. What a sight there would be in only fifteen minutes more.

'A lesson,' muttered Burton-Brown, 'which will spread through all Africa and will show that the white man means business.'

For a moment, although only for a moment, I felt a tremor of repulsion. Burton-Brown, I realized, had not witnessed the scene on the Jubila Plateau. He had no knowledge of what science could now contrive.

Then he added '. . . poor devils!'

Some yards behind us the men were at ease – all except those who had been posted as sentries and were scanning the distance with the care of men for whom scrutiny can mean the difference between life and death.

It was now four minutes past seven. I turned to Burton-Brown, intending to remind him that the troops must be ordered to look away from the crater, even though they remained on the reverse side of the slope.

My reminder was never given.

From a few yards away I heard an agitated whisper from Dobbin who had crawled up to join us on the ridge.

'Sir . . .'

My gaze followed his outstretched arm towards the western entrance to the Basin.

At first I saw nothing. Then, even without the glasses, I perceived a shimmer of gleams as though a grove of bright spear-points was moving upright above the distant scrub. For a moment I could not understand it, even though from our vantage point, hundreds of feet above the crater floor, we could see over the grass which limited the vision of the natives.

Then, as I watched, the gleams spread out into a flickering of points between the cliffs, a long double line of light.

To this day I still believe that as realization dawned I could hear the jingle of bridle and spurs above the continuing background of voices from below.

And even as Burton-Brown turned to me I heard, coming distantly in a thin melodious tone, the notes of a bugle.

Hobday's Horse had arrived.

They had arrived, unwittingly, at the place of our demonstration. They had seen before them an unsuspecting mass of the enemy. And to a leader of Major

Chamberlain's resolute character, only one action was possible.

Hobday's Horse were to be launched on the enemy and in a few minutes would be fighting through them, magnificent in their example.

Burton-Brown, all caution gone, was now standing upright. He had my sympathy.

I looked at my watch and saw that the time was eight minutes past seven. At the same time I felt, even at that distance, a muffled pounding of the ground as the cavalry wheeled into line.

With lances half-drawn from their buckets they started to trot. Now their pennons streamed, and in the light their accoutrements shone. Behind their lines a dust-haze arose.

From a trot to a canter their thunder increased. There was no stopping them now. From a canter they broke to a gallop, stirrup to stirrup, gathering speed.

Again I looked at my watch. I thought of the Light Brigade. This time there would be more than Russian guns. The whole regiment, I estimated, would sweep past my two canisters exactly at seven fifteen.

*

On this same bright morning my dear daughter Julie was meditating on the results of a most adventurous exploit which was to affect not the fate of Hobday's Horse but the consequences of its commander's audacity.

Her letter, which I received before sailing for home in the vessel on which I am writing, explained how Amelia had been taken ill shortly after I had left England. When she had endeavoured to send me the news, my daughter had been faced with the frustrating obstructiveness of the authorities.

Dear Julie divined with a woman's intuition that my recently made acquaintances might know more than was self-evident. Mond was in Germany, Maxim in the United States. She was therefore driven into the bold course of visiting Mr. Zaharoff.

He had been courteous. He had been non-committal. And, as his visitor was about to leave, he had been indiscreet.

'When your father returns, Miss Huxtable,' he said pleasantly, 'the Queen's Indians will have brought him fame and, we sincerely trust, fortune.'

The inevitable question rose in Julie's mind. She bit it back sharply, sensing the indiscretion, fearing to elaborate on it. At the same time the phrase pulled from the deeper recesses of her mind the advice which I had given her when she came of age but which she had never taken seriously.

I had reminded her of our visit to the Queen. And I had told her, in guarded form, of that evening years earlier when Her Majesty had graciously said that if I, or my family, were ever in difficulties, we had but to ask for an audience, and to speak of the Queen's Indians.

I write of my daughter's 'adventurous exploit'. Her actions were no less. For Her Majesty was already at Balmoral; and the prospect of a solitary, unaccompanied journey north, the thought of the long carriage drive out to the Castle, and the presumption of seeking an audience in such circumstances, were all adventurous enough for a young woman of her age, even in our emancipated times. Yet she felt it her duty to communicate with me direct; and if the Queen's Ministers would not help, then there was but one remedy left.

Her first attempt met with frustration. With a confidence which brings colour to my cheeks, she drove past the sentries at the iron gates. She was permitted to enter the Castle. But her request for an audience produced a confusion that arose from the march of history.

'Ask for an audience and speak of the Queen's Indians,' Her Majesty had said; but that had been years earlier. Since those days 'the Indians' had come to signify those Eastern retainers whom the Queen had employed and of whom the Munshi had become the most famous – if notorious is not a better word.

Poor Julie! Her mention of an audience in connection with the Queen's Indians, however it was transmitted, met with a most discouraging refusal, for Her Majesty's servants had by this time gone from Balmoral and from those privileges of which the Royal Household so disapproved. She returned slowly and despondently, to Ballater; any woman of less determination would have returned to London.

Yet within that grey granite burgh by the Dee, she heard, once again, how Her Majesty remained a woman of habit. She heard how the past still seemed to live on in that small body which ruled an empire. And she heard how the Queen still drove up Glen Muick to revisit those happy scenes of more than thirty years ago, an almost regulation visit that was due to be made, if gossip was correct, in two days' time.

A slim chance, indeed! Yet two days later my dear daughter drove six miles up the glen and dismissed her carriage. It was only a little after three, and she had ample time to ensconce herself among the rocks at that very corner where the Queen habitually looked back towards Alt-na-guithasach.

It was almost five when she heard, coming down the glen, the staid hoof-beats of the horses. Some minutes later the royal carriage came into view, open and low-

236

slung, bearing Her Majesty and her Lady-in-Waiting.

Julie judged the distance.

Four hundred yards; three hundred; two hundred yards, and the horses still trod regularly on. Then, a mere one hundred yards away, an imperceptible pull on the reins altered the pace; the carriage began to slow. It halted but ten feet away from my daughter, hidden among the rocks.

She ran down the little slope as the Queen looked back up the glen.

'I must speak to Your Majesty,' she called, forgetting the Indians, forgetting the name of Huxtable, forgetting everything except that this plump old lady ruled a territory on which the sun always shone and would surely know where her father had disappeared to.

'I must speak to Your Majesty,' she called again.

She heard the shuffle of black draperies. Her Majesty's Lady-in-Waiting had already turned, but had been, momentarily, too startled to speak.

Now Her Majesty moved, not turning round, but, as it were, revolving.

As she appeared face-on, Julie saw that her eyes were still of a remarkable, almost crystal-clear blue.

'We are not,' said Her Majesty, 'accustomed to hearing the word "must".'

Julie did her best to curtsy, a little late, among the Scottish rocks. 'It is about Your Majesty's Indians,' she said. 'I think my father has disappeared with them.'

Her Majesty looked troubled.

'But my Indians . . .' She waved her hand as though deploring the fact that her advisers had already persuaded her to dispense with her admirable servants.

'Your Majesty's Indians,' urged Julie, 'but also Professor Huxtable's Indians. They were very important, I think – and to the Prince Consort as well.'

All at once an extraordinary transformation took place. How strange the Queen looked, Julie thought – for a moment not just young, but almost beautiful.

Her Majesty was in fact remembering how gay she had been a third of a century earlier; how often she had asked Albert's advice, how wise he had been, how statesmanlike, how he had guided her so tenderly through her early problems.

'My Indians,' murmured Her Majesty as though they came from a distant world. 'Dear Albert's Indians. No one has talked to me about them for so many years.'

She patted the seat beside her graciously, with a small fat hand.

'Sit beside me, my dear,' said Her Majesty, 'and tell me why you have come.'

*

Colonel Burton-Brown, scanning the cavalry through his glasses, could already recognize numbers of the men, more than a mile away though they were, crouched low over their horses, faces half-hidden by lancecaps.

Each lancer now looked at his future along the slim yellow bamboo of his lance, and where the grass thinned out we could see the red-and-white pennons streaming back from the shining metal tips.

As the thunder of the horsemen reached the natives they turned instinctively to meet the enemy, roughly forming into ranks. Those in front knelt to support their long heavy spears; those behind stood with their throwing assegais at the ready. At the first sound of cavalry they had expected to see an adventurous reconnoitring party. They saw instead a regiment of men which filled their horizon – reinforced, it was now clear, by a party of settlers who had acted as scouts.

Behind them, forgotten in the need of the moment, alone and remote in the long oval of yellow sand, lay my two canisters. Minute and almost invisible at this distance, they yet glinted startlingly in the sun; so did the bright line of the track along which they were to meet their destiny.

For a moment I speculated on the oddness of fate which had drawn me six thousand miles from my London study to meet Hobday's Horse in the African wilderness.

I was naturally anxious that there should be no hitch; yet at the same time I experienced an absolutely contrary sensation. For the destiny towards which the lancers were urging their horses was something different from the chances of battle. For a moment I speculated how grotesque it was that their resolution should be matched against the Indians.

Colonel Burton-Brown did more than speculate. He had no real appreciation of what the new weapon would accomplish. He envisaged at the most an explosion of immense force. But even Burton-Brown realized that the result would be extinction for Hobday's Horse.

His sharp voice shattered my thoughts as I rose to my feet.

He called to the gunners: 'Action front, left-hand canister.'

He called to the lieutenant in command of the infantry: 'Man the ridge, Mr. Martin. Keep your men well under cover. Fire only at response to the artillery.'

For a moment I, a mere civilian, could scarcely comprehend what was happening. Then I craned round to gaze on an extraordinary scene.

The members of the gun-team who had until now been idle men, sunning themselves or casually polishing their metal, moved into action like the parts of a well-oiled machine. As they did so, the infantry responded to the crisp orders of their N.C.O.s, changing in aspect from a huddle of casual loungers into a group of red points which spread out systematically like beads along a broken necklace, left and right from the point of command, up to the ridge, dropping deftly to the ground as they reached their own individual summits, nestling up against the crags, pulling back the bolts of their rifles in a treble score of separate snicks that echoed back and forth around the rocks.

I turned, to find Dobbin stretched on the rocks beside me. His mouth was tight in a glum line as he nodded: 'Trust the cavalry to ruin it, sir.'

I could hardly believe the implication of the moves behind me, but disbelief dissolved as there came the answering words from the gunners' Number One.

'Action front, left-hand canister.'

Then, as his companion tugged at blue metal, a staccato: 'Limber, drive on.'

I watched the horses pulling the carriage downhill away from the gun's new position on the ridge, slewing it round under the controlling hands of the men so that it came to rest in a flurry of dust and small stones at just the best angle.

Beside me, Burton-Brown was continuing his orders: 'Range, three thousand yards plus. With solid shot – load.'

Cambridge might have agreed reluctantly that the Indians should be used; nevertheless, he had agreed.

'Commander-in-Chief's orders,' I shouted across to

Burton-Brown, the dust stirred up by the gun-wheels almost choking me.

Burton-Brown ignored me, intent only on preventing those two shining canisters from meeting, on preserving Hobday's Horse from destruction; and I heard from behind the echoing voice of the gun-team's Number One: 'With solid shot – load.'

There was still four minutes to go.

I saw Burton-Brown signalling with his hands as the calm voice of the gun-leader ordered his men: 'Trail left.'

Looking along the sights he waited as the gunners manhandled the heavy metal, and the muzzle of the field-piece almost imperceptibly moved round.

'This is disobedience in face of the enemy,' I shouted to the Colonel.

He took no notice and called back over his shoulder: 'Fire!'

At the order, Number One responded as though on parade, stepping clear of the gun's wheels as the rest of the team continued with their parts in the elaborate ballet round the gun.

Down below us the cavalry had so stirred up the dust that a faint haze seemed to travel in front of them. The oval arena, now a mere thousand yards or so ahead, could be seen only through a brown veil. And through this veil I saw my canister begin to move forward, a slow and ungainly creature on its little trolley.

'Ready,' shouted Number One as though the crater were the Woolwich grounds.

As a desperate measure, I half-rose from the ridge and called back to the gun-team.

'In the name of the Queen . . .'

The gun-team ignored me.

'Fire!' shouted Number One, and the lanyard was pulled simultaneously.

The noise of the explosion seemed to shatter my eardrums. Drenched in the sandy surge thrown up by the gun as it recoiled, I was thrown on to my knees, face forward, so that with the stench of powder in my nostrils, peering through the spatter of falling sand, I could see a great gout of flame and greyness spurt up by the trolley. But still the trolley moved on.

The gunners had missed!

Behind me I heard Number One's voice: 'Run up – halt – unload.'

Again came the voice of Burton-Brown: 'Range three thousand yards plus. With solid shot – load.'

As the gun roared out, scores of black faces had turned up from the crater floor towards us. Now as many men again were doubling for the foot of the slopes beneath us, ignoring the cover of fallen rocks, dashing forward at the run, arrogantly brandishing their throwing spears.

A dozen yards away Lieutenant Martin gave the order to fire, and an irregular crackle of shots broke out as each man sought his own target.

Beside me a voice said: 'You may find this useful, sir.' Without looking round I held out my hand and grasped the revolver which Dobbin had handed me, the metal still relatively cool from its place in the holster and curiously reassuring.

As the smoke cleared in the arena I saw that the explosion had unseated the rear wheels of the trolley. But the mechanism still worked. As I watched, my canister was still carried on towards its mate.

Only some four hundred yards away, the first line of the lancers tore into the outer bulwark of black bodies, scattering them in a tatter of grotesque shapes and riding on at almost unbroken speed.

For a moment the almost sporting nature of the occasion seized my imagination. The natives below us had been joined by many more, and with remarkable agility they now came up the slopes, taking cover when they could, leaping so swiftly from boulder to boulder that careful aiming was difficult. I moved slightly to get a better view of my stationary canister and, as I did so, heard a curious whistle. I looked round to see a heavy spear rebound from the rocks behind me.

Simultaneously, the gun blazed out again. This time the shot was wide of its mark. Through the smoke I could see that the Indian limped on.

'Trail left,' I heard Burton-Brown shout back, as the man a few yards to my left took careful aim and shot through the chest a tall native only some twenty feet below us.

'Straddle the track. Rapid fire.'

I bent down beneath the sound of the explosions, taking careful aim at the nearest native as the gun roared out. The first shot splintered itself on the rocks this side of the track. The second produced a huge mushroom of smoke some yards beyond it.

I thought of Benson, of England growing mightier yet. I thought of all that we might still accomplish. Then I saw the track disappear into a tangle of upthrown fragments as a third shot plunged into the Indian. The device disintegrated into its natural elements as a violet-blue flash – a mere dozen yards before the first rank of the lancers as they drove through the main enemy ranks.

Immediately below us the natives, only now fully aware of the weight of Hobday's Horse, began to retreat among the rocks. At some isolated places on the veld of the crater floor they surrounded groups of fallen men, lancers and settlers, who fought off their savage attacks. Elsewhere, the cavalry swept on.

Around us the dust died down, and for a moment all I could hear among the smeech was the twittering of small yellow birds which swept out from the crags near our vantage-point, and the slow beat of vultures' wings as the birds circled above in anticipation of the feast to come.

The artillery fire had done more than destroy the Indian. At the crucial moment, when Hobday's Horse was but a score of yards from the enemy, it had provided a diversion in the enemy's rear. Thus more than one of the black warriors, crouched beside his cutting spear, had looked back for a moment. In many cases it was his last.

The lancers had struck the wall of ebony men as the wall itself quivered with hesitation. The riders had gone through, with losses fewer than even the most optimistic could have expected. Burton-Brown had saved Hobday's Horse in more ways than one.

Now they were through the thickest of the enemy groups, broken up at places into smaller segments by the ground or by the defence, yet still keeping coherence.

Among the enemy confusion spread. The arrival of the lancers in force had been unexpected enough; then the artillery fire, brought down near the thickest groups, conveyed only one message.

The spirits in the canister did, indeed, obey only the White Queen.

Like a receding black wave the natives moved northwards, away from the ridge on which we lay, leaving their dead and dying, scarcely troubling to attack the few wounded troopers who defended themselves as best they could.

Away to the east some four thousand yards distant, Hobday's Horse could be seen forming up. A minute later it was clear that they were to repeat the manoeuvre, to sweep back through the disorganized enemy remnants, picking up their wounded as they went, and then leaving the basin by the gap through which they had entered it.

Burton-Brown summoned a trooper.

'This is to inform Major Chamberlain of our position,' he said, scribbling on his note-pad. 'Please ask him to rendezvous with us . . .' He bent down over his map and wrote out a reference.

Then he turned to me. There seemed little for either of us to say. I foresaw our return; I foresaw the evidence which I should have to give against Burton-Brown. Strangely, I found my indignation at the destruction of our great weapon overshadowed. I had lost much; Burton-Brown had lost his future. For all he showed of it, he was less worried than I.

'I suggest that you accompany the column down, Professor Huxtable,' he said. 'I will follow later. I require a few minutes for thought.'

The gunners were now limbering up, the men forming into line. We would soon be about to move off. A feeling suffused me that in another moment Burton-Brown would have held out his hand and wished me goodbye. Before he could do so there was a shout from one of the gun-team.

I looked to where the men were pointing, and at first thought I saw a straggler from Hobday's Horse. Certainly the rider had been pushing his mount to the limit of its speed. Both were in the last stages of exhaustion, but as the man spurred his horse almost cruelly up the slope towards us I saw that he belonged to one of the garrison regiments.

He reined up beside us, almost too far gone to speak. His right hand rose in a faint echo of a salute as he pulled two envelopes from his pouch, handed them to Burton-Brown and half-toppled across the saddle.

The Colonel opened one of the two envelopes – with a steady hand, I noticed – read it slowly and, without a word, passed it to me.

It was addressed: 'Officer Commanding Indian Force'. It read: 'We absolutely forbid any use whatso-ever of Her Majesty's Indians.' It was signed 'Victoria, R.I.'

'Confirmation,' said Burton-Brown, speaking to the near-by men almost as much as to me, I felt, 'confirma-tion of our orders to destroy the canisters.' I wondered how many noticed his slight stress on the first word.

He handed the second envelope to me. I wish I had been able to open it as steadily as the Colonel had opened his.

I knew, almost before I began to read, that the mes-sage would be signed 'Victoria, R.I.'

We are deeply disappointed [it read] that Pro-fessor Huxtable should have left our shores with-out finding it necessary to discuss with us the mission on which he has embarked. He is in no cir-cumstances to allow the detonation of Her Majesty's Indians and he is to return to Britain with all speed. We do not yet know – although we are determined that we *shall* know – how the present situation has been brought about. But we have de-cided that it would be wrong, in the present cir-cumstances, to invoke the powers which have been granted to us, and against this decision there is *no* appeal. Professor Huxtable must remember that when victory comes, as victory surely will come, our enemies will no longer be the savages whose deeds we now so earnestly deplore. They will be led into different ways; these people will be *my* people.

I handed Burton-Brown my message. Like him, I could make no comment.

How, less than an hour later, we met Hobday's Horse is no part of my story; nor is an account of our uneventful trek back to the coast. Throughout the journey, Burton-Brown and Chamberlain argued endlessly on the relative effects of the lancers' action and of the artillery fire which had helped to clear their way – and I was distressed to hear that both talked of my canisters as though they had been filled only with a new kind of explosive, a refined version of dynamite.

Yet there had been one unexpected result of the morning's work. Perhaps the fear of the White Queen's new magic had combined with the slaughter of those few minutes to suggest to the native mind a greater wrath to come. Perhaps they felt that there was, as M'Bambi had claimed, some inexplicably evil eye in my canisters.

Whatever the reason, the chieftains had made up their minds with speed. Runners had been sent on ahead of our column so that, by the time we arrived back at the coast, the Governor was already reading the details of what was a native capitulation.

With the Governor, Dobbin and I remained during many months of exasperating delay, waiting until there steamed up across the horizon the ship that brought Julie's letter and that is now taking us home.

Of all those involved, the Governor alone had been

given some hint from London of the cataclysmic power with which we had been dealing. He alone suspected that the wing of a new angel of death had almost touched the country he ruled for the Queen. He alone believed that he would carry a great secret to his grave.

'What a deterrent you scientists must have constrained within your canisters,' he had exclaimed when we were alone together. 'Even the threat of its use, Professor Huxtable, was enough to cause surrender.'

As we sit here on deck, watching the white bow-wave of the ship, I writing and Dobbin just thinking, it is easy to smile at the Governor. But there is an inner dynamic in military affairs that cannot be stopped. Each step leads inexorably to the next. This time the Indians were deployed on the field of battle; next time they will be used.

There is, of course, the question of Her Majesty. Some of the royal odium will no doubt be passed down to the Prime Minister, to Cambridge as Commander-in-Chief – as innocent of intent as of wisdom – and through him to Wolseley.

But we live under a constitutional monarchy. The Indians are available. And I write confident in the knowledge that the last serious impediment to their future has been swept away.

12 : The Great Decision

Thursday, October 19th, 1899

'Too late, too late' – those words which have been the epitaph of high hopes down the years must also be the epitaph of mine. More than a decade ago, returning from Africa to find my black-robed daughter on the quayside, I realized too late what my travelling had cost me. Just as I realize today how the suspicions raised by Delane's parting questions have been more than justified. They had grown for a decade and a half, and had then been dissipated, as I prepared for Africa, by those thoughts of Imperial splendour in which I had for a moment basked.

The news of my wife's death, a week before I reached England, revived my doubts – illogically, of course, but we are unreasoning creatures. The private storm raised by Her Majesty over Baluba blew itself out, as I had expected, with decreasingly violent gusts down the chain of command. Zaharoff, Maxim and Mond quickly became engaged in more profitable matters. The Indian Committee slid into oblivion.

Yet my past remained with me. When poor Dobbin died I felt that I had lost not a servant but a collaborator. And when I learned from the States that the huge Coon Butte depression in Arizona, six hundred feet deep and four thousand feet across, was simply, as long suspected, a meteor-crater, I was appalled by a frightful possibility.

I thought of Her Majesty and her claim that the Almighty had sent the Crimean storm to wreck the

Prince and its cargo. Had He, I asked myself with self-destructive honesty, also sent a meteorite to the Jubila Plateau? Were Hooker and his grotesque flowers, Godwin-Austen and his monsters, mere coincidences provided by God to compound my arrogance? I remembered how Cambridge had twitted me with having deceived his dear cousin: had I, in fact, unknowingly done so? I thought of Gladstone, and the thought was too awful to bear. Had my belief in the possession of ultimate power been after all but an illusion sent to tempt me – the temptation of which Gladstone had spoken – and one which I had seized with both hands.

When I fought off such fears, they were replaced by others, for my history would not let me be. Thus recently, when I was bearded by an enthusiastic young man bubbling to be off to the war, I began to have suspicions. He mentioned his father. He hinted this way and that. With his constant talk of new weapons he seemed to be trying to draw me. Were there other young men like him, I wondered, who might have gleaned some inner knowledge of the Indians? I never knew, for while I was still evading his inquiries he was drawn away by some high-spirited call of 'Winston'.

I trusted that I would be left in peace. Yet such has been the recent talk that I was prepared for the summons which came this morning. If the subject was ever raised with Wolseley, he had remembered the aftermath of the Baluba expedition and the Queen's scathing words, and had passed on the problem to a higher level. The summons came from the Prime Minister.

I noted, two days ago, that although Her Majesty had remained at Balmoral, the Prince of Wales had called on Salisbury shortly before a Cabinet. There has been tremendous coming and going; Wolseley no doubt doing his best with the resources at his command. And it seemed the most natural thing in the world that I should be asked to present myself.

It was not a Cabinet, and there were only half a dozen men in the room when I entered. Most of them rose and looked at me with interest. Then they half-bowed as though I was the answer to their prayers.

I sat down where they placed me with some ceremony, on the Prime Minister's right hand. I could tell by their cautious remarks, as they told me about the war and the difficult times of our poor troops, just what they were about.

Eventually, and with some embarrassment, for we had been together on more than one platform when he had been President of the British Association, Salisbury raised the subject. He spoke with great care, explaining how he had refused foreign mediation, how he had in mind only the greatness of England, how he detested un-necessary destruction of life, but how he had now decided that he should at last exercise the prerogative of the Prime Minister since, as he put it, 'the Prime Minister was given it by yourself, Professor Huxtable, almost half a century ago. Sir, we must ask you to prepare for us one of your devices.'

Salisbury's plan was quite clear. There was to be a minimum loss of life, perhaps none. A demonstration on some lonely part of the veldt after the enemy had been warned that it was to take place – that was all. I trusted Salisbury, but I did not trust all those present. 'A demonstration – if we must have only that', was a phrase that more than one man used.

Yet I could not readily blame them. They were not bad men; they simply had not the slightest idea of what they were doing.* I nodded briefly, said that I would communicate with them again in a short while, and took my departure. At the end of the corridor a servant was waiting but I waved him aside and walked out into the evening air.

Had I taken a cab instead of walking home, the history of the world might have been different. I do not know. For I was already disconcerted by the attitude of some in the room I had left.

And then, as I walked up Whitehall, I remembered a letter I had read in *The Times* this very morning.† It came from a Major Baden-Powell. He has just returned to England from inspecting General Count Zeppelin's vast contrivance – 'as big as one of our powerful battle-ships'. This is not all. 'Notwithstanding what peace conferences may decide,' he goes on, 'wars in the future will no doubt be decided in the air.'

So another of Tennyson's prophecies is coming true!

I looked up towards the night sky, its stars obscured by the smoke of the capital, and realized that within the lifetime of my grandchildren the Laureate's 'pilots of the purple twilight' might be sailing there. I wondered what they would be carrying.

I walked on, and at the top of Whitehall the crowds were thick. I passed through them and as I listened to their talk I was profoundly shocked. They were, I suppose, like all crowds down the ages. But Britain was already at war with the Boers, and I could sense beneath their honest artisan faces the naked passion of animals

---

*'Although personally I am quite content with the existing explosives, I feel we must not stand in the path of improvement ...' Churchill to the Chiefs-of-Staff Committee, August 30th, 1941, recommending work on the atomic bomb.

†See *The Times*, October 19th, 1899.

baying for blood. They were not, at heart, unkindly people, but they were moved by an unthinking vehemence, and circumstance was beginning to raise them above their biological station in life. I could not but be sorry for them. Yet sorrow was not enough, and I began to consider the consequences for the world if control of my device were ever delivered into their hands.

From Trafalgar Square I looked down the long dark gulf of the Mall, the windows which I knew would be shining in Marlborough House concealed by the trees, and with the Queen still in Scotland not a light showing in the great front of Buckingham Palace. I remembered Her Majesty, not as she is now but as she had been when young, naming her Indians and not yet realizing what they meant. I walked on and saw that in the Club all the lights blazed, and I did not doubt that its members' minds were ablaze too, as confident as ever. The spectacle brought to my mind the memory of John Dalton, almost exactly two-thirds of a century back, and of his warning, so much more percipient than the advice of his educated betters. In Piccadilly, the common people were shouting for slaughter, and I remembered the Duke, steady into old age, and his verdict on the wisdom of the human race.

I walked on northwards, not caring much what I heard or saw but appreciating the smell of autumn which floated across from the keepers' bonfires in the Park. Dear Julie, I reflected, was now happily married and her children were already growing up into a world I would never know. I wondered what that world would be like. I remembered the face of the Prince Consort when I had first seen him at Windsor, a face cut by the line of the green shade – and I realized that most of the human race was still split thus. I remembered Lincoln's words; Gladstone, hard as a fixed rock in mid-stream as my arguments beat round him; I remembered Delane and his decision to withhold the most important story his paper would ever tell; and I remembered the voice of the old Queen and how she had called the black-skinned murderers 'my people'.

As I turned the key in the lock, my mind was made up.

I shall be dead by morning and even the authorities – for I no longer completely trust them – will learn nothing from the ashes in my grate. For now I believe that Dalton and Lincoln and Gladstone and Her Majesty were right – that we cannot exorcize evil by creating a masterpiece of evil. Let us forget it all, like a bad dream. Men may perhaps discover my secret again. But if they do, may the Lord have mercy on their souls.

Postscript

London   *Tuesday, November 5th*, 1985

My dear Richard,

You will remember that following Geoffrey Huxtable's death in 1967, Professor Franklin Huxtable's story of the world's first nuclear bomb was discovered. We both know that even after a long history Professor Huxtable's stroke of genius was not exploited against the Boers or, as would then have been almost inevitable, during the Great War which broke out in 1914.

But an even more intriguing possibility has come to light. I have just found some additional pages – previously missing from the Professor's manuscript – which give his account of some events a few years after 1870. Some pages of explanation still appear to be absent but these additions at least make a coherent tale. They reveal the nimbleness of his mind, and their significance to the 1980s is so great that I am sending them to you both as a comment on history's might-have-beens and as a warning for the future. You may like to add these additional pages as a postscript to any future edition of Professor Huxtable's story.

Once again, it's over to you.

Yours,

RONALD

As so often [begin the missing pages from Professor Huxtable's manuscript], fate was to be guided by luck, that luck which Napoleon always preferred his generals to have. Without it, my ultimate weapon would never have been tested in Britain, with results which could have altered the fortunes of the world.

It was chance alone which brought me to the Club later than usual one night. And I thus found myself kept from my usual chair and seated in another within earshot of an old military gentleman. For once Sir Montague was excoriating the stupidities not of our politicians, his usual target for contempt, but of Continental military leaders, particularly the Prussians, who had been surprising the world with their military weaponry.

'More powerful, no doubt, more lethal no doubt,' Sir Montague admitted, 'but of what use when it becomes necessary for victories to be won, not on the customary fields of battle but within the cities of one's enemies or, worse still, of oneself. Unlimited destruction when casualties alone would make one's opposing forces *hors de combat*. Wasted energy, wasted effort. But subtlety of thought is no doubt beyond the foreign mind.'

Maybe. But such subtleties had not been entirely absent from my own thoughts, although I had previously given them only superficial attention. I had, in fact, considered the work of our own Joseph Swan and the American Thomas Edison who had both – and in what order of priority was to be long disputed – perfected a new means of illumination. It appeared that their invention depended on the movement of electrical currents through inanimate metal wires; but movements of such a character that they had made it possible to extinguish life even though the wires through which the currents passed suffered no apparent change.

Now, mulling over the prognostications of Sir Montague, I gave more thought to the matter. Would it not be possible, I asked myself, so to arrange the details of my weapon that its rays, as I called them, would be in some ways neutral – neutral since, although they would kill living things, they would not affect lifeless matter.

My good wife – even now ignorant of the apocalyptic nature of my work – maintained that I should be devoting my thoughts to what she still described as more important things; but I devoted the next week and more to calculations. Blast and fire would have to be eliminated from the explosion of my device and I soon saw that the size and range of the weapon would have to be measurably smaller than those of the weapon which had wrought its devastation on the Jubila Plateau so many years ago. But even when I had produced an outline for such a device, and for the triggering mechanism which could set it off, one problem remained. I thought it unlikely that the old Queen would relish the thought of allowing me another long and expensive expedition to India. And, however circumscribed the effects of my new weapon might be, it would surely be difficult to find, within the British Isles, a site suitable for its adequate testing?

It was here that chance again came to my aid. For reading a newspaper report of a meeting of an old Scottish society, my memory was jogged by the name of a very close friend of my youth whom I used to call 'the Chief' and with whom I had continued to keep in contact over the years. Donald's ardent Stuart leanings had once again brought him to the notice of what he always derided as 'the Hanoverian Press'. He had been born in the same year as myself, in that part of Scotland that is still one of the least visited parts of the British Isles. His family had left the ancestral home while he was still a youth and had taken up residence further south on an estate situated at no great distance from the Rough

Bounds of Knoydart, where I had been his guest more than once.

The Rough Bounds! Nearby, if anywhere within the United Kingdom, it would be possible to test my new device – Jubila Mark II as I lightly called it – with a secrecy inherent in the situation of Donald's estate, close to Scotland's west coast, accessible by pack-animal rather than wheeled vehicle. There was, moreover, another advantage if Donald could only be persuaded to cooperate, as I had no doubt he could. Not only was he himself a Jacobite of quite exceptional fanaticism; he employed as retainers on his isolated crofts only those who believed as fervently as he did that a successor to the 'King over the Water' would eventually arrive to reclaim his due. Any hint that preparations might be in hand to assure victory in a Jacobite armageddon would be enough not only to secure whatever cooperation was needed but to close their mouths.

All went as I hoped. Donald was apprised of my needs only in the broadest terms. The crofts along one stretch of territory bounded by the Sound of Sleat would have to be evacuated for a short while. And a number of animals of various sizes and ages would have to be made available for tethering at marked spots in the area. It was on this last point that I met trouble from Dobbin. It had been necessary to explain to him that the results of the new device he had helped me to perfect could only be measured by their effect on goats, deer and any other animals that might be available. At this he had blenched and had then explained to me, albeit with some hesitation, that this involved a matter of moral principle. He realized, by a mixture of common-sense and intuition, that all the experimental animals might not be killed but some merely incapacitated or wounded. This offended what he called his moral principles. At first it seemed useless to explain that the outcome of future wars or – as I put it – the limitation of casualties in future wars, could be governed by the outcome of the work on which we were engaged.

After some discussion – in which, I must admit, I was forced to think more deeply on some issues than had previously been the case – we arrived at a compromise, as so often in matters which are first considered as those of immutable principle. Both Dobbin and I would arm ourselves with the latest revolvers and, after making the necessary observations for scientific purposes, would despatch those beasts which had survived the experiment.

Shortly afterwards we entrained for the north, accompanied by a series of boxes, heavy enough in all conscience but weighing merely pounds where my black boxes for Jubila had been weighed in hundredweights. Dobbin had charge of the triggering mechanism I had devised. Based on a muzzle-loading rifle which I had adapted for its special role, it was a formidable weapon in its own right, and had the season been later there might have been speculation among other passengers that we were engaged on some rather un-sporting development of deer-stalking.

Beyond the Border we changed to the carriage I had hired and in this we drove northwards until, at Fort William, that southern bastion of the Great Glen which splits Scotland from south-west to north-east, we found awaiting us the pack-horses. Here also was the Chief, more tartan than George IV had been at his investiture in Edinburgh, a genuine Scot of the Scots, entranced by the muzzle-loader which from his first sight of it he regarded as a symbol of Stuart resurgence.

It was a long drag up the Great Glen until eventually

we struck off westwards into the Rough Bounds. Here it was not only roads that ceased. Tracks were of the roughest, deer-stalkers' paths almost as bad, and both Dobbin and I soon realized that only the long drawn-out evening which kept a glimmering half-light until midnight, would prevent us from being benighted.

Indeed, even the last light was going before we could see in the distance the white waters of Loch Nevis. Here we were nearly at the small group of crofts which were our destination.

Dobbin and the Chief, with such assistance as I could give, now off-loaded and erected the tents and we were soon all bedded down for the short night which ended for me with the smell of breakfast and of the peat fire beneath it.

In the light of morning I could see that the site was as I had remembered it from earlier years, and that the Chief had ensured that my instructions were carried out to a nicety. Our camp-site sloped down to the sandy shore of Loch Nevis, to north and south of which there rose peaks with all the austerity of the Scottish highlands at their fiercest. Beyond the loch, which a few miles on became the Sound of Sleat, could be seen the grand outlines of the Outer Isles. The crofts a few hundred yards away were deserted. Indeed, across the whole sweep of the scene there was not a soul in sight, nor likely to be. If the explosion for which I had made such preparations was to cause a greater convulsion than I expected, then it would only be perceived from afar, if at all. As I had hoped, the weather was already thundery, and once again, as in India, meteorology could be conscripted if necessary to carry the burden of science.

I quickly completed our preparations. Beyond the crofts there grazed a selection of goats, deer and sheep, tethered at what I checked were carefully measured distances from the rude buildings. On the near side of the crofts I now set up the muzzle-loader, the end of its barrel containing one half of my device while the second half rested near the breech, waiting to be shot down the barrel when my timing mechanism actuated the necessary charge.

When all was ready I withdrew with Dobbin and the Chief to our camp-site, nearly half a mile distant. My two companions had been warned to look away from the apparatus, and obediently did so as we all heard the start of the primary actuating device.

At the same time I began counting: 'Ten, nine, eight, seven . . .' and so on. As I was about to pronounce 'zero' two things happened. The Chief, unable to contain himself, let out a triumphant shout of 'Remember Culloden'. Simultaneously, there came a roar from the muzzle-loader, a gout of flame, and a juddering of the ground which resembled if not an earthquake at least an earth tremor.

On my instructions the three of us remained where we were for half an hour. Then, as we slowly approached the crofts, both Dobbin and the Chief were amazed at what they saw. The ground beneath the muzzle-loader was blackened as though it had suffered from a peat fire which had burned out of control but, *mirabile dictu*, only the slightest of scorching could be seen on the walls of the crofts. So one part of my experiment had been successful. But what of the effects on living things?

It was with some trepidation that we walked round the buildings. At first it appeared that nothing had happened. A few of the animals had, it is true, dropped to the ground. The rest still stood in their steps. Only when we cautiously approached them did we realize that none were breathing. On some of those nearer the crofts there could be seen a faint sign of scarring as though they had walked too near an open fire. But all were dead, dead without any other visible trace on their bodies, even those which had been only a quarter of a mile from the explosion.

But it was the scene inside the rude habitations which so greatly intrigued me. To the eye of the observer, nothing had been visibly affected and even the bunches of flowers, which on my instructions had been placed at certain points, looked as fresh as when they had been placed there. Indeed, I had made a delightful discovery, and one which might change the face of warfare.

The experiment which had been carried out so successfully was, as is not always the case, free of awkward after-effects. The dead animals were decently buried in due course and the Chief's crofters returned happy that they had not been present when, as he reported, a fireball had dropped on the area.

My success in this first development of Her Majesty's Indians encouraged me to think harder. It was clear that if I could retain Donald's cooperation I had the means of testing out a whole variety of projects with a secrecy which any military man would envy. The problem was what to try next and I might have been at a loose end for some while had I not attended one particular meeting of the Royal Society. Here Sir Francis Galton, cousin of Charles Darwin of the monkey theory, expounded at length upon some remarkable experiments he had been making. These experiments, aimed at breeding racially pure rabbits, involved transfusions of blood from rabbits of one colour into rabbits of another.* Nothing came of

* F. Galton's experiments about rabbits: 'viz injecting black rabbit's blood into grey and *vice versa*', as Darwin's wife Emma wrote to her

this work, much to Galton's disappointment, but when I heard of it I began wondering whether colour might be not only a matter of inheritance but an indication of subtle differences within the human frame. We know, for instance, that the black races respond to the effects of the sun very differently from the white. What other differences, I asked myself, might there not be. Much was still concealed from us by the blanket of ignorance and even Godwin-Austen's tale remained a mystery to me.

What differences, indeed! As I mulled over Sir Francis' talk that evening I bethought me of my own work, some aspects of which were as little understood as those with which Sir Francis was involved. Was it, perhaps, possible that men and other living creatures, black or brown, reacted differently from white to what I took to be the unidentified rays released by my explosives? Was it not perhaps possible that I had within my power the means of intervening, in some as yet unthought-of way, in the European conquest of Africa in which white men were already competing ferociously with each other? I knew that here I would be raising moral problems of a high order. But I had always believed that Montrose was right – 'He either fears his fate too much/Or his deserts are small, /That puts it not unto the touch, /To win or lose it all'. That was not quite my position now, since I already knew what my Indians would do. But I decided to put my latest idea to the touch – with the Chief's help, that was.

My friend was agreeable, although when I told him that I wished to discover whether my weapon could be

---

daughter, Henrietta Darwin on 19 March, [1870] (see *Emma Darwin, Wife of Charles Darwin; A Century of Family Letters* by her daughter (H. E. Litchfield); Cambridge; privately printed at the University Press, 1904; Volume 2, page 230).

made selective in its application – I would tell him no more – his response was different from what I had expected. 'I will no ask ye upon what lines your selectivity will run,' he said. 'But what a grand thing if your device could pick, so to speak, the sheep from the lambs, the evil from the good. If your weapon could strike down all Hanoverians within its radius and leave unharmed all Jacobites, intent as they will in future be on restoring to his rightful throne whoever the inheritor of Charles Edward Stuart may be when your weapon is ready for battle, then the Cause would have victory within its grasp.'

I had not the honesty to discourage him and some months later he was entering into the spirit of my instructions even more confidently than he had the previous year. His crofters had once again been evacuated to temporary quarters and Dobbin and I had once again met the Chief in the Rough Bounds on what I was by this time thinking of as a proving-range. This time, however, there was one important difference. Sheep and cattle were again tethered at varying distances from the place where the explosion was to take place but this time they were tethered in pairs, one black, one white, so that each would receive an equal fluxion from my device.

I had long debated with myself whether I should confide at least some details of the experiment to Galton. But from the earliest days with the Indians I had followed what I called a 'need to know' policy, confiding to no one any more than was essential. Even to my own dear wife I told no more than was necessary, and in the case of my two excursions to the Rough Bounds I explained, with as little mendacity as possible, only that my old friend the Chief required advice on delicate matters. This was true to some extent since he did his best to discover some details of my work. I knew, of course, that she would not have the temerity to question him personally, particularly as on both occasions I sent her up to enjoy herself among the pleasures of Scotland's Venice of the North while I was absent for the week or so that was necessary.

Once again Dobbin, the Chief and I made the journey westwards along Loch Quoich on the tough little garrons, those horses which can stumble through the heather more efficiently than a Derby winner. Eventually, past Ben Avon and Sron na Ciche, we found ourselves nearing the shores of the Sound of Sleat. And here we found that all had been arranged as ordered. Soon after dawn the next morning our weapon was ready for firing.

As before there was the flash, enormous by conventional standards but a mere firework compared with the sight I had witnessed on the Jubila Plateau. Once again we inspected the results after a due interval. This time, however, I was faced with disappointment. Dobbin, who had insisted on the same details as previously, despatched with his revolver those animals which were still alive. The Chief watched in ignorant wonder, believing only my story that I had again been testing a new explosive at its maximum power. For me there was frustration. For it was clear, even from a cursory examination, that at all distances from the explosion black and white animals had been affected equally. Colour gave neither protection nor added vulnerability. My theory vanished without trace on the shores of the Sound of Sleat – but I must admit that I was in some way relieved. For if my limited experiment suggested anything at all, it suggested that differences of colour in the human species were superficial differences, irrelevant to the great factors that were common to all men.

Moreover, I still had my Indians. Whatever might

arise from future experiments – for at that date I planned
to continue them – I was confident that my magic could
in the future be developed for use in different ways,
perhaps beneath the seas or even, such were my fantasies,
from the air. In the aftermath of those days in the Rough
Bounds I still believed that I could be responsible for a
deterrent which would remove the threat of war from the
human race. But before I could continue my attempts to
adapt the weapon for use in fresh circumstances, there
began a small war in Africa and a demand for my services
as a master-armourer. My efforts on that occasion were
to be frustrated while later, during the last years of the
century, my views changed and I so organized matters, as
I shall relate, that the story of Her Majesty's Indians
came to a sudden end – I now hope for ever.